An Unfolding Trap

by

Jo A. Hiestand

The McLaren Mysteries

An Unfolding Trap

Cover Art by *Angela Anderson*

The Wild Rose Press, Inc.
PO Box 708
Adams Basin, NY 14410-0708
Visit us at www.thewildrosepress.com

Publishing History
Previously published as Rock Song, by Copper Ink
First Crimson Rose Edition, 2016
Print ISBN 978-1-5092-0587-5
Digital ISBN 978-1-5092-0588-2

The McLaren Mysteries
Published in the United States of America

Ross leaned forward, closing the distance between them. "You're sure you didn't get angry when you found him this afternoon?"

"*Of course* I got angry! Who the hell wouldn't? The bloody git killed a man, frightened a dozen others who were there, kidnapped Miss Skene, held her hostage—" He stopped before saying Lanny had knocked him on the head and left him for dead in the marshland along the loch, or that he was a threat to Neill McLaren. He took a deep breath. "But I didn't kill him. I tied him up so he wouldn't escape, then phoned you when I could."

"An hour later." The voice was flat, unimpressed.

"Yes. An hour later. Maybe ninety minutes. I didn't write down the bloody time, but I phoned here, in the village."

"Why wait so long to ring us?"

"Pardon?" The suspicion that things were turning horribly wrong whispered to McLaren.

"Why didn't you phone right then? Did you want to put some space between you and the killing so you could establish an alibi?"

Dedication

For Babette, Bill, Peter, Christopher and M-H.
Who knew what would result from a gift?
Thanks for the concert and the setting.
~*~
And for Kathy,
the eager reader who had to wait 290 days too long
to see what McLaren's up to next.

Acknowledgements

Since I'm not an imbiber of beer, I had to ask someone I consider an authority. *Slàinte mhòr agad!* and a tip of the glass to Ian McCalman, who created the brewery's beer name and supplied information on the beverage. He also de-Anglicized my Scottish conversations, turning them into something real Scots would say. I thank him for this immense undertaking.

A hug and my thanks to Paul Hornung, St. Louis-area police officer, for reading the manuscript and catching police problems.

My gratefulness also goes to Kaitlin West, my editor, who did a super job and didn't blink an eye when she came to the Scottish dialogue.

Gabe Maichel, Kevin Cheli and Nathan Pence...what can I say about their recording of "The Braes of Balquhidder"? The song is important in the book and they gave it a lilting jazz rendition. I'm so thankful it's saved for posterity on CD recordings.

Thanks to David McLaren, who provided me with the description of Loch Voil and The Boar's Rock—all very important to Michael and the story. I also thank Chuck Lawson, Vice President of Clan MacLaren Society of North America, Ltd, for steering me to the song so pertinent to Michael and the Clan. Barbara Gard, President of Clan MacLaren Society of North America, and Gloria Shellenbarger, Commissioner for the Mid-West Region of CMSNA, both pointed me in the right direction when I'd lost my way. Without their compass I'd still be stumbling in the dark and would not have met people with the detailed knowledge I needed.

More gratitude than I can ever convey to Donald MacLaren of MacLaren, Clan Chief, for supplying details of Balquhidder and the area, for the suggestion of the song "The Braes of Balquhidder," for enduring my seemingly unending emails and questions, for giving me some Clan history, for supplying a story point, and for his general enthusiasm for reading about another McLaren.

Any errors that may have crept into the story are solely mine.

Jo Hiestand
St. Louis, MO
February 2016

Cast of Characters

Michael McLaren: former police detective, Staffordshire Constabulary

Gwen Hulme: McLaren's sister

Dena Ellison: McLaren's girlfriend

Jamie Kydd: McLaren's friend and police detective, Derbyshire Constabulary

Neill McLaren: McLaren's grandfather

Brandon McLaren: McLaren's uncle

Karen Overton: Brandon's girlfriend

Jean MacNab: owner of Saltire Guest House,

Hurd Dowell: research librarian

Liza Skene: accident witness

Stuart Forbes: owner of Arthur's Seat Insurance Company

Lanny Clack: car mechanic

Fowler Ritchie: businessman

Frank Papadakis: Yank Army soldier in World War II

George Roper: British Army soldier in World War II

Tam Innes: British Army soldier in World War II

Ross Gordon: Constable, Central Scotland Constabulary, Stirling, Jamie's colleague

Charlie Harvester: former colleague of McLaren's, now a detective in the Derbyshire Constabulary

Words You May Find Unfamiliar

Balquhidder: village (actual) in Scotland, pronounced *BalWHIDder*

ben: mountain peak

brae: sloping river bank, a hill

burn: stream

close: small lane branching off a street

couldnae/didnae: could not/do not

dreich: drawn out, tedious, dreary (describing weather)

goldie: whisky

havenae: have not

heavy: a strong, dark traditional beer of Scotland (similar to the English 'bitter') sometimes written and referred to as 80/- which denotes the old currency system of 80 shillings. Beers were priced according to their strength, the lighter beers perhaps selling for 54/- up to 90/- per cask or barrel

Hogmanay: the Scottish celebration of New Year's Eve

kirk: church

lang: long

linn: a waterfall, pool of water at the base of a waterfall

loch: a lake

muckle: great, much

Saltire: the flag of Scotland, a white St. Andrew's cross on a blue field

Sassenach: Highlander for anyone "from the south"

shieling: a rough hut on summer grazing land in which shepherds, livestock tenders, and/or their families stayed for the season

sporran: type of purse/pouch worn with a kilt

wasnae: was not

wouldnae: would not

Chapter One

Dreams woke him that night. Not nightmares. Not exactly. More like flashes from his past. Mingled, as happens through the power of dreams, with foreshadowing of the future. Except he didn't know that yet.

Michael McLaren sat up in bed and threw off the duvet. November's chill had no affect on him; his fantasies consumed his attention as he stared into the darkness. Moonlight gilded the edge of the clock on his bedside cabinet and threw a shadow across the top of the furniture. The sweep second hand caught the light and accented the swift passage of time. Three fifteen. Halfway between night and morning, as far as he was concerned. Too early to get up and he was now too awake to lie down.

He sank against the headboard. The wood lay cool across his back. What had wakened him? He rubbed his forehead, uneasy, trying to remember. Something about the letter in the morning's mail, the invitation from his grandfather. That was real. But the dream took that and twisted it, turned the invitation into a funeral notice.

The transformation had frightened him. He had stared at the black-edged envelope as through gauze or in the distortion of a funhouse mirror. His breathing still came shallow and fast as he regained his sense of normalcy. Why would a letter hold such terror in his

1

dream? He took a deep breath, trying to slow his heart rate. Because he would soon be out of his comfort zone? Because he'd be seeing his grandfather for the first time in thirty-six years?

McLaren switched on the tableside lamp, got up, and rummaged about in the wardrobe. He found the family photo album and sat cross-legged on the bed as he leafed through the pages.

Photos of his mother and dad, smiling in their home in Auchtubh, Scotland, crammed the early part of the album. McLaren's uncle Brandon appeared in few pictures, away at school for most of his formative years. When he was older, he spent time on the Continent touring breweries. With McLaren's father out of the family business, the responsibility to grab the helm would eventually fall to younger son Brandon. So education and hopes were piled on Brandon with all the weight and solemnity of one of his university tomes.

Neill, McLaren's grandfather, stared from a few sepia-toned snaps, gruff-looking and Auld Scotland in his kilt, sporran, and tam o'shanter. In every photo a pipe stuck from the side of his mouth, spewing white smoke that at times hid part of his face. A dog—whether a terrier, setter, or deerhound—always appeared at his side.

Photos of outings and church plays came next, then suddenly stopped when his parents moved away.

He eased the book shut, the leather binding cracking and flaking, the pages angled at various degrees from the cover. It was a different world, that life in Scotland. He had no recollection of it, no warm feelings of connection. His grandfather was this old-time photograph, an image without a voice, a piece of

Jacobite Rebellion in the twenty-first century.

McLaren returned the album to the wardrobe, flipped off the bedroom light, and got into bed. He lay awake, watching the moon inch across the black sky and disappear behind the hills. The Pennines was his recollection of his childhood here in Derbyshire, forming part of his parents' property. The house had cradled and nurtured him until he'd left to make his own life. Now that he'd bought it, settled in it for his adult years, he felt the ties of this branch of the family. He was content in his part of England. Why even contemplate traveling up to Edinburgh to meet his grandfather, a sepia tone and a mere name? Because he was curious about the older man, had heard the stories of his childhood and wanted to see if they were true?

Because he wanted to accept the olive branch the man held out.

McLaren rolled onto his side and fell asleep, dreaming of a Scottish winter and a frigid drowning.

****

"You're a liar. I never sent for ye. And if I had, it wouldnae be to receive ye in my home. It'd be me standing on soil and you in a thistle patch." The elderly man paused to catch his breath, his face red, his green eyes throwing daggers. He bowed his head as a cough shook his body.

McLaren sensed that his grandfather hated the show of weakness. He didn't know much about the family, but he'd heard enough stories from his parents to know his grandfather'd been reared to emulate the Scottish chiefs and warriors of the past, the bravest of his brave clan. Yet as McLaren looked at him now he could see that age and illness reduced the man's stature.

And he probably hated that. Just as he hated anything that pulled him down to McLaren's level and handed him a one-upmanship that he couldn't change for all his desire and money.

When the spasm passed, the grandfather glared at McLaren, staring as though he saw a mirror image of himself fifty years ago—tall, muscular shoulders, thick blond hair. Now he was bent as a comma, with sparse white hair. The change must madden him.

McLaren stood erect, nearly at attention. His throat threatened to close, but he tried not to struggle for air. It would be a sign of weakness. "I don't mean to contradict you, Grandfather, but you did invite me. You mailed me a letter." He returned the slip of paper on which he'd written his grandfather's name and address to his jacket pocket, then fumbled for the piece of stationery. It wasn't there. He patted the pockets of his jeans, hating the display of forgetfulness and confusion. Another point for his grandfather.

"Tell me why I should have ye here." Neill McLaren's fingers clenched the edge of the front door. He leaned on it, as though it was a second cane, ignoring the December wind that whipped into the entryway. "Why I should break my oath and foul the air in my house with ye? It's enough that ye're tainting the village with your self. I'll not have ye contaminating the house of my family. Now, out with ye." Neill grabbed the doorframe and steadied himself with his walking stick as he struggled to stand straighter. The shock that he stood a head shorter than his grandson was obvious in his expression. Perhaps feeling disadvantaged, he sought the intimidation of volume. "Get ye gone now or I'll call your uncle to throw ye out."

McLaren's fingers slid over the lump in his back pocket. He drew out his wallet, opened it and removed the folded piece of paper. Smoothing it flat, he held it in front of Neill. "Here's the letter, Grandfather. And the envelope. See? Postmarked in Edinburgh. I wasn't making this up. You wrote it middle of last month, if you recall. Look." He stepped forward so Neill could see the handwriting.

"I've no need to look at it. It didnae come from me and it's not my handwriting. Ye've forged it, a skill ye no doubt perfected with your police job."

"But it was mailed in *Edinburgh*." McLaren's voice rose and he tapped on the envelope. "How could I have maneuvered that?"

"I dinnae know and I dinnae care. If ye dinnae leave my house—"

"Please, Grandfather. I don't know why you're saying you didn't invite me, but I came. A two hundred fifty mile train trip. I want to patch things up between us. I-I don't like this rift in our family and if I can heal things somehow, you've only to say."

Neill angled his head, his gaze directly falling on McLaren. "I've only to say, eh? I say for the last time, get out or I'll ring for the police. How will that look, do ye think? A copper arrested for trespassing." A hint of a smile flickered at the corners of his mouth before anger erased it.

"But you reserved my room at the bed-and-breakfast. I checked in yesterday afternoon. It was made in your name. Ring up the owner if you think I'm making this up."

Despite his obvious desire to end the conversation,

Neill paused. McLaren's voice held the urgency of wanting to be believed. "Where are ye staying?"

McLaren's tone lowered in pitch. Had he convinced the old man? It was easy enough to check out the reservation. "At Saltire Guest House. In Edinburgh."

Neill blinked. "I've not heard of the establishment name, but I give ye that it may exist."

Sensing a chink in Neill's armor, McLaren rushed on. "Would I have bought a train ticket and hired a car for some kind of joke? For what purpose? If I made this up, I'd know you hadn't booked the room for me. Or would see me. I traveled up here because I want to be part of your family again. That'd be the best Christmas gift I could ever receive."

Neill glanced outside. December settled over the village of Auchtubh in a smothering blanket of gray clouds and stinging cold wind. The hills, usually heather-covered and alive in green, purple, and pink, lay barren in outcroppings of rock and patches of early snow where the sun had not found them. A burst of wind rattled the wooden casement and stirred the edge of the curtain as it seeped into the neighboring room. Neill drew his woolen jumper closer about his neck.

McLaren tapped on the letter once again. "Then who did? It says in your letter—someone's letter—that you couldn't put me up due to that wing of the house having construction done on it. You stated that I shouldn't phone because Brandon usually answers and my visit was to be a surprise to him. You stated that the bed-and-breakfast room was paid for, I was to be your guest for the week and to email you in care of this email address so you'd know when to expect me." He pointed at the paragraph in question and held it steady so his grandfather could read it.

"I didnae call ye up north and I didnae book ye a room." The voice and stare matched the wintry wind's chill.

"Can't we talk, Grandfather? I've come all this way."

Neill turned slowly, his cane serving as the compass' spike and marking the center of his arc. He remained facing away from McLaren, his gaze on something beyond the window.

"For my father's sake," McLaren added, grasping at anything that might soften the older man. "Can't I talk to you for a bit?"

Neill's words bounced against the stone wall, sounding as hard as the man's resolve. "Get out, ye bloody Sassenach. Get out before I set the dog on ye."

Chapter Two

The drive back to the guesthouse contrasted sharply with the good humor and hope that filled McLaren on the journey up. He drove in silence, the radio and CD player turned off, the hum of the tires on the road echoing the questions that plagued him. It was unlike him not to sing in the car or at least listen to music. It was a part of him as much as his Scottish ancestry. Yet, music didn't interest him now. Any sad song would heighten his looming despondency.

He left the portion of the A90 hugging the Firth of Forth and turned onto the street leading to the guesthouse. The smell of approaching snow, unmistakable in the air, normally lightened his spirit. Right now it merely emphasized his anxiety. He had faith in the car he'd hired in Edinburgh—a metallic black Land Rover Defender with four-wheel drive— and knew he'd get around even if it did snow. But the darkening sky mirrored his darkening hope of visiting with his grandfather. Why such a turnabout in three weeks? Was the old man forgetful, or was he lying?

McLaren climbed the steps of the bed-and-breakfast, the cold air sharp in his lungs. The guesthouse sat a mile from the Royal Mile, the town center comprised of the stretch of the High Street and Cannongate bookended by the castle and Holyrood Palace. Clumps of snow and ice clung to the north side of buildings, lampposts, and tree trunks, remnants of last week's early snow. Most had melted and run off in cold trickles or lay in puddles on the pavement. Water dripped from eaves, splattering onto the concrete below or hitting pedestrians' heads and shoulders. Seagulls soared overhead and seemed not to mind the cold, taking it as a part of life. McLaren watched two birds fight for a discarded slice of bread on the pavement before hurrying inside.

The Saltire Guest House on Minto Street echoed its name, for the blue and white Scottish flag hung from the entryway's high ceiling. In case the visitor still did not associate the name of the national flag with the bed-and-breakfast, bunches of smaller flags crowded glass vases on the dining room sideboard and on a side table in the guest lounge. The common areas were painted sky blue with white woodwork, and photos of the flag in many events adorned the walls. Jean MacNab, the owner of the establishment, appeared to be fiercely proud of her country.

"You find your way, then, luv?" The female voice brought McLaren to a stop.

He turned on the stairs, quickly eyeing the two flights he had yet to climb, and nodded. He had no intention of sharing the catastrophe with a stranger, so he stuck to noncommittal replies. "Yes, thanks. Your directions were spot on."

"I hope you had a chance to stop at Callander. It's a lovely town. Those row houses are so classic. Did you pop into the fudge or the antiques shops?" Jean raised her eyebrows, and McLaren wondered if she expected an enthusiastic recital of the shops' merchandise. Her black hair and eyes caught a shaft of sunlight angling through the round window over the front door. Before she moved out of the light she looked younger than her forty-five years, for the blush in her cheeks showed clearly. Her hands, though, betrayed her middle age and the hard life of a guesthouse owner. Too many dishes to wash, bed linens to launder, and tile floors to scrub. Yet, she held herself straight, and she still had a spring to her step. Perhaps the hard work would betray her later.

"No. I didn't get a chance to stop this time."

"But you'll be returning, I'm guessing. What with your grandfather close by in Auchtubh, and you coming up to see him." She let the sentence dangle, as though hoping McLaren would fill her in on his itinerary. When he didn't respond, she picked up a brochure from the wooden rack near the front door. She crossed the floor and handed it to him. "You won't be with the old gentleman every minute of your stay, no matter how fond of him you are. If you've a mind to, here are a few suggestions of events and sights around the area. St. Giles Cathedral is worth a visit. Or, if you're not of a religious or architectural bent, there's the Scotch Whisky Heritage Center and the Writers' Museum. But perhaps you're the one for the outdoors. The Trossachs and the lochs can more than take up your week." She turned toward the door, as though she could see through the frosted glass inset. "You've the transport for it. I've seen your Defender. You doing a lot of off road exploration?"

McLaren nodded. The Trossachs, a wild yet beautiful spot where the Highlands and Lowlands met, was one of the more picturesque areas in Scotland. Rough hills and serene lochs epitomized romantic folk songs and poems. "I really don't know right now, Mrs. MacNab. My plans are quite flexible."

Jean straightened the stacks of brochures in the rack, squaring all the corners. Everything correctly in their place evidently was the motto for the house. "Aye, it's best to be that way. Fewer ulcers in the long run."

"I *am* interested, though, in the area around Auchtubh. The village of Balquhidder, in particular, and Balquhidder Station. I hear that's no longer a train depot, that it's been developed as accommodations for people on holiday. Is that correct? Seems a pity, if it is…about the discontinuance of the train, I mean."

"Aye. It closed in the mid sixties, I believe. I'm not that familiar with it, being as it's not really a tourist destination. Will you be wanting tea later?" She looked like she would run into the kitchen that moment and put the water on to boil.

"Better not count on me, Mrs. MacNab. I'm not sure where I'll be at four."

"Just as you like. Well, I'd best be getting on with my baking. Call out if you need anything."

He thanked her and climbed the stairs to his room.

He shut the door and leaned against it. The heavy wooden slab muted sounds of the vacuum cleaner and conversation of a couple talking on the landing. On top of the dresser the gentle tick of a wind-up clock faded under the sharp clicking of the radiator as it turned on. He resisted the urge to warm his hands on the heated surface, too emotionally tired to give up the door's support.

The room lay in a half-light, the sunlight from early morning long gone. McLaren looked around the space. Spartan seemed the best word to describe it. Or tired. Someone had chosen brown and orange for the color scheme: neither cheery nor restful. Two bedside cabinets sat along the sides of the twin beds, while a plastic wood-veneer wardrobe claimed the opposite wall. A small sink nestled in one corner, an equally small back splash across the back. Chairs were nonexistent. The electric kettle, teacups, packets of milk and sugar and teabags sat on a metal tray on the window seat.

The facility had probably been a closet before the fashion for en suite accommodations took over. The toilet was jammed between the sink and the shower. Worse than that, the seat had no lid, so items were in danger of falling into the open bowl. It was impossible to fully open the bathroom door; the edge of the sink stopped it. To access the sink and the towel rack beside it, McLaren had to squeeze through the door, close it, and then shuffle past the toilet to get to the sink. Standing a bit over six feet tall with broad, muscular shoulders, he wondered how a heavier person could manage. Perhaps all the rooms weren't as confined.

He slid out of his gray suede jacket, draped his tartan muffler over the back of a chair, and rolled up the sleeves of his blue shirt. The room was overly warm, close to stifling. He cracked the window open and stood there, breathing in the cold, crisp air, and looking down at the street. It was dressed with Georgian townhouses as far as he could see; all of the same tan stone; all three stories, with large windows peering out from the cupolas lining their roofs. Individuality asserted itself in the colors of the doorways and fences running along the pavement. Other than that, the smear of tan presented nothing extraordinary, hinted at no life inside. It was as if everyone were away at other guesthouses in other cities.

The sides of the curtains fluttered faintly, and he abandoned his fantasizing. He pressed his right palm against the windowpane, feeling the swirls of etched ice beneath his flesh. He withdrew it and ran his other hand over his palm, scraping off the flakes of frost. After brewing a cup of tea he returned to the window, sat on the window seat, and stared outside. His breath created foggy patches on the cold pane. Nothing made sense. Why would his grandfather invite him, pay for a room at the guesthouse, and then deny he'd done so? Had he changed his mind after he mailed the letter, regretting the olive branch he extended? Had someone else extended the invitation, either to aggravate Neill or to embarrass McLaren? But that meant both men had an enemy willing to do that, and the letter sender knew it.

McLaren slumped against the windowpane, his head pounding. The cold glass kept him focused on reality. It was easy to believe he was walking through a nightmare. All he needed was the appearance of the monster.

He shut his eyes, shifting his head position, his thumb massaging his forehead. Dena was good at doing this. He pictured her brown eyes smiling at him. Dena Ellison, his fiancée, who'd stayed with him during his years near hermitage, who waited patiently for him to make up his mind about marriage.

He sighed heavily as her image faded, then swallowed the last of his tea, yet held on to the cup. If someone had played a trick on Neill, why involve McLaren? Surely the prankster could've used someone nearer to Neill than McLaren. He lived in Derbyshire, a good two hundred fifty miles. A week's lodging at a guesthouse seemed an expensive joke.

But was it? Logic pointed out how daft that was just by common sense. No one targeted Neill; they were targeting McLaren.

Chapter Three

McLaren lunched at Oink, a small sandwich shop on Victoria Street in the Old Town of Edinburgh. He'd been aimlessly walking, thinking through the new scenario, when he saw the whole pig roasting in the window. It intrigued him, hinted at a different type of fast food, so he went in. The establishment was crowded with diners, but he got a place just as a man left his seat. While McLaren ate his pork and applesauce sandwich he scribbled his thoughts in his notebook.

He eliminated Neill as the focus of the prank. The older man hadn't been inconvenienced, just annoyed with seeing McLaren again. So that left himself as the butt of the joke.

But why and who would have set it up? The Edinburgh postmark guaranteed some local hand in this. So, who had the means and the motive to lure him to the city and make it look authentic?

McLaren took another bite of the sandwich but nearly choked on it as Charlie Harvester's grinning face hovered before him. Charlie Harvester, McLaren's former colleague when they worked for Staffordshire Constabulary in England. The sniveling whiner, the conniving Daddy's boy, incapable of making a career for himself, needing his father's high rank and tacit threats so son Charlie could make Inspector rank. And to make McLaren's life a misery.

He forced down the bite with a swallow of his drink. The years of frustration and envy over McLaren besting Harvester erupted one night on a case. Harvester arrested McLaren's friend, a seventy-year-old publican who defended himself, his wife, and his property from a burglar. The injustice of the situation so angered McLaren that he assaulted Harvester and resigned from the Force. Since then, the two men saw each other sporadically, were marginally polite. But McLaren never trusted Harvester, never forgot the underhanded tricks he pulled to gain the spotlight or his superior's praise. Using McLaren's grandfather as bait had some deeper purpose than a mere laugh.

But motive aside, it rested on the Edinburgh postmark. Did Harvester know anyone in Edinburgh who would do him that sort of favor? Could he have gone to Edinburgh to post it? That seemed far-fetched, though. Travel two hundred fifty miles to post a letter.

But Harvester had a colleague. Derek Parry, an inspector with the Lothian and Borders Police. They had worked on a case two years before McLaren left the job. They'd been quite chummy, even visiting each other on holidays. This letter prank seemed just the sort of thing Parry would do for cohort Harvester. He might not have known what he was posting. Harvester could've had someone write the note, enclosed it in a large envelope along with his own letter to Parry asking the colleague to pop it into a convenient letter box. Harvester could've told him anything about the letter; it wouldn't have made any difference to him.

Of course, Parry could've written the letter. McLaren wouldn't have known his handwriting any more than he knew his grandfather's hand. What might Harvester have told his cohort? That he was playing a joke? But was it? Was there something sinister behind it? Why bring him to Edinburgh? To involve him in a crime? If so, that meant setting something up and making absolutely certain McLaren was charged with the crime. Not impossible, but why do that in Scotland and not in England?

The speculation was getting him nowhere. Nothing made sense. Even if Harvester had done something like that, he'd want his hands on the reins, to be close by to oversee the operation.

McLaren pitched the sandwich wrapper into the trash bin, zipped his jacket, and left the shop. Victoria Street was crowded with workers and tourists, all seemingly eager to find lunch. He crossed to the Christmas shop. Someone'd had a brilliant idea, painting the shop front red. It screamed the holiday and its location in the neighboring facades of gray stone. Finding a spot out of the flow of the pedestrian crush, he opened his mobile phone. He turned his back, trying for a bit of privacy, and punched in Jamie's phone number. He'd barely had time to examine the shop window display of ornaments, snow globes, and nutcrackers before his friend answered.

"Mike." Jamie's voice sailed into McLaren's ear with a hint of surprise. "You're not home already, are you?"

"No. I'm still in Edinburgh."

"You meet up with your grandfather? How'd it go?"

McLaren exhaled slowly. It wasn't that he minded giving Jamie a play-by-play of what had transpired.

Lord knows the two of them had done that often enough in their men's nights out and poker games. Shared over a pint at the local or while either man helped the other with some physical labor. Jamie and McLaren had been best mates since childhood, had gone through police school together, had worked their first year after graduation in Staffordshire Constabulary. It'd been a learning year for them both, with numerous phone calls and discussions over meals. Then Jamie transferred to Derbyshire Constabulary in Buxton, and McLaren felt as though he was stumbling through the darkness. They still were best buddies, still downed a pint and fished, but the immediacy of advice was missing.

He waited until a group of chattering teenagers passed before he spoke again. "Where are you?"

"Where am I? You in trouble?" The question wasn't flippant. McLaren frequently had run-ins with less than cooperative witnesses and suspects. Although he wasn't investigating a case in Scotland, that didn't preclude him from ending up in some situation that called for Jamie's help. "Why'd you ask? What's going on?"

"Everything's just smashing. I'm over the moon."

"Yeah? I've heard better lies from first time offenders. Something's wrong, Mike. What?"

McLaren related the morning's scene at his grandfather's front door, pausing frequently for Jamie's expressive comment, and added his suspicion about Harvester planning it as a joke.

"He's the type who thinks a rubber crutch is hysterical." Jamie's voice grew bitter.

"That and unscrewing the cap on the salt cellar. I think I've been set up. That's why I rang you."

"Sounds rather odd, I admit. As you said, who'd play that type of joke on you?"

"And, as I said, where are you? Can you talk without being overheard?" McLaren envisioned the station's open room of desks, the close working conditions, the police constables and sergeants walking around. He'd worked in similar environments; everything said bounced off the walls and into everyone's ears.

"Sure. I'm walking to my car."

"You just finishing up your day?" He glanced at his watch. One o'clock wasn't the normal time to start or end a shift.

"No. I'm on my way to interview a witness. What can I help with? I assume that's why you rang me."

"Can you give me Harvester's work and home phone numbers?"

"Are you serious?"

"Better yet," McLaren said, not wanting to be that close to Harvester, even if it was only the man's voice, "could *you* ring him?"

"Sure, but what's this in aid of?"

"I've a feeling Harvester's behind it all. I don't think he's here, but I want to make sure."

"Seeing him in a dark alley isn't my idea of a delightful surprise either, Mike."

"It won't eliminate his hand in setting it up, but at least I'll know if I should expect to see him at the guesthouse or on the street. Can you do it now and ring me?"

"Give me a minute. I'll call you right back."

"You better. If you don't get an answer, ring up the local Edinburgh nick. I'll probably be there."

Which wasn't far from the truth, McLaren thought as he rang off. But he stood there, his mind conjuring a dozen scenarios. If Harvester had engineered the elaborate hoax, the reason was either to ridicule or devalue him. To make his name a laughing stock, a person who could never be trusted again. If that happened, McLaren's job of delving into cold cases would dry up, along with the accompanying fees. Worse than that, the idea suddenly frightened him. He'd lose the dry stone wall work. He'd have nothing coming in, nothing on which to live.

Yes, Harvester could've arranged the hoax. He had the hatred, the pent-up frustration, and the connections to set the scheme in motion. But if anything went wrong, Harvester's involvement could be exposed, and that would end *his* police career. Even if McLaren bested Harvester during all their work years, it couldn't still be bothering Harvester, could it?

McLaren let his head fall against the wall and shut his eyes. His head pounded. The whole thing would be difficult to set up if Harvester were in England. But who said he was?

McLaren opened his eyes and stared at nothing in particular. Sights and sounds whirled in front of him. Best to wait until Jamie called back; then he'd know what to pursue.

He nodded and slipped the phone into his jeans pocket. Jamie would get the information or die trying. Even though McLaren constantly warned Jamie about researching and emailing information on police cases, his friend kept doing it. Anything to give a hand up for justice. "After all," he'd say, "it's for the victim's good and doesn't hurt anyone but the criminal." So he continued to hunt down facts so McLaren could hunt down the offender. Jamie was like that—diligent, trusty, single-minded. A loyal friend who'd not hesitate to risk his life for McLaren. Sounded rather like a Boy Scout. McLaren allowed himself a smile. Or a faithful dog. Jamie had always come through. The situation at the moment wasn't a case, he reminded himself. But Jamie wouldn't work any less hard to supply the data.

But the help went beyond research. Jamie had an uncanny knack of showing up when McLaren was in physical trouble: lying unconscious on the ground or outnumbered in a fight. Jamie's sixth sense about McLaren had proven true time and time again and it wasn't confined to police work. During a fishing trip, Jamie woke in the night, sensing something was wrong. He evacuated them from the angry, swollen river lapping at the door of their tent. Career and life saving tends to bond people for life, yet McLaren knew that was all secondary; they were best mates without the drama.

McLaren wandered up the hill and turned onto The Hub. He paused, briefly considering touring the Scotch Whisky Heritage Center. Jean MacNab had suggested it, but he wasn't in the mood. He walked to the Lawn Market and turned right, following the street to the corner of George IV Bridge. St. Giles Kirk loomed ahead in its creamy-colored stone glory, but he kept walking along Bridge Street, finally stopping near a bus queue. Trash seemed to be everywhere: cigarette butts, wine bottles, Styrofoam cups, paper bags, candy wrappers, plastic straws, newspapers. Most were wet from the melting snow and lay in a near-shapeless mass in the puddles. Several dogs were tied by their leads outside shops; men stood in doorways and closes, smoking.

Tucked between the multi-story tan stone buildings of commerce and government were tourist meccas of tartan, Scottish gifts, and entertainment. An array of posters announced ghost tours, bus tours, literary tours, history tours, architecture tours, castle tours... The queue at the bus stop grew and reshaped itself into a lazy J shape. McLaren shifted his gaze from a poster to a woman beside him, her face barely visible above the thick plaid muffler encircling her neck.

"Excuse me." He gestured toward the poster advertising The Real Mary Kings' Close. "Is that interesting, do you know?"

"The Close?" The red-haired woman nodded. "It is, if you like history, dark places, and being underground. I would add my usual joke about that all describing the residents of Greyfriars Kirkyard, but I won't. I don't want to scare away a tourist."

"Greyfriars...is that the haunted cemetery, and the one where the dog is buried?"

"Yes. I have some information on it, if you'd like to read about it." She dug into her handbag and passed him the brochure. "The information about the Kirkyard is included in there, since the pamphlet is on Old Town. I don't normally walk around with these things, but I had it to mail to a friend."

"I don't want to take it, then."

"Nonsense. I can get another."

"Please, I'm uncomfortable about taking it away from your friend."

"Then we'll do this." She tore off the lower corner, handed it to him and took back the brochure. "That's the info on Greyfriars' goings-on. I'll send the rest of the Old Town info to her. Feel better?"

McLaren laughed and slipped the printed material into his pocket. "Your friend won't wonder about the pamphlet's odd look?"

"I'll explain it in the letter. But she would never go there, so she won't mind the kirkyard's exclusion."

"Well, thank you. Now I've got two spots to explore, if I do the Close."

"You thinking of touring it, then?"

"I've got a free day. Just wondered if it was worth my time and cost of admission."

She smiled and tapped her handbag. "I can't answer about the money 'cause I don't know either the price of the ticket or the worth you place on your wallet. But I'd say it was worth your time."

"Have you toured it?"

"No. But I'll get around to it one o' these days."

"Spoken like a native of any city. We never act like tourists in our own patch. How old is the Close?"

"That I don't know. You'll find out on the tour, I'm sure. But you can ask Hurd. He's a walking encyclopedia."

A gray-haired man standing near the woman turned slightly and looked at McLaren. He seemed to be nothing but gray, dressed in a gray, mid-calf length overcoat, darker gray trousers and shoes, and a gray peak cap. "Normally she refers to me as something a bit less complimentary, but I'll accept that. I'm Hurd Dowell. This is Liza, by the way." He nodded at the woman.

McLaren introduced himself and shook hands with the man. "I admit I know nothing about the Close other

23

than the bit I heard just now. It sounds fascinating."

Hurd smiled. "Aye, it is."

"You can thank Liza for firing my imagination."

"She's missed her calling. She should've been a novelist or a tour guide."

"Look who's talking," Liza said. "I've heard some of the yarns you've woven. You've nothing to be ashamed of in the storytelling department. I keep saying he should be a guide for one of the city's walking tours, like the ghost walk or the Close, but he complains he'll not have the time." She looked at Hurd, as though sizing him up for a suit fitting. "You'll be retired in four months. What's going to consume your hours?"

"Pay her no heed, Mr. McLaren," Hurd said. "She's always hustling some project or cajoling us to do something. We work in the same library, by the way. But to answer your question, the Close dates from the 1600s, I believe. It was home for hundreds of people in the middle ages, and continued in that capacity until the early 1900s."

McLaren blinked, surprised by the information. "I just heard of it on the telly, since I've been up here. There's something about people living underground, right?"

"Yes. Edinburgh, as you may have discovered, is built on an incredibly steep hill." As though tired from the walk, he shifted his briefcase to his other hand. "It was also a walled city. As the population increased, there was no place for people to build homes but upwards, if they wanted to live within the protective walls. Dwellings were built stacked on top of previous ones so that skyscrapers developed to around fourteen stories."

"And we think skyscrapers are a modern invention."

"What's the saying? Everything old is new again?" Hurd winked at Liza. "Imagine medieval, cramped, narrow streets…then imagine fourteen stories' height to these buildings. Hardly any sunlight would fall to ground level. Must've been dreadfully gloomy."

McLaren was about to reply when his mobile rang. He excused himself and turned slightly as he answered his phone.

"Mike. It's Jamie."

"Did you talk to Harvester?"

"I tried his home first. He didn't answer so I rang up his office. Same thing there. He didn't answer. Then I rang the station, thinking he might be out and they'd know his work schedule."

"Good news or bad news?"

"For you, bad, I'm afraid. Harvester's on holiday all this week."

"And it's Monday." He rubbed his forehead, trying to make sense of the whole thing. Which he couldn't. Harvester had never acted rationally about anything, at least not the occasions when the two of them had been thrown together. Discounting their classic run-in that led to McLaren's job resignation, McLaren really couldn't fathom the man. What thinking would prompt Harvester to focus on one suspect only and ignore the others despite evidence to the contrary? Why would Harvester use the desk phone at a murder scene, possibly destroying fingerprints? Why disregard a CCTV video of a suspect buying a possible murder weapon, or look through a vehicle without a search warrant? Or use his personal mobile phone to photograph the crime scene—which, technically speaking, made the phone police property. "He could've come up as I did, on the train this past weekend. He still could've set up everything and be here, waiting to implement the next phase."

"*Next* phase? How many parts to it are there? What do you think he's going to do next?"

McLaren grimaced and shook his head. "I haven't the bloodiest idea. Maybe I'm making too much of it all. Maybe Harvester's not involved. But someone had to have arranged everything. I can't see my grandfather breaking his silence, inviting me up here, then deciding this morning that he didn't want to see me. He's had thirty years to think about the reunion. If he really wanted to welcome me into the fold, he wouldn't do such an abrupt about-face."

"He might. You don't really know him, do you?"

"Well, no. But it seems odd."

"Odd to you, but it could be in character with him. You don't know if he does that stuff all the time or not. Abruptly change his mind, I mean."

McLaren admitted it could be true.

"Just be careful. Watch your back, Mike."

He rang off assuring Jamie he'd be cautious. "Sorry for the interruption," he said to Hurd. "You were telling me about the Close."

"You're interested, then." Hurd's eager expression spoke of his delight at finding a kindred spirit.

"Yes."

"Of course, I am, but it sort of comes with the territory. I'm a research librarian. I tend to yammer on when I get talking on favorite subjects."

Liza squeezed his arm. "You're always saying you

have underground connections and I believe it. The details you know about the Close...one would think you lived there."

Hurd laughed. "The underground is a different way of life. It was hard for them to escape once they were thrown into that culture. Just as hard for anyone doing it today. Era makes no difference. People are people and situations don't really change." He shrugged, the humor gone from his eyes. "Some look at it as an out, a place to hide from the law. Whether you view it as a criminal haven or a community of poor people doesn't matter much. They were still trapped."

"Sounds as though the cycle of poverty hasn't altered much."

"It has its advantages, just as it has its disadvantages. But it's who you hang around with that really decides your life, don't you think?" He looked at McLaren, expecting an answer. When McLaren shrugged, Hurd held up his hand. "Sorry. I put you on the spot. Didn't mean to bore you."

"On the contrary. You've just made my decision for me. Is the Close open today?"

"Seven days a week, I believe. But I don't know their hours. Still, it should be open—"

McLaren yelled, cutting off Hurd's sentence. A car broke from the line of traffic, aimed at them. McLaren grabbed Liza's arm and pulled her with him as he dodged left. Shouts and screams rose above the groans of bus and car motors, the yapping of excited dogs and shrieking of seagulls. A confusion of running bodies and ear-splitting noise seemed to smother him as the scenario played out in slow motion. Later, he recalled the cacophony of honking car horns, but no screeching brakes. The car appeared to ram into the crowd, oblivious to anything in its path. As Hurd fell to McLaren's right, McLaren wrapped his arms around Liza, pulling her farther to the left. The car jerked to the right, hesitated briefly as the driver straightened the wheel, then zoomed down the street, its roaring engine underscoring the higher pitched yells.

Chapter Four

"The driver hesitated," McLaren explained, watching the police officer take notes. The ambulance arrived; Hurd Dowel's body had been taken to the morgue, the street area cordoned off, and photographs taken. Curious people bunched in small groups at shop doors and near the bus shelter. Several officers kept them back from the scene while others rerouted traffic.

Officers still interviewed others at the scene. Their chartreuse-colored slickers stood out boldly among the more somber-clad civilians and reflected in the puddles of melted snow. A yellow-and-blue checkered police vehicle drove up, parked near the bus stop, and two officers got out and melted into the contingent of other police, the handcuffs on their black belts catching the sunlight.

A young female constable nodded to one of the new arrivals, then adjusted her black hat more firmly on her head before slipping out of the corralled area and following them. The majority of onlookers jockeyed for best vantage point; something big was obviously about to happen and the murmurs increased in volume.

McLaren exhaled loudly. Nothing much changed, no matter where one was.

He shifted his gaze from the blinking blue lights and tried to recall where he'd been standing, just when he became aware of the car. He confessed to the officer the entire event took mere seconds, that he'd thought only of grabbing Liza and diving out of the car's path. "I have the impression he was looking for something, and took his foot off the accelerator for an instant. And if he had slowed, I should be able to give you his description, but I can't. The whole thing's a blank." He admitted it frankly but slowly, embarrassed and mad. He'd had his moment; he'd seen the vehicle and driver. Why couldn't he conjure an image in his mind? He exhaled heavily, nearly overcome with frustration. While a police detective, he'd interviewed hundreds of witnesses; now the role was reversed and he was astonished to find his memory shaky.

The officer sympathized and told him to contact the police station if he later remembered anything.

He said he would and watched the officer move on to another witness. McLaren found it interesting, yet slightly surreal. How many times had he mimicked the officer's actions and words when he was in the job? How often had he muttered under his breath that witnesses were nearly useless because their observations weren't quick enough. And now he was doing the same thing, feeling the same disappointment and failure as police officers and witnesses did. Like viewing himself in another dimension and another time.

Like seeing himself go through it in slow motion.

Which, in McLaren's mind, the driver of the hit-and-run car appeared to do. Odd that he had no clear impression of the person behind the wheel. He'd been a trained police officer; he should have been a better witness. The realization that he had failed tore at his ego. Had it been a fluke that he was a good witness? Was it different when it pertained to him as a civilian?

McLaren jammed his fist into his pocket to stop his hand from trembling. The significance shouted at him, laughed in his head, taunted him. Maybe he wasn't the blue-eyed boy his colleagues and mates had led him to believe. Maybe he was as fallible as anyone. As Harvester.

The comparison to his adversary stopped his breath. His throat closed up and he stared past the crime scene tape, not seeing the crowd or hearing the confusion of noises. Harvester had climbed the career ladder through trickery and knowing the right people. He hadn't failed but he hadn't soared with accomplishments. He'd achieved what McLaren had, though more slowly and with greater difficulty. No. McLaren shook his head and unclenched his fist. He wasn't like Harvester. Even failing now as a witness, he wasn't like Harvester.

He waited while Liza finished her statement to the police, then escorted her to her residence, a two-story stone house that blended with the others lined up on Cluny Gardens. She insisted she was physically fine, even if she was still shaken from her near miss. "I have great faith in my guardian angel, Mr. McLaren," she said.

He believed her, for her voice was steady and the color hadn't drained from her cheeks. Still, he brewed a pot of tea for her, wrote his name on one of his business cards before handing it to her, and insisted she phone if she needed to talk. "I can come over or meet you some place if the personal presence is required. I'm not that far away. The Saltire Guest House on Minto. I'll be over in the time it takes to brew a cuppa." He smiled, hoping he'd convinced her he could be trusted, that he cared. "You don't have to suffer through this…alone."

"Thanks. For some reason, that helps just knowing you're available. Why that is, I couldn't tell you. It's not like you're my best friend. I don't know you."

"Maybe it's realizing you're not in this alone. There's a great comfort in experiencing upheavals and tragedy with someone."

"That's true, but there's something about you. Dependability, strength, integrity…" She flushed and cast her gaze downward. "It sounds so sappy when voiced, but you've a moral strength about you, something that speaks of absolute trust and help."

"I was a police officer, if that explains it."

"It does. But you were more than a bobby, I think. Not that there's anything wrong with being a bobby. But you have an air of making decisions and directing."

"My best mate is a bobby, so I agree there's nothing wrong with the rank. I was a detective-inspector."

She nodded, returning her gaze to his face. "You still carry that with you. You must've loved your work very much, Mr. McLaren."

He took a swallow of tea, not wanting to open the story of his resignation from the force, and said he hoped his former job wouldn't stop her from ringing him up if she wanted to talk.

"Not at all. But I still can't believe any of it." She leaned forward, resting the teacup on her thigh. She seemed impervious to the heat of the china, as though all she could feel was her grief. "All I see is Hurd and that car. It was—" She broke off, turning her head so he couldn't see the tears in her eyes.

"I know." McLaren handed her a facial tissue. "It

was a hell of a thing to happen." He eyed her as she nodded and faced him again. "Can I phone someone to stay with you? A friend or relative?"

She shook her head and forced a smile. "I'll be fine. It's just the shock, the rapidity of the whole thing. You know."

"Yeah. Bloody awful way to die."

"The worst thing is I can't remember anything about the car." Her voice quivered and she grabbed the arm of her chair. It was modern and sleek, as was the other furniture in the room. Black, lime green, and silver. Solid splashes of color against white walls. Uncluttered surfaces for an uncluttered life. Her muffler was the only incongruous item there, the tartan's bright colors of red, green, and blue stating her link with a long ago Highland life. "It came right at us and I don't remember what it looked like. How can I not remember?" Her voice broke as tears streamed down her cheeks. "How can I help the police find Hurd's killer if I can't remember anything about the car?" She dabbed at her eyes and looked at McLaren. "Do you recall the car?"

"No. I'm angry that I don't."

"I guess it all happened too fast." She nodded slightly and averted her gaze to her hands. "Like deer in the headlights. I don't mean to sound flippant…sorry."

"I didn't take it that way. But I think it's true. We stared at it without it registering on our consciousness. I won't be surprised if someone has a video of it, taken on their smart phone. Even if they don't turn it in to the police, it'll pop up somewhere on the internet. Everything of a sensational nature seems to, eventually." He leaned forward, looking as though he would take her hand, but merely clasped his hands and rested his forearms on his thighs. "Maybe we'll recall something later, when we're over the initial shock—"

"Sure. We'll remember then." She said it slowly, half-heartedly, as though she were repeating a poem she'd memorized or learning a mantra she didn't really accept. Or reassuring him in order to convince herself. "I don't know what the driver looked like, either. I suppose it's the same reason I can't remember him, I mean."

"Don't force it, Liza. From what I've always heard, it'll come back. It's bound to."

"Like in the middle of the night or when you're doing something else. Yes." She gave him a half smile and leaned back in her chair. The sunlight fell on her face and McLaren saw the redness in her eyes and the wet streaks down her cheeks. They were the only flaws in her otherwise china-smooth skin. "But I've got to remember! I can't let the driver get away with this! Hurd was such a brilliant man, so talented. It's indecent he's killed and no one knows who did it."

"There were too many people there for him to escape detection. We can't recall any descriptions because we were so closely involved in it. But people standing farther away, on the edge of the crowd, may've seen something that will prove beneficial. Don't give up hope just yet. It's just happened."

"I can't help but think I might've been lying there instead of Hurd." Liza shook her head and moved slightly. The sunlight fell on a small brooch. It looked to be a clan crest badge. He could just make out an arm, the cloud where the shoulder should be. The hand held a crown. The clan Skene. She shifted and the badge slipped into the shadows. "Thank you again for pulling me out of the way, Mr. McLaren."

"I was lucky. Anyone would've done that. And our experience was a bit too personal for you to keep calling me Mr. McLaren. My name's Mike."

"Thank you. The point is, Mike, *you* did it. I'm not likely to forget your bravery."

"We were both lucky, then."

She looked around the room, her eyes holding the vacant stare that comes with concentrating on something else. Her gaze rested just to McLaren's left, as though something on the other side of the window fascinated her.

He turned, wanting to know what held her attention. Nothing presented itself but a vacant street and bare-branched trees.

"I suppose I should call someone at work." Her voice sounded flat and mechanical. Perhaps she couldn't think, McLaren reasoned. She grimaced and avoided his gaze. "You know. Let our boss know what happened to…" Her hand went to her forehead, as though it could stop the pounding of her headache. "It's unreal. Hurd and I were just talking together. He'd just shown me his latest photographs last Friday."

"Photos?"

"Yes. A hobby of his. Nature and landscape things. They're quite nice. He'd been to the Trossachs the previous weekend and took…" She exhaled slowly and looked at McLaren, perhaps aware she was rambling, aware she was about to become hysterical. But talking helped, not only to release her emotions but also to make sense of the tragedy. "As I told the police, Hurd lived alone. He was divorced, no children. Still, that doesn't make him less mourned, does it?"

"Not at all. His friends will certainly miss him."

Liza nodded, her expression blank. Perhaps she hadn't really taken in McLaren's words, the grief numbing her to everything but her own thoughts. "We worked together for little over a year. At Charles II Library. He was senior research librarian. I just came on staff." She took a sip of tea, holding it as an anchor in this nightmare. "He was working on a large project. I don't know who'll get it now."

"Were you working on it with him? Might you oversee it?"

She stared at her fingers gripping the cup. The knuckles were white. "It'd be nice to think so, but I doubt it. I haven't the experience."

"And the project calls for experience? You can't just look up information?"

"I don't know. Hurd worked in private sometimes. Other times he'd ask me for help. I don't know what our boss will do."

"It's from an important client, then."

"I never heard. A man would come in weekly to confer with Hurd and see how the work was going. But I don't know his company or business."

"If it's that important, your boss will probably request that you continue on it. You know a bit about it and he wouldn't want to break the continuity. Someone new would have to be brought up to speed."

She nodded and set the cup on the side table. "He had smaller projects. Perhaps I'll get one of those. Not that they were all confined to business hours. He'd work on some during his off hours. You know. Any extra income is nice."

"Smaller projects...like what?"

"Oh, individuals or civic groups would hire him to work on things in his free time. He'd just finished a current job and was about to tackle one for Mary King's Close. Something about digging into a particular aspect of the place's history. Maybe it was a resident of the Close, like Robert Fergusson."

"The poet?"

"Yes. You know of him?"

"Just that he influenced Robert Burns."

"It's things like that, history of people, that Hurd liked to work on outside his normal job hours. He was quite good at it, and he was well known among the city."

"He'll be sorely missed by many people."

Liza sighed heavily and blotted her eyes. "I hope the police catch that maniac. They have to put him in jail, make him pay for what he did. He didn't even stop after...what he did. He knew he hit someone. Couldn't help but know, with all of us at that bus stop. And he didn't even stop to help." She wiped her cheeks but her eyes still glistened with tears. "Do you think the police will find him?"

McLaren hesitated. She wanted assurance and comfort, wanted a storybook ending. How could he guarantee the car driver would be caught and convicted? He flashed a smile and patted her hand. "They took our statements, Liza. They talked to everyone else there, people at the bus stop, pedestrians, and shopkeepers. They'll get the thing pieced together."

"I suppose so. Hopefully the CCTV cameras caught it. They can get the car plate number from that, I guess."

"That will help, of course. Try not to worry. I know it's easy for me to say it, but the police can work miracles."

"Sometimes, yes." She nodded, as if controlled by a puppeteer.

McLaren glanced at his watch. The afternoon was slipping by. "Well, if you're sure you'll be all right on your own…"

His words seemed to snap her out of her reverie. She smiled, wiped her cheeks again, and nodded. "Perfectly fine. I'll be right as rain tomorrow. Or the next day."

"You'll keep in touch, let me know how you're getting on?" He meant it purely in regard to her health and hoped she didn't take it incorrectly.

"I'll ring you daily with my progress. Cross my heart and swear on a stack of Bobbie Burns poems." She smiled but he felt the sincerity beneath her jest. "Thanks for taking an interest in my wellbeing."

"Things can develop later. Things you're not expecting. It's best to have…someone you can report to on a regular basis." He left unsaid in case she suffered from a concussion or other life-threatening event.

"I won't forget. Every morning until I'm my old self again." She got up and escorted him to the door. "And thanks for being so thoughtful and seeing me home. The police didn't seem to—"

"The police were busy with the scene. They hadn't time to—" He stopped, aware he almost said they hadn't time to babysit emotional witnesses. He'd come close to losing his emotions, too. But fear hadn't threatened to engulf him as it had Liza. Anger gripped him, and he had difficulty shaking it off. Not only from the senseless violent act but also from the disturbing suspicion that the driver had meant to kill him. McLaren took a deep breath and continued. "The police hadn't time to see to anyone other than the victim. He's top priority. It was nothing personal."

But as he left the house, he thought it was personal. Besides the lack of squealing brakes, the car had left no tire skid marks. The driver seemed to change direction as McLaren dodged, aiming straight for him.

****

He took a taxi to Blackwell's, a bookshop on South Bridge in Old Town Edinburgh. South Bridge, the northern end of the A7, was a section of a main artery that changed names through the city. He had a cup of coffee and a sandwich downstairs in the shop's café, an airy space separating two sections of the building. Light conversation and aromas of warm bread and soup filled the air, and McLaren found himself relaxing and thawing from the chill that stiffened his body. People around him chatted or read, and he jotted a few things in his notebook. Although situated in a popular store, the café gave the feeling of an independent establishment, for it sat in a corner of the bookshop, several steps below the main floor level, several steps above the neighboring section. Perfect for a relaxing meal or perusing a book purchase. He preferred the store's environment and busyness to his lone room at the guesthouse.

It had just gone five o'clock, several hours after Hurd Dowell had been killed, but already the television newscasts carried the news; the video of police statements and witness concern played out on the telly above the food counter. The newspapers no doubt would have an article about it.

McLaren finished his meal and browsed through the books on local travel. He chose one on the Trossachs, determined to stay a few more days and see the area, and left the store.

Outside the streets were dark and choked with workers and shoppers making their way home or perhaps to an after-work event. Evening settled at four o'clock at this time of year, giving the wintry landscape more hours of frosty temperatures. He ignored the urge to catch a bus or taxi, and walked back to the guesthouse, his shoes crunching on the re-freezing puddles of water and cracking them into shards. The patches of snow still clinging to the northern sides of the roofs stood out in ghostly contrast to the dark surroundings, the streetlamps' glow throwing amber-colored orbs onto the puddles uncovered by other feet. Great clouds of frozen breath rose briefly before dissipating into the black night. Ahead of him, rooftop high, the moon shone intensely, illuminating the edges of the neighboring clouds.

Minto Street appeared to be wrapped in sleep. No cars traveled the artery; no pedestrians strolled along the pavement. He glanced at the windows of the townhouses as he passed, curious to see if the inhabitants were still up. Several rectangles glowed with yellow light but no black silhouettes implied residents within. There were enough dark areas along the street to imply people were elsewhere.

He pushed open the wrought iron gate of Saltire Guest House, aware of the resistance of the rusty hinges, and eased it shut behind him. The catch clanked firmly and echoed sharply against the building's face.

Someone had cleared the pavement to the front door during his absence, the concrete merely damp now. Clumps of snow still snuggled against the house foundation in spots, but the soil was nearly free. He wiped his shoes on the doormat, walked into the residence, and up to his room.

He sat on the window seat, busying himself with the book he'd bought, making a list of potential things he'd see in the next few days. Then he made a similar list of places in Edinburgh. At six o'clock he turned on the telly for the news. The hit-and-run was the second story.

The police had the car number plate information, attained from a CCTV camera, but they appealed to the public for help in identifying the driver. The car, a Ford Kuga SUV, midnight blue, had been stolen, and the car's owner had an alibi that cleared him of any involvement in the incident. In fact, Stuart Forbes, owner of Arthur's Seat Insurance Company, had recently bought the car and was shocked at his car's involvement. A photo of the driver showed a man probably in his early twenties, with dark hair and mustache, wearing a dark-colored jacket with a skull design. Anyone having information about the driver... McLaren clicked off the set.

There it was again: the man behind the wheel and he had fostered as much recognition as a blank sheet of paper. McLaren had stared at the television screen when the CCTV still photo came on, had looked at the mustache and the hair as he tried to recall if he'd seen it around the city before the incident. But nothing had flashed across his mind.

He gave up forcing a recognition, exhaled sharply,

and threw the television remote onto the other bed. Nothing connected. Not the face or the car or even the reason for the mishap. Had the police accepted it as a hit-and-run, a tragic accident? Had the driver been ill, drunk, or on drugs, as sometimes happens, and was scared to turn himself in? Had he just got his driving license and feared that he'd lose it? The newscast hadn't mentioned alcohol, drugs, or a possible medical condition, but it wouldn't until police could find the driver. Still, the car had come at him, Hurd, and Liza straight enough. If the driver hadn't had a seizure or been unable to distinguish the crowd at the bus stop, perhaps that's what would happen.

McLaren cursed the situation and the driver's disappearance, and brewed a cup of tea.

Of course the car was stolen, he thought. Expressly to run him down. But was he the target? He'd thought so earlier, yet perhaps Hurd Dowell's research fingered him as the intended victim after all. Which would mean that Hurd's project was important. But important to whom? And enough to kill him? Which meant some rival company, if that were correct.

McLaren sipped his tea, his long legs propped on the edge of his bed. It didn't quite add up. If the project were that sensitive, why take it to an outside, public source for research help? Why not hire someone and have the work done at the firm?

He leaned his head against the windowpane and shut his eyes. Faint sounds from the street seeped into the room and mingled with the sounds of the car incident. Nothing made sense, not his grandfather's invitation, not Hurd as intended victim. He opened his eyes, his gaze falling on his wallet. He'd given one of his cards to Liza, telling her to phone him. She'd mentioned Hurd's hobby of photography. Was he well known? Could that be connected to his death?

McLaren thumbed through the Edinburgh phone book, found Liza's number, and rang her up. After a dozen rings and no answer, he rang off.

He finished the tea and rinsed out the cup. He flipped open his notebook, grabbed a pen, and punched Jamie's phone number into his mobile. Seconds later Jamie answered.

"Mike. Two calls in the same day. I thought you were on holiday to leave all the dreary daily grind behind."

"If wishes were horses," he began, doodling in his notebook.

"So what can I do this time? I assume that's why you rang me up."

"You still semi matey with that constable in Central Scotland Constabulary?"

"Don't tell me. You're in the nick and want me to pull strings. What did you do? No, don't tell me. Ignorance is bliss and I'd like to sleep tonight. Anyway, I didn't think you were there on a case. Something happen?"

"Something happened." McLaren related the hit-and-run incident, ignoring Jamie's sporadic exclamations. "You never told me your cohort's name. I need to talk to him."

"Why? You've no authority in Scotland, Mike. Leave the investigation to the police."

"I will. I just need to ask a question. Now, your mate's name, Jamie."

Jamie knew when he was beat. "I think I better ring

him up. He'll talk more readily to me than to a private party."

"Are you really going to phone him, or is this just a way to get out of it?"

"Daft question. When have I ever let you down?"

"All right. You've got me."

"You're not in any trouble, are you, Mike?"

"Not that I know. Other than disturbing my grandfather's peace."

"What do you want to know?"

"If they have a name for the driver of that car."

"Tell me you're not going to hunt him down."

"You've got my promise. But don't forget I have a personal interest in this, Jamie. I could've been killed, too."

"What makes you think it's anything other than an accident? The victim wasn't specifically targeted, was he?"

"Not that I know of. But he was doing some research on a big project, and—"

"And you're envisioning spies and gangs and underworld schemes. Drop it, Mike. You'll live longer. You'll also be welcomed back if you return to Scotland. Your face looks bad enough in the flesh. I don't want to see it on a wanted poster."

"I don't know what your wife means when she says you have a sense of humor. Look, I'll be fine. Just ring up your mate and ask him that one question. I swear I won't even show myself at the police station."

"It's not the station I'm worried about. It's those people standing with you at the bus stop."

"Ring me tomorrow when you've talked to him." McLaren hung up and phoned his sister.

Gwen was twelve years older than he, so probably remembered their grandfather. McLaren waited impatiently while the phone rang, doodling on his sightseeing list.

"Hello?" Gwen's voice burrowed into his ear.

"Gwen, it's Mike."

"You decided not to go to Scotland?"

"I'm in Scotland."

"Grandfather's house?"

McLaren snorted and walked over to the window. A bus labored up Minton Street and past the guesthouse in an exhale of engine exhaust. A dog walker ambled down the pavement, the end of his cigarette glowing red whenever he took a puff. "In my dreams." He told her about the encounter, aware he sounded tired. "You were fourteen when we moved to Derbyshire. Is his behavior in character with him? Do you remember what he was like?"

Silence greeted him and he could imagine Gwen on the sofa, her legs curled beneath her, coffee mug in her free hand. He assumed he was at least partially correct in his assumption when he heard her take a sip of something. "Even when we lived near him, Mike, I didn't see much of him. He was always at the brewery or in his office or shut up in his castle."

"Castle?"

"Well, his house. It seemed like a castle, with all that stuff from the clan dotting the walls."

"What about *him*? Did that sound like him, the way you remembered him?"

"You mean, he invites you to something, then changes his mind? I don't know, Mike. Mum and Dad would've known. They'd be the ones grandfather would've extended invitations to. I was just there, as it were."

"Right. You just tagged along to dinner or whatever."

"Though I must say it sounds a bit odd, doesn't it?"

"That's why I wanted your expertise, Gwen. You knew him. I was too young."

"Careful. You're treading on thin ice, laddie. I don't need to be reminded I'm fifty."

"I wasn't going there. I simply meant you were a teenager when we left, so you'd been around him, knew him."

"I'll take your implied apology, then." She swallowed a mouthful of coffee. "He was larger than life. That's the way I remember him. Tall and barrel-chested and Scottish with a capital S. I was always slightly afraid of him, he was usually so serious and had little time for any of us. But on the occasions when we did get together, a picnic on the moor or a birthday celebration, he could be charming. I think it depended on his mood."

"How the business was going, perhaps?"

"That I didn't know about. I just remember my awe and trepidation. Not that he did anything physically to frighten me. But his manner. His way of talking, his orders to his staff, the purposeful way he walked. Like he measured time in seconds and rushed to get things accomplished."

"We'd label it a workaholic today, probably."

"Could do, but I think, at least I had the impression, that work didn't really rule him that much. I think he was rather an angry man. Maybe hurt by life and people, and so he threw a shell around him, as a protection against future wounds." She stopped, and McLaren had the feeling she'd just described his personality and behavior last year. The teaspoon clanked against the side of the mug, rather longer than usual. Was she hoping he would think she stopped to stir her coffee, covering up her near *faux pas*?

McLaren pressed her for details. "When did Grandmother die? Could that have affected him?"

"Could have done. Anything could have done. But we left thirty, thirty-five years ago, Mike. Grandmother's been gone only twenty."

"So something else colored his outlook on life, then."

"This might just be his personality, you know. Not everyone's as easy going as you."

McLaren conceded the possibility.

"But it is odd that he'd send for you and then change his mind on seeing you. You didn't make him mad, did you? Like, insult him or something?"

"I didn't have time! He wouldn't let me into the house. Besides, I wouldn't insult him."

"I know. I'm just trying to think of a reason for his about face."

"Yeah, well, think of something else. Something that makes sense."

"Do you look like someone?"

McLaren coughed and leaned forward to get his breath. "What the hell's that mean? Of course I look like someone. Me!"

"Mike, I meant maybe you look like a family member. You know, Uncle Aengus, or Cousin Muira. Someone who's a black sheep or on grandfather's hit list. Figuratively."

"I don't know. I could do, I suppose. I've got that old family album."

"Well, there you are, then. Leaf through it and see if you resemble Cousin Sinclair or whomever. It might explain his action."

"Like, he originally thought it a good idea to invite me up, but I turned out to resemble Aengus or someone, and he changed his mind. Wouldn't have been able to have me around because I stirred up old memories."

"Don't pooh pooh it, Mike. Stranger things have happened."

"Well, little good it does me right now. I'm in Edinburgh and the photo album's back home."

"We all have our cross to bear, dear."

"I'm surprised he hasn't asked you to learn the brewery business, Gwen. With dad gone, you're next in line."

"Grandfather's too old school for that, Mike. Oldest male type thing. You know."

"If he's desperate for a family member to take the helm, he might not be too picky."

"Thanks."

"You know what I mean, Gwen. I don't know his plans, of course, but Uncle Brandon might not have any children."

"You think that's why grandfather invited you up? To talk about the brewery and you taking over? You're awfully old to start learning the brewery business. No insult intended."

"Like I said, I don't know his plans. But it's possible."

"Well, when you get home, Mike, you can see if you look like a masculine version of Cousin Gemma. It could explain a lot."

"She had to have been gorgeous, then."

"In your dreams, dear brother."

McLaren rang off, drank another cup of tea, and went to bed.

Chapter Five

Neill McLaren sat over his dinner and pushed the last bite of Welsh rarebit around the plate with his fork. He seemed not to have the appetite tonight for his usual heavy fare; tension knotted his stomach, making swallowing difficult. Brandon faced him at the other end of the long table, setting them up like lord and lady of the manor. Except the lady in Neill's life, his wife, had been in the churchyard these past twenty years. A space waited for him, too, his half of the headstone blessedly empty of engraving. He'd join her soon enough, but not just yet. He was too cantankerous to die right now; he had things to do, to set right.

Brandon laid his fork on his empty plate and asked if the older man was feeling well. "You haven't eaten much, Dad," he observed. "Shall I ask the cook for something else?" He started to get up but Neill waved him back into his chair.

"It's not the food. I havenae the appetite this evening."

"If you're sure…"

"I'd think by this time of my life I know my own mind, Brandon. Ye've no need to question me."

"Sorry, Dad." Brandon folded his serviette and laid it beside his plate. "I understand Michael was here today."

The room grew deathly quiet and the older man's

face reddened.

"Is he in the area?" Brandon felt his face growing red in the panic for something to say to relieve the sudden tension. "Is he coming back? I'd like to see him. It's been years since he left...after Colin—" He broke off and glanced at Neill. The man's face had drained of color and his fingers choked his table knife.

"He's not coming back. He wasnae invited here and he didnae stay."

"That's too bad. I'd have liked to talk to him. Is he still here...Edinburgh, perhaps?"

"I don't know where he is. He can be with the devil for all I know or care."

"I'm sorry, Dad. If I'd known you felt like this I wouldn't have mentioned Michael. I just thought he came up here to see the brewery, to come back to us."

Neill pressed his lips together and snorted. The phone rang in the hallway and was promptly answered. "He's abandoned the business, just as he's abandoned us. Three hundred years of work, and he's turned his back on all of it: his ancestors' struggles, his family, our dreams. Not a letter or phone call these past thirty six years—that's how much the brewery and we mean tae him, the bloody Sassenach."

"He's got his own life in Derbyshire, Dad." Brandon tried to smooth the waves. He'd experienced his own choppy water with Neill; he knew the anger that ran as deep as the sea, as unrelenting as the tide once the older man chose to hate someone. "He's certainly got his own career. Even if he thought of returning to the business, he couldn't do it overnight. Perhaps he wanted to come back first, see how we felt about him before he quit his job and moved up here."

"He didnae get the prodigal son's welcome, if that was his intention." Neill leaned forward, his chest against the edge of the table. Now that he was closer to Brandon, the light behind Neill haloed his head and threw his face into shadow. "You know what I think? I think he needs the money. I think he's run into debt or lost his job and he needs the steady income the brewery could hand him."

"Dad, you can't be serious!"

"I think he believed he could waltz through the front door, I'd throw open my arms and put him on the payroll, add his name to the company stationery. Well, he learned this morning that it was a bloody daft idea. If he wants to make amends for the past, he'll have to do something a might better than appearing on my doorstep."

"But Michael's kin, Dad. He could take over the brewery when I...when it's time. We need him. He's a McLaren, a part of you through Colin. You can't just turn him away."

Neill slammed the hilt of the utensil onto the table. "He's no longer any relation I recognize. That woman—"

"Michael's mother's name was Elaine, Dad. She married Colin legally, regardless of your insinuations then and now. A church wedding with dozens of guests and two clergy to perform the ceremony. Elaine deserves to be referred to as a decent person."

Despite Brandon's reprimand, Neill roared on. "That *tart* took my grandson and my son out of my house, out of the business, away from our land. Growing up in that...south of the border wasnae my idea. Michael turned his back on us and on Scotland. If either of them had wanted to make amends, to come back, they had thirty-six years to do it. But they did nothing."

"You can't blame Michael, Dad. You don't know how he was reared, what he was told. He might not have known about the brewery or you. You can't just erase him like that. The brewery—"

"The brewery survived world wars and poor economies and staff turnovers. It'll still survive, without Michael McLaren."

"But can it survive without a McLaren to guide it?"

The silence again seeped between them, lying heavy and oppressive. The tick of the clock barely made itself heard, muffled as draped drums for a funeral. Indeed, Brandon felt as though he'd heard his nephew's death knell as regards to the family business. He eyed his father, preoccupied with staring at his beer. It had cost the older man to voice his feelings, to admit to his fears. His dad faced seeing the McLaren business dying out with him. Three hundred years of McLarens and he was seeing its end if he didn't relinquish and eventually turn it over to Michael. Brandon was the last of the line if Michael didn't step in. When the time came for Dad to pass, would he really hold to his opinion and watch the company gasp its death rattle in his hands? Will he really let the tradition die—let the creation from more McLarens than they would ever know pass away?

Brandon pushed his plate back and reached for the platter of cheese and oatcakes. He held it toward Neill, who shook his head and glared. Brandon set the platter on the table and considered another topic of conversation. He didn't feel like talking. His dad was behaving like an old-time clan chief, the supreme head of the extended family. When would he realize it wasn't the 1700s? Oaths of allegiance and blind acts of fealty no longer mattered. The clock broke into the quiet, striking the hour.

"I've no need for ye to sit and hold my hand, either. We're both too old for that. Go about your business." He excused Brandon, making it sound more like a command than permission, and slumped back in his chair.

The chair legs scraped across the flagstone floor as Brandon rose from the table. He picked up the chair and replaced it noiselessly in its spot. Nodding to his father, Brandon left the room, the heavy door closing with a *whoosh* as the air rushed into the space.

Neill stared at his plate, suddenly tired of fighting and tired of struggling. The beets had been easy to eat, as had been the green beans. But the beer caught in his throat, produced a coughing fit that had turned his face red and given Brandon a fright. All of which puzzled Neill. Especially the beer. He'd always been able to drink pints of the stuff, non-stop. Why could he not even get one swallow down tonight?

The fire crackled and a log settled into the thick bed of glowing coals, sending sparks up the chimney. A blast of wind rattled the casement windows and a wisp of cold air seeped into the room. It brushed against a small tapestry hanging near the window, moving its edge in a slow undulation.

Neill inched his chair closer to the fire. The flames fascinated him, mesmerized him. He stared at the yellow and red tongues lapping the logs, the embers winking from the blackness beneath the logs. Did they wink because they knew his secret? He'd told no one of his feelings, not even Brandon. He shared most things with his son, feeling the family business would be handled more efficiently and profitably if Brandon knew of problems or acquisitions or daily operations. Especially in the office. But Neill had never revealed that part of his heart that held his grandson, Michael. It was difficult for Neill to acknowledge the truth right now, so how could he talk about it to Brandon?

Neill grabbed his glass of beer and raised it to his mouth. He was getting soft in his old age. He'd damned his daughter-in-law after she convinced Colin to move their family to Derbyshire, to take over the family farm from another branch of the family. She'd broken up the McLaren business, all because she felt sorry for a distant relative. With Colin in England, working the land instead of working with hops and yeast, the family business depended on Brandon. And Brandon had no heir, so everything the McLarens had worked for these past three centuries meant nothing.

He tilted back his head and downed a mouthful of beer. He gritted his teeth as he swallowed it. Damn his grandson. Showing up unannounced, lying about it. Michael hadn't turned out well. He wouldn't, being reared without his grandfather's strict hand to guide him. He had the blond hair of his mother, the hazel-colored eyes of her father, the speech of her people. If Michael had been reared in Scotland, he'd be a different man. One not concerned with other people's problems. He'd not have time: he'd be too busy with the brewery.

Neill rested the glass on his lap and looked around the room as though seeing it for the first time. Or after a return home after a long trip. What would happen to the family heirlooms, the furniture and silver and paintings? Brandon would take them over on Neill's passing, but who'd get them when Brandon passed?

The mantel clock ticked into the silence, as though commiserating with Neill. Or mocking his life. *Tsk tsk tsk.* The taps drummed over the snapping of the fire and reverberated around the room. There *was* someone to whom he could pass the business, the pounding seemed to remind him. During the war. Had he forgotten about that girl, about their baby?

He stared at the fire. The flames wove themselves into Liesbeth's blonde hair. Long and sleek. It'd nearly reached her mid back. She'd had a habit of kneeling over him in bed and letting her hair fall around his face, like a curtain. He'd never experienced such softness and sweet scent as Liesbeth's hair.

Neill stirred uneasily, the memory growing stronger. He'd forgotten about her until now. A Dutch girl barely seventeen. They'd met in Kleve, a town on the Germany-Dutch border when he'd been stationed with his regiment. They'd been thrown together during a bombing raid by the Allies. Whether the war had accelerated their attraction, urged them to seek what comfort they could, or whether they'd merely sought some sanity in the midst of the horror exploding around them, Neill didn't know. Hadn't stopped to analyze his feelings. The glory and adventure he'd enlisted for had quickly turned to revulsion. He remembered only that he'd found her exquisite and shy and needing to be loved.

Needed love as much as he did. Two lonely, scared teenagers—he, who had never been out of his village before the war; she, whose world had been invaded by foreigners who took her normalcy and replaced it with a nightmare.

They'd met many nights after that, whenever he could get leave or she could sneak away. He hadn't thought about their future, didn't even know if she was engaged or not. He knew her name and that she was the most beautiful woman he'd ever seen. That was enough for him for the present.

When his regiment prepared to pull out, they met one last time. He remembered that plainly enough—her dingy basement apartment, the one working light fixture, the ersatz tea and smear of jam on week-old bread. They sat in candlelight, not because it was romantic but because the power wasn't on. She was dressed in a blue blouse and black floral skirt, and her hair was done up in one long braid. As she opened a tin of pears she told him she was pregnant with his child. No grand announcement, no joy on her face. Just a piece of information, as though she were a television news reporter.

He'd accepted her word as fact. She could have lied, told him she carried his child in order to procure a husband, a more comfortable life, and a way out of the dinginess of war. Just another British war bride. But her voice held a tone that suggested the sadness of the truth. The baby would be another mouth to feed, another body to keep clothed, another handful of guldens or Reichsmarks or bartering reciprocal work for babysitting.

Neill had asked what she wanted; marriage was impossible at the moment. But after the war...

Liesbeth looked at him gravely, her blue eyes mirroring her hopelessness. She'd have the baby, keep it. If he felt the same after the war…

They'd parted after exchanging home addresses. He recalled hesitating, about to write down a fictitious house number and street in Glasgow. The pencil point made a dark, deep mark on the paper, underscoring his hesitation, then the smooth, even flow of his penmanship took over as he wrote out his Balquhidder address.

He swallowed, suddenly ashamed he'd contemplated leaving her alone with her burden. He had prided himself on being a man.

Neill saw combat in other European occupied countries and escaped being wounded. When the Scots Guards were demobilized, he wrote to Liesbeth, pouring out his constant love and wish to be married. The letter was answered months later by a relative, saying Neill's daughter was being reared by Liesbeth's sister and husband. They'd decided it was best for the child to be kept in Holland. He could never discover their names or whereabouts.

The wind touched the tapestry again, shifting his gaze to the McLaren clan crest badge. A crowned lion's head surrounded by two laurel branches. The clan motto *Creag An Tuirc* stood out in stark white thread beneath the crest. The Boar's Rock. A rallying cry. A place of gathering.

Neill shook his head. He hadn't gathered Michael into his embrace nor rallied around him when he'd come to make amends for the past, for something not of his own doing. Was he living a lie? Was he so useless that he was allowing Michael to slip out of his life again? He'd done that with Liesbeth, with his baby.

Was that why he'd grown so hard and unforgiving?

He'd not always been so. In his youth, during his war years, he'd been fun-loving and outgoing, wanting to explore the world and gather friends to his side. He'd wanted to be popular and loved, unconcerned what others thought or how the world ran. Had losing Liesbeth and the girl changed him, made him bitter for his loss, determined to wall his heart against human emotions so he'd never be hurt again?

Had his fanaticism about the family business developed to take the place of his lost love? Wasn't he cursing his elder son for doing what he, himself, was doing? Colin had taken over the farmstead, keeping it in the family. Was that different from taking over the brewery?

Neill got up and went to his desk. The wood shone in the firelight, dark and distressed and satiny from centuries of use and polishing. He pulled a pen and a sheet of stationery from the drawer and sat down. The paper lay large, white and intimidating before him, waiting for his words. He chewed on the end of the pen, suddenly unsure of what he would say, unsure of his motive. His and Liesbeth's daughter would be in her sixties now. Ten years or so older than Brandon. Would he be able to find the girl? She had a lifetime of living somewhere else, of growing up Dutch, of having different values. Even if he could locate the girl, she was probably married. She wouldn't want to leave her husband and family to live in Scotland. Or want to learn the family business. Anyway, where would Neill start to find his daughter? Her last name would have changed when she married. How would he ever find anyone after all this time? Did wartime records even exist?

His right hand slowly fell onto the stationery and drew it into a wad. The paper crackled as he squeezed it into a ball. He laid the pen on the desk and walked to the fire. He tossed the paper onto the logs and watched as the flames devoured it. A charred wisp remained, fragile and cobwebby against the log. He blew on it and it disintegrated into ash and floated up the chimney. A clean death, he thought. A closed door on the past. Ashes to ashes. Fire purges many mistakes.

He reclaimed his chair and grabbed his fork. The Welsh rarebit had grown cold, the cheese tough and stringy. He pushed the plate aside and picked up the beer glass.

Beer. Rannoch beer from Strathearn Brewery. His brewery. The brewery he could not pass on beyond Brandon.

He stared at the glass, lifted it shoulder high, and threw it into the fire.

****

Tuesday morning after breakfast, Jamie phoned McLaren with the information. "I had to lie through my smile," Jamie said. "I told Ross Gordon, my contact in Central Scotland Constabulary, one of our probationary constables was looking through Scotland and northern England reports for a black Ford Kuga that might've been used in a robbery here in Derbyshire."

"You will be rewarded in heaven, my son."

"I could feel my face getting redder by the moment, but I got what you wanted."

"Good thing Ross couldn't see you, then. You're a rotten liar, Jamie."

"Probably why I'm not a good criminal. The hit-and-run bloke's name is Lanny Clack. He's got a history of theft, robbery, assault, and domestic violence."

"Well known to the local coppers, I take it."

"I'm sending his photo to your mobile as we speak. My contact up there sent it to me, thinking to help me with my…inquiry."

"Good lad."

"You probably won't want to keep it after you leave Edinburgh, Mike."

"That bad?"

"Let's just say he's no contender for the next romance novel cover. He has a job as a car mechanic."

"Bloody hell. Is that where he got the car? The news report said the car'd been stolen."

"He evidently picked it up at the owner's house. That's Stuart Forbes."

"I remember."

"The car was parked on the street."

"An expensive car like that? It must cost between £22,000 and £27,000."

"Same old story. Forbes got home from church service Sunday afternoon, was going to go out again in two hours, so he left it outside. He discovered it had gone around three o'clock when he stepped out of his house."

"And no one saw anything." McLaren exhaled loudly.

"At least no one's come forward yet. The police suspected Stuart Forbes of dumping the car somewhere or paying Lanny Clack to steal the car so the insurance company would have to pay on the claim."

"Does Forbes have a history of insurance fraud?"

"No. But he does own Arthur's Seat Insurance

Company, so that raised a few red flags for the cops. So far, nothing's been proven against Forbes or his company. Lanny Clack was ID'd by the CCTV photo. One person rang up the police station to give the face a name. Right after the newscast, in fact. So those appeals do some good, it seems."

"Maybe he merely wants to blame Lanny for this incident."

"The jacket was the best lead. Five people phoned in to mention that skull was a gang design."

"It's probably a few hundred gangs' design. Why are these callers so certain it's associated with Clack?"

"This little gem includes a few neck vertebrae with a knife stuck in it."

Chapter Six

The face looked at McLaren from his smart phone Tuesday morning. Jamie had been right: Lanny was better suited for a novel's villain instead of the hero. Black eyes glared at the viewer from beneath a thatch of spiky black hair. An equally vigorous mustache hid his upper lip and bracketed the corners of his mouth. All this seemed to be connected to a tattoo that blanketed his chin, beginning where the mustache left off. But McLaren had never seen a tattoo such as this. Rather than teardrops or a dagger or other picturesque graphic, the design was abstract. It was comprised of black swirls and curves, the skin between the geometric figures as much a part of the pattern as the tattooed flesh.

Lanny might've been known to the local constabulary, but evidently the tattoo had muddied the identification waters a tad. Which was why the coppers put out the television appeal. Lanny had acquired it after his most current prison stay. Probably some sort of rite of passage, McLaren thought, knowing some gangs marked successful candidates or rewarded successful fetes with these visible badges of honor. If so, those six conscientious citizens must be extremely familiar with Lanny to be able to name him even with a fresh tattoo.

The coppers got their break when, according to Jamie's Scottish colleague, the helpful citizen even trotted a photo by the station. The photo was Lanny with the tattoo. Something new to the police. But technology stepped in where the human eye failed; the photo was scanned and the tattoo was eradicated on the computer screen. Gazing back at the graphic artist who accomplished this "before" likeness was the Lanny Clack known to the police.

The problem with the CCTV was that the image was too small and the driver's head had been partially obscured. The photo from the concerned citizen cinched the ID.

McLaren stared at it, trying to recall where he'd seen something similar. It looked Hawaiian. Or at least Polynesian. But Lanny Clack didn't appear to be of that race. Was there a rule that designated only tribal members were allowed to sport such a tattoo? Like tartans of Scottish clans. The wearing of the tattoo or tartan established kin and pride of belonging.

He abandoned his speculation. It did nothing to explain Liza Skene's silence. He called her home phone again but still got no answer; he rang up her work place. Her boss hadn't seen Liza that morning, nor had he heard from her. He was not amused.

Neither the boss' report nor the unanswered phone calls comforted McLaren, so he drove the mile to Cluny Gardens, near the Royal Observatory. As he parked in front of the cream-colored stone building, he eyed the front windows and door. Nothing looked different from when he'd been there yesterday.

He walked up the pavement, aware of the sharp tap of his shoes on the concrete. Behind the row of houses curving along the road, fragments of the comma-shaped lake peeked out from the mass of trees. Their bare branches nodded in the slight breeze that brought the chill off the frozen lake. Diverting his eyes from the painful glare of the iced-over water he knocked on the front door.

The house was deathly quiet. No dog yapped at the intrusion into the silence; no voice responded. He pressed his left ear against the door. No conversation issued from behind its protective buffer.

He peered into the windows of the front room. Nothing looked out of place or suspicious.

Leaning against the wall, he pulled his mobile from his jeans pocket and punched in Liza's phone number. The house came alive with the sharp resonating of its phone, and McLaren again stared into the front room. It was odd standing outside, listening to the ring sounding inside, looking at the phone he wanted Liza to answer. The room appeared gloomy and foreboding, as though it had gone into mourning or held a terrible secret.

McLaren shook the fanciful scenario from his mind, told himself he was overly concerned. After all, Liza might be seeing a doctor, still suffering from emotional trauma. Or perhaps she was at a friend's house, unwilling to stay alone after the experience. She could even be on her way to work, having overslept. He called up the library and this time talked to one of her co-workers. Liza Skene was still absent.

The now familiar urge to break into her house or talk to neighbors threatened to overpower him. He walked back to his car, telling himself he was not hired to find Liza, he had no jurisdiction in Scotland even if he were still a cop, he would receive no warm handshake or slap on the back from the local authorities if he investigated. He had to stop inventing trouble, stop creating drama where none existed. Why did he think drug dealers or gang members or spies had kidnapped her, done away with her? Nothing at all hinted at such people; it was a simple case of an accidental hit-and-run. The driver, Lanny Crank, had probably been on his mobile, distracted, and unfortunately lost control of his car. Those things happened.

He drove back to his guesthouse, parked the car, and walked into town. He needed the exercise, needed the physical activity that would calm his galloping imagination.

The suggestion of snow hung in the air, more an aroma than flakes. Gray clouds bunched in the west and overhead, but the eastern horizon held a slash of blue sky. A wisp of wind curled down from the slated roofline, stinging McLaren's face with the bite of cold and a few pelts of frozen rain. Two seagulls huddled together in the protection of a dormer window, their feathers fluffed against the chill. McLaren stepped over a patch of frozen water as a bus threw a spray of slush across the road.

He turned left off South Bridge and meandered up the High Street. Aptly named, he thought. Edinburgh Castle sat farther ahead, like a prize on the crest of the hill, beckoning the footsore to plod just a bit farther.

He passed the police information center, and shop windows displaying readymade kilts, leather goods, cheap souvenirs, bottled drinks, Scottish food, and knitwear. Christmas specials, the placards announced in large red and green print. Unique gifts; make her happy; free gift-wrapping; overseas shipping available. Cheap flights to the Canaries, Crete, or the Caymans for a never-forgotten Christmas gift! McLaren glanced at the lettered proclamations and considered a heathergem and silver necklace for Dena or a kilt for himself. Of course he was entitled to don the Clan tartan, but would he ever wear it? Was it merely a rebellion against his grandfather's treatment, needing to declare and cling to his Scottish heritage? He sighed heavily, letting the moment and the link slide by before going on.

St. Giles Cathedral loomed ahead, its gothic exterior bright in the sunlight. He hesitated, the architecture whispering to him to explore, his aversion to organized religion whispering to go elsewhere. As he turned, ready to walk to the castle, he stopped short. Lanny Clack sauntered toward him.

Before McLaren could move, Lanny crossed the High Street. McLaren ran after him, determined to detain him for the police. Lanny seemed to be headed for the City Chambers, the U-shaped courtyard holding governmental apartments from the 1750s. Fearing he'd miss Lanny in the maze of doors and alleyways, McLaren yelled. Lanny turned around. Either recognizing McLaren or fearful of the man running toward him, Lanny dodged down a tiny lane. McLaren bolted after him.

The lane, a few dozen yards long, contained a courtyard cafe on the left, but by the time McLaren got there Lanny had disappeared. Ahead was the entrance to The Real Mary King's Close, the seventeenth century underground labyrinth of residences and alleyways of which Hurd Dowell had spoken. McLaren yanked open the attraction's door and hurried inside.

A well-lit, well-appointed gift shop greeted him, not at all what he expected. Upscale souvenirs and books claimed most of the area, the ticket kiosk in the center of the floor. A voice announced the group had left on the tour and McLaren looked around wildly. Lanny wasn't in the shop.

McLaren dashed to the ticket kiosk. A young woman sorting brochures looked up, smiled, and asked if she could assist him.

He glanced at the sign proclaiming the start times of the tours, then at the wall clock. "Am I too late to catch this tour?" he said, his voice urgent and sharp.

"They've just gone." The woman gazed at the open doorway at right angle to the shop entrance. The stairwell descending to the warren of lanes below was dark. "You've missed the first two minutes where the history is told if you join them now. Anyway," she added, looking slightly hesitant, "there *is* the safety rule. It's black as pitch down there. The tour leader has the light. You might get hurt if you were to join them now. We can't risk that."

"Safety regulations," McLaren leaned closer and lowered his voice. "I won't sue you. I'll sign something to that effect."

"There's another tour in an hour, sir. I think it'd be best if you joined that group."

"I haven't the time to wait. Please." He opened his wallet and pulled out the admission price. He handed it to her, closing her fingers over the pound coins. "I'd really appreciate it. They can't have gone too far ahead. I'll catch them up."

"Well…" She looked at the money, as though considering the man's urgency and the darkness below them. "There *are* pockets of light down there, of course. It's not *pitch* black. Many of the recesses and chambers are theatrically lit." She printed out a ticket and gave it to him. "Through that open door and down the stairs. You'll find them."

McLaren thanked her and dashed into the chilly gloom.

The upper landing was dimly lit, so as not to spoil the theatricality of the underground scene. But tiny strips of lights shone from beneath the stair treads, defining the path to the bottom. His left hand slid slowly along the metal railing, gripping more firmly as he paused to find each successive step. He felt the small torch in his jacket pocket but didn't remove it. He needed his eyes to acclimate to the darkness.

He came to the second landing and the railing snaked back on itself, yet still angled downward. McLaren could see a small pool of light at ground level, a dozen stairs below. It seemed to come from a small door to the right. He took a deep breath, steeling his nerves, and descended.

At the bottom of the spiraled staircase he stood for moment, letting his eyes become accustomed to the near darkness. The ceiling was not much more than head high and seemed to mock his fear of confinement. Ahead he heard a voice relating the Close's history. The voice sounded thin, bouncing off the hard walls.

He took a few steps past the bottom landing and looked around. The gloom intimidated him, threatened to suffocate him. Ahead and to his right pinpricks of weak yellowish light displaced some of the gloom and defined the areas through the maze, but murkiness filled the majority of the expanse. He moved slowly, his feet gliding over the rough ground, his hand skating over the wall. His fingers touched the bumps and small protuberances, skimming over them as though he were reading Braille.

He passed a small chamber on his right. A mannequin dressed in the uniform of a foul clenger, a person who cleaned plague-infested living quarters, gazed out from behind his spotlight. McLaren started at the life-like dummy, disquieted at his first encounter with the tableaux. He dropped his hand and wiped his forehead of sweat before rounding the corner and joining the group.

There were more people than he'd thought, perhaps one and a half dozen. The darkness made it difficult to get an exact count. It didn't matter. He was certain Lanny Clack was among them.

McLaren stood in the back, hoping his arrival hadn't been noticed. The guide was explaining about the creation of the underground city and held everyone's attention.

"These stacked 'skyscraper' buildings ran uphill, giving each one a slightly different ground level. Because they could not continue building upward, due to the unsafe foundations of the buildings, the poor people burrowed into the side of this hill. By digging horizontally into the base of the building, they created rooms at right angles to the building. As more and more people burrowed into the underground, they connected their one-room dwellings to each other via underground "streets." Again, imagine being underground and living like this—an entire family confined to one room, no windows, no fresh air, no light. The smoke from their cooking fires, odors from the bucket in the corner... They lived their entire lives below ground, died below ground for the most part, going outside to work or beg or empty the bucket, which was allowed only twice a day at specific times."

McLaren glanced around the group. He could make out individual faces in the ochre light, distinguish clothing. Lanny Clack stood near the guide, the white skull on his jacket nearly glowing in the light, his tattoo easily discernable.

As the guide moved to the doorway, the group shifted to follow. Instead of darting out the door and waiting, McLaren hugged the back of the party, turning with them as though directed by a sheepdog. He kept to the shadowy section of the chamber, for the first time thankful for the dim light.

Several chambers on, the guide gestured to a tableau of a family. The woman mannequin held a small child in her arms. A young boy lay on the bottom mattress of a bunk bed. "If a family member caught the plague, the mother had a heartbreaking decision of whether to keep that member with the family—thereby practically ensuring the entire family would catch the plague and die—or seal that member in a separate room, still here underground, confining the person to the dark, locked in area so that the rest of the family could survive. Most times it resulted in a certain death for the quarantined victim, although food and drink were brought to the room. One young girl even had her doll with her, her only bit of comfort as she died."

The tour emerged into a wide alley. The low, cramped quarters of the rooms gave way to multi-story-high space hewn from the bedrock and, with it, the darkness of that confined area. The light, though still not daylight, was brighter here. At least one story above them a line of wash stretched across the alley, the bed linen looking oddly ghostly with outstretched arms.

Another line of wash hung one or two stories above that, nearly indiscernible in the dimness. The light lessened at the top of the structure, plunging the upper-most windows into near blackness.

McLaren clung to the back of the group, feeling vulnerable in the half-light, praying Lanny wouldn't see him. The group inched along, listening to the guide and craning their necks to gaze at the nebulous roof of this subterranean world. Puffs of breath floated upward, vanishing into the murkiness above. He bent forward slightly and made his way slowly up the steep incline. The guide talked of the last inhabitant of the close, pointing out the man's dwelling and stating he resided there until approximately 1900. He talked of the children used as chimney sweeps who often got stuck in chimneys. Of the cows and other animals that were boarded below ground with the inhabitants. Of the unbreakable cycle of poverty. Of the perfect criminal hideout the twisting alleys, tunnels, ill-lit chambers, and black recesses became for the thousands of people who resided and hid there.

At the top of the enclosed alley they turned, ducked through an arched doorway, and instantly plunged back into the blackness of the cavernous city. The group paused as their eyes readjusted to the dark, then the shuffling feet increased their pace. The sound mingled with the murmured comments of the group. McLaren still kept to the back. As they came into the original passageway, McLaren realized Lanny Clack was no longer in the party.

McLaren hung back, trying to recall when he had last seen the man. Had he left the group in the first few minutes? He couldn't have; that would have necessitated lagging behind so the tour guide wouldn't see him leave. And McLaren had been in the rear of the group the entire time. Which meant...

McLaren fell farther behind, letting the group walk on. The guide's voice faded to a low-pitched drone. Left alone in one of the chambers, the walls and darkness seemed to close in on him, the sound of distant footsteps turning into the imagined scurry of dozens of mice. He sagged against the wall, his heart rate galloping, his forehead beading with sweat. The voice and footsteps were nearly inaudible. If he didn't move now, he'd be alone in the blackness.

He took several deep breaths, then forced himself forward. He passed a group of mannequins when one appeared to move. In the near dark his childhood fears transmuted into monsters. A faint stirring of air hinted that the group had recently passed this point. He pushed himself past the display, heading toward the voices at the bottom of the steps and the sanity of light.

Chapter Seven

Lanny wasn't among the group members ascending the stairs, nor was he in the gift shop. McLaren dashed out the door and into the courtyard. No one lingered in the area or in the doorways. He hurried back into the shop, thinking he might have missed Lanny, but the room was square, devoid of alcoves or person-wide columns. Admitting Lanny had eluded him, he left the Close.

He got a table in The Elephant House, a combination café/gourmet coffee and tea shop on George IV Bridge. Lunch for him usually was something grabbed and eaten on the run, but after his experience in the Close he needed to sit for a while. Plus, he wanted to think through the Lanny Clack connection.

He ordered a chicken burger, green salad, and a concoction of hot chocolate and Cointreau crowned with whipped cream. Although the list of gourmet coffees and beers looked good, he wanted something hot to chase off the cold that penetrated his body. Creeping about underground had done nothing to placate the city's wintry temps. The Chocolate Orange was a necessary indulgence.

Lanny's agitation at seeing McLaren chasing him on the High Street seemed as good as verbally confessing he was the driver who killed Hurd Dowell.

Why else run off and hide? Or was he afraid he'd be recognized and ultimately linked to something bigger than the hit-and-run? What could be worse than killing someone?

He brought up Lanny's photo on his mobile phone. There was no hint of a smile in the lips pressed together; the eyes glared at the viewer, conveying disdain for anyone outside the gang and smugness with his position. All in all, the snap showed a young man who saw himself superior and invincible.

****

Fowler Ritchie made the phone call as he swallowed a spoonful of his barley soup. He'd made it the previous weekend, expressly to take to work. But events had progressed faster than he had anticipated and he was now home, trying to keep his blood pressure from soaring and his head from splitting. His boss hadn't pried into the reason for the immediate request, and Fowler suspected the man had no desire to become a bosom chum or want to know anything personal of his life. Fowler knew he wasn't popular, but he assumed it was jealousy that kept his cohorts at arm's length. Same held true for his boss. Working with Fowler was probably as close as the man cared to get. There were no fishing trips or nights out at the pubs.

"Hello?" The voice was soft from a near-whisper.

"It's Fowler."

"I thought you knew to ring me up only in an emergency."

"Yeah, I know." Fowler laid his spoon in the soup bowl and leaned over the table. His heart thudded against his rib cage. "Don't get excited."

"Excited? What the hell's that mean? What's going

on, then?"

"Bit of a cock-up, but nothing unfixable."

"Then why waste my time and phone? If you can fix it you better. I'm not paying you if the job's not complete. That was our deal, or do you need reminding?"

Fowler's finger curled around the table's wooden edge. There was something about the man, something in addition to the anger in his voice that hinted he wouldn't be pleasant if he were crossed, so Fowler steeled himself. They'd never worked together before, but he was already marking this as their last joint effort. The man needed handling with kid gloves. "I just thought I should inform you of what's going on. In case you want to give different orders."

"Look. I'm paying you to be the man in charge up there. You know what the situation is. You know the people. I could've come up and done it, but for various reasons it's best that I stay here right now and be seen. If you can't handle the situation or the people, I'll get someone who can."

"Sure, sure. I just thought you'd like to know about the glitch, so you don't come back at me later and say I should've done something else."

"What does that mean? It got there, didn't it?"

"Got here and already gone. With no one the wiser."

"So the package arrived at its destination."

"I observed the arrival myself."

"And?" The voice on the other end of the phone turned threatening.

"And after a bit of debate about its acceptance, it was rejected. Return to sender, you could say."

A deep exhale blasted Fowler's ear. The voice took on a bored tone. "So, what's the problem, then? You said there'd been a slight cock-up."

"It occurred afterwards. The following day. One of the drivers had an encounter of a rather unpleasant nature. The package turned up unexpectedly and we're wondering if we should depart from the schedule."

"Why? Is it still returnable?"

"Oh, I've no doubt of that, sir. Maybe the box will be a bit dented, but nothing to damage the value."

"Not yet. This minor damage…do you have everything you need to…ship the item?"

"Not an issue at all. Even if it's a bit worn around the edges I'll firmly stamp it myself."

The voice dropped slightly in pitch. "Any idea when this will be sorted out? I've left it up to you, if you need reminding."

"Don't get your knickers in a twist…sir." Fowler added the title as an afterthought, hoping he wasn't sounding too familiar to his employer. After all, he'd not been paid yet. "Nothing to worry about. You know our reputation."

"That's why you were recommended to me."

"Well, then, you should know we always deliver. Whatever shipment you want, we deliver." Fowler hesitated momentarily as he wondered if he should up the price.

The question on the other end of the phone line came forth slowly as Fowler considered the consequences of the pay hike. "Same as we spoke about previously, right?"

"Sure," Fowler answered hurriedly, feeling he should let well enough alone. "Unless you've changed your mind, sir."

"Why would I do that in the middle of the transaction? You don't change horses in mid-stream, Fowler. If the package is going to meet its final destination in a day or so, that's what I want, what I paid you for. I'm not changing a thing."

Fowler murmured that the man made a wise decision. "We charge extra for change of plans."

"You're costing me an arm and a leg already, mate, so I'm not about to cancel or change a thing. Just get it done."

"You know our company guarantee: one hundred percent satisfaction with the delivery or you don't pay us a bleedin' quid."

"And this will be concluded…"

"Tonight or tomorrow. Next day at the latest."

"It better be. Stick to the timeline we agreed upon. Your schedule has to coincide with mine in order for my alibi to work. If you do a cock-up you ruin more than the simple package delivery. You deliver me into the hands of the authorities. And if that happens, I've got mates who will see to it that you join me before your next meal. Got it?"

"You'll be notified of the destruction of the package very soon, sir. Think of that and have a good night's sleep."

Fowler rang off over the man's muttered "Hell", wondering if *he* would be able to sleep come night. He was that nervous.

****

McLaren played the tourist for two hours before stopping at a pub for dinner. The building was in keeping with the Old Town section, a blackened stone edifice squatting on the street corner. Its leaded windows glowed yellow against the night and threw strangely warped rectangles onto the outside pavement. He pushed open the wooden door and immediately felt embraced by the aromas of hot meat pies, fried chips, and coffee. The atmosphere of the establishment sang to him above the mix of music and conversation, appealing to his mood—restrained camaraderie.

He sat at the bar, a heavy wooden rectangle that showed its age via its dark mahogany and dented surface, and perused the list of beers on tap. They were listed in two columns of type on large sheets of cream-colored paper, and given alphabetically. Near the bottom Rannoch Heavy seemed to leap from the encompassing black frame, its name bolder and shinier than the others. The beer was the original beverage Ian MacLaren had developed three hundred years ago, the beer on which the family brewery was based. Other eighty-shilling beers had been developed and their recipes either forsaken or added to the growing number of products under the Strathearn label. Whether heather-based, heavy, or export varieties, many brews proved popular and were widely available in Scotland: Kilsyth Export and Devil's Tub Heavy deserved the awards heaped on them. But tonight he needed the link with the past. He ordered a pint of Rannoch from the publican, ignored the conversations and music, and munched on his fish and chips as he thought about his grandfather.

The older man was fiercely proud of their clan association and of the brewery. Both deserved his admiration. But McLaren thought his grandfather acted more like the chief than he should. Traditionally, a clan included everyone living on the chief's territory and on territory of anyone owing loyalty to that chief. Other families, even without the tie of surname or fidelity, could join the clan if the chief wished. But he also had the lawful power to bar anyone from the clan. Even members of his own family. Which grandfather'd done to McLaren.

It hadn't been his fault he'd been reared in England, he thought as he sipped his pint. His parents had seen to that. But he could've moved back to Scotland when he finished school, could've joined the police there instead of in Staffordshire. Why hadn't he? Because he didn't want to leave his mates? Because he was afraid to become Scottish, didn't want to imply his parents had been wrong in leaving their ancestral country?

The song ended under a smattering of applause. The musicians propped their guitars against the back wall of the alcove and picked up their pints at the bar before sagging into chairs at a corner table. Now that the competition for being heard had been removed, talk lowered to a buzz.

McLaren glanced at the instruments, thinking better guitars would improve the group's sound and possible future bookings, then paid for his food and left the pub.

The thick oak door thudded firmly behind him, abruptly cutting off the pub chatter. He paused outside the door and breathed deeply. The cold evening air hit him nearly as sharply as his grandfather's scathing words had done.

He rearranged the muffler around his neck and jammed his fists into his jeans pockets. The coldness subsided slightly but still seeped through his jacket. Hunching his shoulders slightly, he headed for the guesthouse, his footsteps as hollow sounding as his hopes of ever reconciling with the older man.

He turned onto the main road and passed sleeping buildings, their darkened windows shielding their silent interiors. Passageways between buildings loomed black and threatening, squatting in the areas where the street lamps' light couldn't reach. He hurried past these holes, knowing what could lurk in their gloom. His quick pace offered no safety from the odors that wound downwind to him, however. Damp stones and cigarette dog ends, stale beer and urine, wet newsprint and gravel pronounced their presence in breath-holding assaults. He hurried on, his gaze fixed on the next stretch.

The blocks reached as far as he could see, merging with the darkness to the west. Storefronts and street corners had a sameness that only distinguished themselves by different names: MacDougall's Electrical, East Meets West Grocer, Dusty Treasures, Montague Street, Lufton Place, Nicolson Square.

Cars sped to their destinations, buses lumbered toward the town center, their headlights bringing fleeting life to the blackness. The silence and gloom settled at their leaving, making McLaren feel more isolated for the withdrawal of the light. He hurried past a passageway between the shop row, aware of the stillness. Nothing moved, not even the abandoned newspapers scattered on the pavement and bunched at the bases of the building. The street wallowed in the appearance of neglect.

The stretch of buildings ended abruptly at the outdoor seating section of a cafe. He'd passed it each day on his walk or drive into the city center, but he hesitated before walking past. It held a sense of foreboding or danger.

He stopped at the corner of the building, scrutinizing the tarped tables and chairs, separating the known from the unknown. He had no reason to linger, no proof anything was amiss. Nothing but his copper's sixth sense, and that had never betrayed him. Yet, he delayed his journey to the bed-and-breakfast and peered into the darkness.

A slight movement at the rear of the patio and a scrape of iron against flagstone drew his attention. He took a step forward, his hand on the corner of the building, and felt in his pocket for his mobile.

A heartbeat of silence flooded the space before the scrape multiplied into a crash and shout. A mass of black moved at the far end of the tables, separated into two blobs and merged again into its original single shape. A scream, quickly silenced, and a yell soared above the clatter.

McLaren stepped past the first table grouping and stared ahead. He could just discern the black lump against the dark. "What's going on? Do you need help?"

Shuffling footsteps and another scrape of iron answered his question.

He moved into the middle of the eating area, his concern outweighing his caution. It was a public place, and while not exactly drowning in passersby, it was an open area surrounded by residences. Nothing untoward would happen there, would it? He drew his phone from his pocket, undecided whether to call for help. Maybe the woman had merely fallen.

"Are you hurt? If you can tell me where you are—"

The indistinguishable shape rushed at him, hitting his right side and pushing him into a table. A hint of floral perfume floated over to him, confirming his suspicion of the one person's gender. He grabbed at the tarp but it slid with him onto the ground. Cursing, he threw it to one side and struggled to his feet. The form rounded the corner of the building and merged with the dark.

He called out, not caring if he were disturbing the quiet or waking people. He leaned against the table as he debated about ringing 999 or running after the miscreants. But he realized he'd dropped his mobile in his fall, so he stopped and palmed the area where he'd been. He lost precious seconds in the search but located the phone beneath the tarp heap.

He shoved the phone into his pocket and raced to the corner. The street extended into the murkiness with no indication of movement or sound. The sporadic dots of light that broke the darkness at regular intervals did nothing to reveal who'd lurked in the patio. He considered walking back down the street in hopes of locating them but realized it'd be a futile quest. They could've ducked into any of the dozens of buildings, hidden in the alleys or behind parked cars.

On his way back to the patio he paused under a streetlamp. His police training whispering that he needed to look through the scene, so he opened the torchlight app and made his way to the patio. At the rear, where he calculated the people had hidden, he angled the beam at the ground and stooped, walking slowly, looking for anything that seemed out of place. A piece of silver winked at him and he grabbed it as he straightened up. It wasn't until he looked at it closer in the full light of the torch app that he realized he held a clan crest badge. It was a two-inch long pewter brooch. A buckled belt encircled an arm that was shown in profile. He stared, disbelieving. It was the symbol of the clan Skene.

****

Back in his room, McLaren read the motto engraved on the belt. *Vertutis regia merces*. A palace the reward of bravery. He laid the brooch on his lap, feeling the strange coincidence. Yes, he was in Scotland, where clan accessories were as common as pasta in Italy. But he'd seen the badge on Liza, and she'd gone missing. Had Liza been the second figure, dragged away by someone after she'd screamed?

He tossed the jewelry piece onto his bed. It caught the light and stared at him. The pin was bent and free of the clasp, and hung open. Had it come free in the struggle? He knew he was fanciful at times; Jamie never tired of reminding him. Besides, what would Liza be doing a half dozen blocks from his bed-and-breakfast? She didn't know where he was staying and her abductor, if there was one, would hardly plant her on McLaren's doorstep. What would be the purpose of the kidnapping, then?

Unless it was to frame him for her murder.

The idea stunned him. Why'd he think of that? He had no evidence she'd been abducted or that she was in danger. For all he knew, she was at a friend's or relatives to recuperate from Hurd's death. She had no reason to let him know where she was; they weren't mates.

But she would've let him know. She'd agreed to

ring him up every day to inform him how she was feeling. Her promise couldn't have been merely to get shed of him, could it? And she did know where he was staying. He'd given her the name of the bed-and-breakfast, insisting she could come over to talk to him in person.

Great, he thought, massaging his forehead. She also had his mobile number. It was on the business card he gave her. Her abductor, if there was one, could've been heading for the Saltire Guest House to dump her on the doorstep after all.

But she'd accepted his offer of help so sincerely. She hadn't impressed him as the type to say something without meaning it. The joke about swearing on the poems had been just that; he'd felt the sincerity beneath the words.

Realizing he could do nothing about it at the present, he leafed through the book he bought at Blackwell's. The Trossachs and the Braes of Balquhidder held his attention not only because his clan came from that area but also because it was magnificent country. Lochs, heather, moors, and brooks trickling out of rocky hillsides aside, he couldn't deny the ancestral ties. A call, actually. Perhaps the invitation from his grandfather had stirred the nearly dead embers. Perhaps he merely was approaching that age when history and ties became more important. But he'd be a git to go home without seeing some of the area. He might not ever get back.

He found himself singing the old Scottish ballad *Braes of Balquhidder* under his breath. He'd never sung it before, either solo or with his folk group, and the song choice surprised him.

Will ye go, lassie, go,
to the braes o' Balquhidder
Where the blueberries grow,
'mang the bonnie bloomin' heather;
Where the deer and the ram,
lightly bounding together,
Sport 'he lang summer day
'mang the braes o' Balquhidder?

~*~

Will ye go, lassie, go,
To the braes o' Balquhidder!
Where the blueberries grow,
'Mang the bonnie bloomin' heather?

~*~

I will twine thee a bower
by the clear silver fountain
an' I'll cover it o'er
wi' the flowers o' the mountain;
I will range through the wilds,
an' the deep glens sae dreary
an' return wi' their spoils
to the bower o' my dearie.

~*~

When the rude wintry win'
idly raves round our dwellin',
an' the roar o' the linn
on the night-breeze is swellin'
sae merrily we'll sing
as the storm rattles o'er us,
till the dear shieling rings
wi' our light liltin' chorus.

~*~

Now the summer is in prime

wi' the flowers richly bloomin'
an' the wild mountain thyme
a' the moorlands perfumin';
To our dear native scenes
let us journey together
where glad innocence reigns
'mang the braes of Balquhidder.

When he finished the last verse, he sat for a moment, letting the sound fade with the image of his grandfather. He held his breath, afraid to break the spell. The clock on the bedside table ticked into the quiet and pulled him away from the heather-clad hills. He jotted 'village of Balquhidder' at the top of his list.

McLaren next wrote down the Boar's Rock, the local hill serving as the Clan's rallying point and war cry. And of course the Braes. Maybe Ben Ledi, too, he thought, his gaze wandering south of Balquhidder and his finger sliding slowly down the map. Hadn't he read something about a beer festival around there?

There was. But it was held at the end of August.

He glanced at the rest of the book and added a few more places to his list, then closed his notebook. The itinerary was long enough: varied and manageable.

But he didn't know how to manage his own feelings. He lay in bed, the room light fixtures off and the darkness hugging his emotional bruises. He mentally went back to the scene at his grandfather's door. The older man was getting up in years. Had he forgotten that he had extended the invitation? Was senility catching him?

McLaren considered the possibility of each question. It was impossible to answer. He didn't know the man. Perhaps he was making too much of the whole thing, creating a mystery where nothing existed.

McLaren rolled onto his side and stared at the moon, which sat in the bare branches of a rowan tree. He wasn't one to take much stock in fables and omens, but noticing the tree seemed fortuitous. The ancients called the rowan the whispering tree, believing it held secrets. A grove of rowans sheltered the mausoleum of MacLaren chiefs near the clan village. Was he exaggerating the importance of his grandfather's feud, his ancestral village and this tree in Edinburgh?

Should he try one more time to bridge the gulf between them? He was going to Balquhidder anyway; why not extend his hand?

He rubbed his head, attempting to stifle the ache building at his temples. Of course he'd been too young to remember, but his mother had told him that part of the family history often enough. Like a bedtime story. Except she'd made it plain it was no fairytale. She and his father had gone to the aid of a distant McLaren relation, buying the ancient house and land to keep the man solvent. And keeping the estate in McLaren hands. Neill had been more than furious at their departure from Scotland: he had cursed and disowned them, yelling that they had thrown his every good deed in his face. McLaren grew up with an English accent, English friends, English middle class attitude, and English outlook on life. But he acquired knowledge about Clan McLaren on his own, in secret. And he consciously broke from the three centuries of McLaren owned brewery to go into the police for his career.

He got up, downed two aspirin with a swallow of water, and went to the window. Moonlight angled through the pane and pooled at his feet, as though throwing him into a spotlight. He sighed heavily, recalling the reaction that decision caused. His mother had been proud and a bit apprehensive, loving his need to help others yet worrying about his life. His sister didn't much care; she concentrated on establishing herself as an artist and getting married. His father had offered no advice other than every man had to choose his own way, even if it meant hurting hearts. As he had, in turn, done to his father when they'd left Scotland. So McLaren grew to manhood with a sense of needing to protect others who were abandoned and trodden upon, who felt the pain of injustice, as he did through his grandfather's condemnation of his abandonment of the family business and his desire to remain in England.

McLaren's career choice had more consequences than just the threat of being harmed by criminals. Going into the police meant he broke the link in the McLaren ownership tradition, forcing his grandfather to consider someone else to inherit the business after McLaren's uncle dies. He also realized that he, his mother, and father were seen as traitors in his grandfather's eyes. But he gave up years ago expecting his grandfather to be different from whom he was. So why couldn't grandfather accept McLaren for his self?

His mobile rang, startlingly loud in the quiet room. He glanced at the display panel. The name Liza Skene shone in large letters.

He answered the call immediately, hardly daring to breathe or wonder where she'd been. "Hello? Liza? Are you all right? Where have you been?"

A male voice muttered something unintelligible before the line went dead.

McLaren stared at the phone, then replaced it

against his ear. "Hello? Liza? Are you okay?"

Silence filled his ear and he yelled into the mouthpiece. "LIZA?"

He listened for a dozen seconds before accepting no one was on the other end. He cursed Liza, the phone company, and his general state of affairs before tossing the phone onto the bedside cabinet. He would've written it off as a wrong number except that Liza had called.

Or had she?

Did someone have her phone? If so, who? Why hadn't Liza spoken to him just then? If she was too sick or injured to speak, why hadn't the other person talked to him just now?

He got into bed, staring out the window until he fell asleep, and abandoned himself to dreams of rowan trees, underground passages, and missing women.

****

The next morning McLaren finished breakfast and wandered into the entryway. Jean was speaking on the phone in the back room, her voice muffled by the closed door but still understandable. In the hall, early sunlight streamed through the glass transom and threw a yellow rectangle onto the linoleum floor. A guest book topped a small wooden stand just inside the double doors and he leafed through the book as he waited for Jean to finish with her phone call. He'd decided during his meal to check out even though he had the room until tomorrow. He could return to Edinburgh after his day in Balquhidder, the village being approximately an hour's drive away, but his itinerary took him farther north, to Rannoch Moor, Ben Nevis, and Fort Augustus. It would be daft to drive back to Edinburgh just for one night.

The conversation droned on and McLaren idly glanced at some of the signatures in the book, curious to see the array of cities and countries of her guests. Many people were from Scotland, with English and Welsh addresses running a close second. Altrincham, Sale, Caddington, York, Norwich, Aberystwyth, Buxton. McLaren stared at the town name, then at the signature.

Charlie Harvester.

The light in the room seemed to dim and the floor slanted up to meet him. It had to be the same Charlie Harvester, the nemesis from his police days. Harvester lived in Buxton. There couldn't be two of them.

His curiosity up, McLaren flipped through several more pages, the dates becoming older. Harvester's name appeared three more times, each date approximately five or six months apart. The penned comment after each entry implied more than a casual lodging; it suggested friendship.

McLaren closed the book. Jean's voice gave no indication of the conversation ending soon, so he tiptoed into the guest lounge.

The blue-and-white color scheme prevalent to the other public areas of the bed-and-breakfast continued in the lounge. But the far wall held McLaren's attention. It seemed to be wallpapered in framed photographs. He slowly walked its length, staring at the pictures.

They were a mixture of black-and-white and color, of various sizes. He gave them a cursory look, wondering what he was trying to prove, when he stopped abruptly before an 8x10 inch group shot. Charlie Harvester's face grinned at him from the confines of the wooden frame.

McLaren stared at the face, unwilling to believe he looked at the man who'd been responsible for his leaving the police. But it was he. Harvester had his left arm draped over Jean's shoulder. They were on a picnic, the basket of food beside them, the blanket spread on the ground. Harvester's jeans were rolled up mid-calf length, his feet bare. Jean wore shorts and an off-shoulder T-shirt. Hardly the attire if the two were not friends.

He was about to move on to the other photos when he looked at the third person in the snap. The man was smaller and younger, probably in his late teens, with dark hair and a mustache. And a tattooed chin.

Chapter Eight

McLaren hurried from the room as Jean ended her phone conversation. She walked into the hallway and smiled as she saw McLaren moving toward the staircase. "You about to leave for the day? Have something nice planned?" Her voice sounded light and friendly.

"I'm about to go out, yes. I will be leaving tomorrow, as originally planned when the booking was made." He smiled, hoping he looked sincere.

"I was hoping you'd stay on a bit. Edinburgh's so lovely decorated for Christmas, with the white lights strung across the High Street and all. Maybe do a bit of your shopping. So many things that you can't get in Derbyshire."

"It's a temptation." McLaren nodded, envisioning the area at night. Strands of white lights seemed to float in the darkness; lighted decorations and red ribbons adorned street lamps. The snow and crisp wind added to the festive feeling and, if he would admit it, it tempted him to stay for the holiday. "I've got other business, though, and will be leaving, however much I'd like to extend my trip."

"I do hope you found everything fine…with your business here and with the room. Nothing wrong with either, is there?" Jean glanced up the flight of stairs, as though she could see up to the landing.

"No." McLaren paused, the lie hard to swallow. The room itself wasn't that bad, but the bathroom was ridiculously cramped. A small radiator opposite the toilet took up several precious inches of space, forcing him to lean over the toilet to reach the sink. Since the curtains in the bedroom couldn't be closed fully, he dressed in the shower cubicle. He'd decided if he ever wrote a travel book he'd title it *Dressing in a Shower Stall and other Traveling Challenges*. That just about summed up his whole Edinburgh experience. So he lied, wanting to avoid confrontation. "I'll be concluding my business here by this evening, and I want to do a bit of sightseeing farther north before I head back home."

"Well, I'm sorry you won't be staying on, but I do hope you enjoyed your stay here in the city."

"It's a trip I'll not soon forget."

"Your first time here?"

"In Edinburgh, yes."

"Well, now that you know where I am, I hope you'll not be a stranger. I've enjoyed having you as a guest."

"Thank you. If I come back, I'll look you up." He climbed the stairs, but he couldn't shake the curious feeling that she was watching him.

In his room, he sat on his bed and rang Liza Skene once more. The woman still didn't answer her phone. He glanced at his watch. Just gone nine o'clock. He rang up the library and asked to speak to her. Again he was informed that Liza had neither phoned in nor appeared for work. He rang off concerned something was definitely wrong. Where was she? What had happened? She hadn't been physically injured, so a hospital stay was unlikely. If she were with a friend or family member, as he'd first surmised, wouldn't she have informed her boss? Just walking off like this had the aroma of three-day-old fish.

Not knowing what else he could do about Liza, he punched Jamie's number into his mobile. His cop's sixth sense about the photograph niggled at him, and he'd been in the job long enough to realize he shouldn't ignore it.

Jamie answered the phone with a sleepy "Hello?" but forced a bit more life into his voice when he realized it was McLaren phoning. "Mike?"

"Yeah. Did I wake you?"

"Just coming off nights."

"Sorry."

"That's all right. You didn't know. What's going on?"

McLaren described the photo of Harvester and Lanny, and of Harvester's multiple stays at the guesthouse. "What's it sound like to you?"

"Sounds like they're all chummy, for whatever reason. Kind of coincidental you staying in the same bed-and-breakfast your mate Harvester frequents."

"Glad you're of the same mind. I thought I might be making too much of the link."

"With Harvester involved? You're joking."

"So, what's it mean?"

"You'd have a better idea of that than I would. I hardly know the man."

"You don't know when you're well off, Jamie."

"Look, Mike. Something's rotten in Edinburgh. That man you were standing next to is hit and killed by a car; that girl, Liza, is missing; you trailed Lanny Clack to Mary King's Close and he magically disappears. Now you see that your landlady, toughie Lanny, and Mr. Personality Harvester all know each other. What's it take to convince you you're in the enemy camp?"

"You forgot my grandfather's invitation that wasn't an invitation."

"More proof. How much more do you need?"

"Before I learned that Harvester is involved in some fashion with Jean MacNab, I couldn't make heads or tails of my grandfather's surprise at seeing me, but now I believe Harvester set up the entire thing, got me up here with that fake binding-of-the-family-wound thing, and booked me into this place." McLaren chewed on his bottom lip as he thought through the last few days. "It's Harvester's style. He steps over obstacles in his way, eliminates perceived problems. He did that in police school and he did that when we worked together. Got a problem with a witness? Get rid of him or apply the strong arm stuff."

"I'm surprised he's on this side of the law."

"His inclination is more like a criminal's, I'll admit. He's a thug in a copper's uniform."

"You always told me he was a control freak, never trusting anyone to follow through, wanting to do everything himself. Sounds more and more like a dictator all the time, even down to arranging your and your grandfather's meeting."

McLaren stretched. "I'll say this for the man: it took a lot of planning."

"But what's it in aid of, Mike? Why would Harvester lure you up there and pay for your room?"

"Perhaps I'll discover that before I leave here."

"I think you can eliminate a joke. He wouldn't

spend that kind of money just to laugh at you."

"Then we've more in common than I thought. I'd not spend one pence on him. Now, the reason I phoned you... Could you call your police pal again?"

Jamie yawned vocally before replying to the question. "Ross Gordon? Sure. What do you want?"

"I want to know what the connection is, if any, between Lanny and Jean."

"You think something illegal is going on at the guesthouse?"

"Not necessarily. But Lanny's a criminal with a long history of robbery, gang association, and violence. He hasn't changed in the ten years he's been in and out of prison, so I see no reason for him to suddenly change his spots now. What's he doing with a supposedly reputable person as Jean MacNab? Especially now that Harvester's in the group."

"If he gets suspicious about all these phone calls I'll tell him the earlier information on Lanny didn't help, that it must be another bloke we're after."

"Just make the story believable. And rehearse it so you don't stumble."

"I'll ring you back when I've got it. Could be a while. I don't know if he's working right now."

"Thanks. I owe you."

"Your tab's getting awfully long, Mike. You better start paying it off soon."

"Soon as I get back."

"When's that?"

"Oh..." He glanced at the date on his smart phone. "Today's Wednesday. I've got a few places I want to see before I leave but they won't take long. I ought to be on the train Saturday evening."

"If you don't answer your home phone Sunday I'll have Ross call out the sniffer dogs." He signed off with the assurance he'd call back soon.

McLaren had had every intention of checking out in a few minutes. There was really no reason for him to stay. But discovering that Jean knew Harvester and Lanny altered everything, not only his feeling toward the woman but also about his personal safety. Surely Lanny wouldn't try anything here: there was the chance a late-returning guest would see Lanny and identify him later. And it was ludicrous to imagine Harvester here. The man would have to be hidden for fear that he'd be seen.

If Harvester had set all this up, and McLaren assumed he had, what was the man's next step? If he had wanted Lanny to run him down, and that had failed, would Harvester personally try something, his faith in Lanny gone? Harvester was not one to delegate important jobs lightly. He liked to control every possible thing. So did that mean Harvester was in Edinburgh?

McLaren rang up the station where Harvester worked. Detective-Inspector Harvester wasn't in, wouldn't be in the rest of the week, but if the caller would like to leave a message…

He closed his phone and slipped it into his pocket. Just because the man was on holiday didn't mean he was here. There were a million places he could be, but none of them made as much sense as Edinburgh.

McLaren glanced at his watch. Nearly nine thirty. Sighing, he got up, slipped into his jacket, and left the guesthouse. It was going to be a long day.

He breathed in a lungful of cold, dry air and

stepped off the porch. A bank of gray clouds clung to the western horizon but the sky overhead was clear. Perhaps it boded well.

His confidence faded quickly, however, when he spotted one of his business cards on the pathway. He picked it up, staring at his handwritten name sprawled across the card's face. The ink had feathered slightly, the paper stock damp from the wet walkway, but "Mike" was unmistakable. As was the card. It was one of his. Probably the one he'd signed before giving it to Liza. He wrote on cards only when he gave them out, fitting the signature or additional information to the recipient.

He straightened up slowly, as though he'd suffered a jab to his stomach. As if he still harbored a doubt about the card, the date in the upper left hand corner confirmed it belonged to Liza. But why was the card here, and where was Liza? Perhaps more importantly, he thought as he strode down the street, whose blood was smeared over the white surface?

The corner café was busy with breakfast customers dining in or picking up orders. The air was thick with low-volume conversations, the ring of the cash register, and recorded classical music. The air also held the scents of hot coffee, hot apples and cinnamon, and pine boughs.

He stood in line, his mind trying to sort through the recent events. He didn't hear the cashier call "Next, please," and was nudged into taking his turn at the counter.

"Yes, sir. Good morning. What may I get you?" The soft Scottish burr tore his mind from the card in his jacket pocket.

"I'd like…a coffee." He said it quickly, needing an excuse for his visit and feeling he'd get more cooperation if he were a customer.

"Very good, sir. White or black? Which blend?" The cashier stepped to the left so McLaren could see the menu on the wall.

Not really caring, he read off the first choice that he saw. "Flat White."

"Perfect choice, sir." The clerk grabbed a small ceramic cup and turned to the espresso machine. The whir masked the music and nearby conversations until it was shut off and the steamed milk poured into the coffee. McLaren watched the clerk move the jug as she created the latte art. She set the cup in front of McLaren, careful not to disturb the spiral-caged heart floating on the coffee's surface.

McLaren commented on her skill, paid for the drink, and sat at a corner table. He sipped the beverage, considering what he'd do. The blood did nothing more than suggest Liza had been hurt. Running a DNA test against hair strands in her brush, for example, was as ridiculous as it would be expensive. Besides, even if he got a court order allowing the police to collect samples from her house, the lab results would take months. He hadn't that much time; Liza needed his help now. And even supposing he got the lab results in a day or so, what good would it do? She would still be missing, with no clue as to where she was. No, the card held no significance other than hint at someone's injury.

The Christmas carol "God Rest Ye Merry, Gentlemen" filtered through the café noise. Should I take that as a hint, he wondered. Give this whole thing a rest, stop imagining spies and crooks in every alley and bus stop? But he couldn't deny events had turned odd the minute he'd knocked on the family home door. His grandfather hadn't sent for him; he'd been the target of a botched hit-and-run; the woman he'd been with had gone missing; a phone call from her had ended abruptly; and now he had his business card decorated with a bloody smudge.

He withdrew the card from his pocket. The partial thumbprint was well defined closest to the card's interior. It turned into a smear near the edge, as though it'd been yanked from the holder's hand. Yet, if that were so, did that suggest the two people had been on the walk of the guesthouse? Or had Liza run from her abductor, getting as far as the porch and leaving it as a clue before she was recaptured?

He rubbed his forehead, listening briefly to the carol. Yes, he should give it a rest. This whole thing didn't make sense. If Liza had run from her kidnapper, why hadn't she screamed? Surely someone, if not he, would've heard that and come to her rescue.

The carol ended and he finished the last of the coffee. He got up, shoved the card back into his pocket, and walked up to the cashier.

She smiled and asked if he'd like something else.

"Yes, but not another coffee. My friend and I were walking around last night and she lost her ring."

"Sorry to hear that, sir."

"Sorry to have to say it. I know you weren't open, but we did pass the café and the outdoor section. I wonder if anyone found the ring this morning and turned it in? It's gold, rather small, with…" He took a breath, biding for time, thinking wildly. What could he say? "With a clan crest on it. Skene. The writing's very small, but it's of a dexter arm coming out of a cloud." He looked hopeful, wondering if he'd sounded convincing. Dena always said he lied more smoothly than anyone she knew. Must be his police training…

"Nothing was given to me, but perhaps one of the other staff members received it. Let me look." She walked over to the counter behind her, stooped, and opened a door. After rummaging through several articles and looking into a drawer, she closed the door and came back to him. "There's no gold ring here, sir."

"Perhaps it's not been found yet. Would you mind if I looked in the courtyard area?"

"Not at all. Good luck." Her voice faded under the explosion of Manheim Steamroller's drums and the whine of the espresso machine.

One hardy soul sat at a courtyard table in the sun, his newspaper spread before him, a coffee cup in his hand. A plate, empty except for crumbs, had been shoved away from the paper. Several sparrows appeared to be eyeing the leftovers from their perches on a nearby tree.

McLaren walked around the patio, peering beneath the tarps covering the chairs and tables, using a tree branch to poke through the few remaining clumps of snow. When he finished one length of the area, he returned, covering a new section.

Except for some patches of snow, the patio held nothing foreign. Several depressions in the snow had thawed into irregular shapes, some exposing the flagstones, but he couldn't swear if they were footprints or merely melting clumps. He found no indication that anyone had hidden there last night, and he began to wonder if he'd imagined it.

A slight movement attracted his gaze and he walked over to the far corner. A bird's feather stuck vertically in a lump of snow, pale gray against the dingy whiteness, twitching in the breeze. He jammed his fingertips into the cold mass but felt nothing suspicious.

He moved on, searching the remainder of the courtyard. He found no other items connected with Liza. The clan brooch was still his only clue she'd been there.

Or *someone* had been there. Skene kin other than Liza could lose items just as easily as she could.

He silently cursed the brooch and the business card and walked back to the guesthouse.

****

"The infuriating thing about this," McLaren exhaled sharply into his mobile, "is that I know Liza's in trouble, but I can't prove it."

Jamie's reply was slow in coming. "You can't go to the police with what you have, at any rate. That's for certain. Did she say anything about visiting a friend? Maybe she decided to go off somewhere to get over the trauma."

"I thought of that, but she didn't say. I need to find out what happened to her, Jamie. I need to do it now, not tomorrow. If she's hurt, she needs help. I can't just wait around. I have to do something to find her, and do it *now*."

"Short of going on the telly to ask if anyone's seen her, I haven't a clue as to what you could do."

"If I could get into her house and look at her address book—"

"First of all, how many people do you know who

still have an address book? They keep all that contact info on their mobiles or on their computers. Second, I'm not going to ring up the constabulary so they'll let you inside. Third, you don't know the woman last night was Liza and you don't know a bloody thing about the circumstances of the tossed business card."

"But you said it's damned weird."

"I can say the sun rises in the north but that doesn't make it so, Mike. Sure, this is all very odd, but you said it yourself—you can't prove a thing."

McLaren muttered that he'd get better results from a sniffer dog than from Jamie. "Isn't it weird, though, that these two people last night didn't say a thing and rushed right by me, and I find a brooch like Liza's after they leave? And isn't it odd that the card I give her ends up where I can conveniently find it a few blocks from the café?"

"I grant you it's weird, but maybe you interrupted a drug deal last night. Or they were about to do a lift."

"A burglar wouldn't react like she did. The woman screamed."

"Maybe her male accomplice stepped on her toe in their hurry to leave the crime scene. Hell, I don't know, Mike. You've got to give it a rest."

"This is the second time I've heard that today," he mumbled, thinking of the carol in the café.

"Then follow the advice. I'm not saying you shouldn't be concerned about Liza, but you can't do a thing if you don't know where she is or what's happened to her. When you know something definite, ring up Ross Gordon at the Stirling police station and get some help. Better yet, play the tourist and visit some places. Like the city's Old Town Jail. I hear it's quite interesting."

"If you're not in the nick, it might be."

"Anyway," Jamie yawned, the clink of a spoon sailing into McLaren's ear, "you'll know what to do and do it when the time comes. That's your second best quality, Mike."

"What's my first?"

"Patience."

McLaren rang off, unsure if he felt better from talking to his friend. He considered talking to Ross Gordon to get the man's view on Liza's disappearance, but quickly abandoned the idea. As Jamie said, without any evidence, he'd come off looking a right nerk.

He checked his notes, debating about the rest of his day. He wondered if he could ring up the house and meet his uncle somewhere for lunch or a pint, but the way his day was going his grandfather would probably answer. And that would fuel his frustration.

He'd just about decided to disguise his voice and phone the family home when his mobile pinged. An email from his sister. He sat on the bed and read her message.

From:GwenHulme <him.and.me@GBlinked.TL

Subject:granddad info

Date:10 December 10:54:52 AM

To:Mike McLaren

Mike—I've had to root around but I found the old journal I wanted. Dad must've packed it by mistake when we left Auchtubh for England. At least, I can't figure out any other reason why he and not granddad would have it. I doubt he would've willingly parted with it or given it to dad as a keepsake. Gran was extremely dejected when we left and although that doesn't match granddad's anger, it must've made for a gloomy household. Be that as it may, perhaps he didn't even know it was gone. He doesn't seem the type to bring out the Auld Reminders to reminisce over, but I haven't seen him since I was a teenager, so what do I know?

Anyway...you sounded so frustrated and confused the day we spoke that I thought this might help you understand granddad and thereby clear up some of your hurt. Not that I condone his treatment of you in all this, but perhaps knowing him better will shine some light into the darkness. Let me know if the attachment doesn't come through—I scanned it, and we all know the limitations of my technology knowledge.

;-) Ta. Your sister

He smiled, recalling the times he'd had to talk her through various things like programming the VCR or hooking up her computer. He didn't fault her for her shortcoming. Her brain didn't work that way. She was an artist, not a techie.

He opened the attachment and was surprised to see a multi-paged handwritten document. Larger than a traditional girl's memoir, it had probably been written in a ledger. The writing held the hint of past generations, the letters firm and rounded by hours of practiced circles filling the pages. McLaren noted the year at the top of the page—1949—and quickly lost himself in his grandfather's jottings.

20 April

Gillian sent word that she couldn't come to tea. Thrice this month, now. She declares she's not sickly, but I suspect she's trying to spare me grief if she's terrible ill. Can it be serious?

Lambing continues, though most of the ewes have

delivered. Gillian's suggestion last month, about selling the entire flock to her brother, have led to many hours of contemplation, I must admit. But the sheep tend to themselves, for the most part, and the output of cash is minimal, so I'll wait a bitty to make my decision.

23 April

Gillian came to tea, though she couldnae stay long. She looks to be in good health but for paleness to her face. At times the flush came to her cheeks and she would lower her head. At such a time she would consult her timepiece. Powell saw her off and we talked about the brewery until he left.

30 April

Powell couldnae make the appointment with the bank this morning. He had the financial figures so I had to postpone the meeting for another fortnight. I'm anxious to get the loan so we may begin our expansion. But I must be patient, for I havenae the facts.

Had the man in to quote a price for the roof repair.

Gillian will have a flower arrangement at the village fete tomorrow. I must remember tae get someone else tae judge that event.

1 May

Rained for most of the May Day fete. Many exhibits could be moved into the kirk hll. The flower arrangements, bakery entries and artwork already were safe inside, which eliminated a disaster.

The singing went well. Miss Lennox took First in violin, while Master Ewan succeeded in capturing his fourth consecutive First in piping.

I couldnae find Gillian after the judging so I had tea with Lady Murdock.

Cousin Alec accompanied me to the fete. He

agreed with my purchase of the Coloured Ryeland ram—the winner in its division—and made arrangements to transport it to the farm. I feel the new bloodline will greatly improve my stock, if for no other reason than to sell next year. The sheep have been an interesting sideline, but am needing to focus on the brewery.

Laurel's Crown placed first in the stallion judging. I'll increase his sire fees.

6 May

Rained all afternoon and into the evening.

The church was broken into last night. Dogs and men searched the area but no evidence has been found as to the culprit's identity. Nothing was taken other than a Hymnary. The sheriff found footprints in the soft ground, but the men and the dogs lost both the prints and any scent on the rocky ground on the ben.

Word from Powell is that he's been called to London to deal with his cousin's estate. He's postponed the bank meeting until the end of July.

8 May

Beryl accepted my offer to tea, which we had by the fire, since the rain spoiled my planned outing. She arrived punctually, which I put down to her father's drilling and not her character. Still, she's pleasant enough company, if not as handsome as Gillian. She commented quite sensibly on the foals in the paddock. She knows horseflesh and rides well. I may include her in the next ride, as she sits a decent saddle.

Received a letter from John in Auckland. It's unbelievable he's been there four years already. He says he's doing well, is married, and the sheep station is returning money. The land appears to yield bounty to

those who seek it.
10 May

The rain hasn't abated much, if at all. There are fears the road into the village may wash out due to flooding. I've instructed the staff to lay in provisions for all of us, as well as for the animals. We may very well be cut off from the town for some time if the road goes.

15 May

No word from Gillian despite my phoning her house and then riding over. The butler assures me she is well, but indisposed, which I take to infer too busy to see me.

I've had a few words with Cousin Alec about the brewery expansion. He cannae fund the work, so I must wait for Powell to return from The Smoke. He's stayed longer than his fortnight and cannae say when he'll be back. I'm very disheartened.

The Sheriff has canceled the search for the church burglar.

Priority has been given to the theft of one of my stallions from the northern paddock.

4 June

Cousin Alec informed me this evening that Gillian and Powell were wed on 29 May. Alec received the information from the Reverend Dunbar, who happened to be visiting his uncle in London. The uncle performed the marriage ceremony. They will be immigrating to New Zealand in two days. Powell has a position in a bank in Wellington.

I will return Grandma's jewels to the bank tomorrow.

5 June

Beryl arrived this afternoon with a bouquet of

heather and laurel, as well as a Dundee cake. We took the horses for a ride until dusk and she stayed for tea. I saw her home.

McLaren smiled, envisioning a ribbon tied around the plants' stalks and the shy way, perhaps, that Beryl presented it. Heather was an obvious choice for a proud old-world Scot, and laurel was a stroke of genius. It was the clan badge, the plant denoting victory. But in this instance, was it the MacLaren bloodline or Beryl who was the victor?

He turned back to the writings.

6 June

Beryl accepted ma marriage proposal. She seemed happy. I dinnae know if she realised I didnae say I loved her. Whether love will develop in time isn't important right now. She's an undemanding companion and will run the house well; I'll have time for the business. We set the date for 6 August. Her brother and father are advancing me the money for the brewery expansion. I'll talk to the bank tomorrow.

10 June

I met with my solicitor to begin proceedings against Powell. I'm ignorant of the laws regarding criminal flight to Australia, but I do need my money, especially now that Beryl's father and brother cannae come up with the funding after all. Powell took every quid I'd set aside fir the brewery.

McLaren looked up from the computer screen. The images of the house in Auchtubh and his relatives' faces floated before him. His grandfather had suffered a lot—his fiancée running away with his business partner, his money for the brewery tucked away in some Australian bank, his future wife's relatives reneging on the expected money.

McLaren sat back, his throat tightening. His grandfather's life had been defined by betrayal. No wonder he had suspected a trap when McLaren appeared on the doorstep. Every time the man had opened his heart to love or friends he'd been double-crossed. Just because the face before him was different didn't guarantee he wouldn't be betrayed again. The man had built a shell around him to deflect potential hurt. It wouldn't be easy for McLaren to crack that shell.

He scrolled down dozen of pages and stopped at a page approximately a year farther on. He read slowly, his eyes tearing.

30 September

Beryl miscarried of a son this morning. We had him baptized immediately before the burial. I named him Michael.

McLaren leaned his head back and shut his eyes, ignoring the tear trickling down his cheek. Michael. My Christian name. Was that part of the reason for Granddad's hostility? Was he looking at me as the son he would've had, the boy on whom he'd wanted to place his future and dreams, yet who betrayed him by forsaking the family and business?

He wiped the back of his hand across his eyes and fired off an email to his sister.

From:M McLaren <boars.rock.walls@GBlinked.TL
Subject:inquiry info
Date:10 December 12:14:02 p.m.
To:Gwen Hulme

Dear Brilliant Sis—I read most of the journal pages. I'm still reeling...from shock, joy, grief, pride. Of course I had no knowledge of any of this, neither gran's being married on the rebound, her less than love-filled life, the brother that could've predated dad... And the misery granddad dealt with through the betrayals. I can't quite comprehend it all. It'll take me a few days to absorb it. But it explains a lot about his personality, so even though I'm despondent about his life, I empathize with the man. He's suffered a hell of a lot, and none of it from his own fault, evidently.

I'll read the rest later. Right now I have a few other things to get done. Thanks again for scrounging through the dust or attic or the horrors of your dresser drawer to find this and send it along. All kidding aside, Gwen, I'm very grateful to know about The Auld Laird. ;-) Ta. Mike

He remained where he was, his back sagging against the headboard, his head throbbing. The sunlight had shifted in position and color, the deep yellow of afternoon slanting into the room. His stomach complained that breakfast was too long ago, yet he made no attempt to get up. The sins heaped upon his grandfather angered him. It was unjust. And he fought injustice.

And maybe he needed the reminder of the laurel. He might get through all the problems after all.

He got up, grabbed his car key and mobile, and went out to look for a lunch place and Liza Skene. Not necessarily in that order.

****

McLaren spent the hours after lunch talking to Liza's colleagues at the library before explaining to the police about the hit-and-run accident and his suspicion that Liza was a bona fide missing person. The session hadn't gone well, as he'd privately bet with himself as he entered the building. He'd sat for nearly twenty minutes in the lobby before a sergeant led him into an office replete with wanted posters, missing persons appeals, and prints of nineteenth-century police uniforms.

When McLaren had finished his explanation, the officer asked for a photo of Liza, which McLaren couldn't provide. The officer then wanted details of her friends, relatives and coworkers, none of which McLaren knew and, therefore, had no information. Nor was he helpful with particulars of places Liza frequented.

The officer was less than enthusiastic about looking at hours of CCTV video for a sign of her possible abductors or a street accident. Had McLaren any suggestion which camera tape to view or on what time span to focus? And as for a possible medical condition and hospitals to phone…

The officer's irritation poked through his practiced poker face as McLaren recommended a search of her home, stating an appointment notation or phone message might direct the investigation. His suggestion that a constable procure her DNA from her toothbrush, hairbrush, bed linen, or fingernail clippings was quickly nixed; besides needing a crime scene, suspect, or body for the genetic match, the DNA sample would require entering Liza's home. And the officer, at least at this time, had no motivation to do so, unless McLaren wanted to provide a mouth swab or fingerprint inking to match to anything found in the home, should they need to collect such items later… McLaren readily agreed to do it, saying he'd been in her home just the once, and that was in the front room and kitchen, but to go ahead and look if that would propel the hunt for her. When the officer asked which relative would grant them search permission, McLaren could only shrug and say there must be a relation *some* place, and if they'd only look for a card index or Christmas card list or perhaps a scrapbook or box of cards…

The officer had thanked him for his ideas, and kindly but firmly dismissed him, saying he'd record Liza Skene as missing and provide the information to other constabularies within the next two days. McLaren had left the station, angry and frustrated and feeling an utter fool.

He drove around the city, half determined to break into Liza's house despite the officer's non-cooperation, half determined to let it go and see as much of Edinburgh and the area as he could before he left for home. He berated himself for failing to convince the sergeant to instigate the search, and tried to ignore the man's parting statement that Liza Skene was an adult and, as such, had every right to leave the city, should she desire, without contacting anyone.

McLaren slammed his fist onto the steering wheel. He'd rattled off that same phrase often enough when he was in the job, trying to console distraught kin—didn't need the officer's reminder. But it echoed in his head the rest of the day.

It whispered so loudly at one point that he nearly missed seeing her in the crowd.

He was in the outside lane opposite Greyfriars Kirkyard. A red head sporting a red, green, and blue muffler hurried from the pavement toward the churchyard. Even though her back was toward

McLaren, he recognized Liza.

He jerked the car out of the traffic lane and screeched to a halt along the curb. She was a hundred feet or so in front of him and about to disappear around the corner of the graveyard's east wall. The car barely halted before he was sprinting through the iron gates and onto the path.

The snow offered little help with his pursuit, having melted from the sexton's liberal casting of salt. McLaren dashed in the direction of his last sighting, desperate to glimpse the red plaid muffler against the gray stone monuments.

The cemetery was more crowded than he would've thought for a Wednesday, but it *was* a tourist destination, he recalled. Several clusters of people were scattered about the area, no doubt on a tour, and he jogged past them. When he came to the northeast corner, he stopped.

Liza had disappeared.

He dashed down the path curving between the headstones, then paused as he came to the Y-branch. Which way to go? He saw no indication of her presence or her having come this way. He ran back to the corner and dashed several hundred yards down the opposite path before he again stopped. A group of old age pensioners stood around a monument but harbored no one resembling Liza.

He cursed his bad luck and raced ahead, thinking she might be on the other side of the kirk.

A woman wearing a red muffler sat on a bench opposite a large marble tablet. McLaren paused for breath, then jogged up to her. She turned to look at him, and in the first second it was evident the woman wasn't

Liza. She laid a camera on her lap, her expression questioning his sudden appearance, and asked if he wanted something.

"Sorry," he said, disappointed and apologetic at once. "I thought you were someone else. Someone I've been looking for."

The woman shrugged and glanced around her. "What's she look like? Maybe I've seen her."

"Rather like you, which is why I thought you... Well, she's a trim, fairly short, redhead, maybe your age. The last time I saw her she wore a muffler in the Skene tartan."

She glanced at the wool scarf dangling from her neck. "I'm afraid I'm not familiar with that sett. I should be embarrassed, not knowing a part of my Scottish heritage, but clans and things never appealed to me. Are the colors like this, then?" She held up the garment, its red-and-black checks as regimented as a chessboard, and stared at him as if expecting him to transform it into the correct pattern.

"Not really. It's red, blue, and green. A plaid woven in intervals."

"Kind of difficult to tell at a distance. Dark blue and green often are indistinguishable."

He nodded, feeling foolish and impatient at the waste of time. Liza could be anywhere in the churchyard by now. "Well, thank you. Sorry for the intrusion on your photography."

"Not at all. I'm just waiting for the light to shift."

He nodded and walked on, thinking a shift in light might help him see Liza's disappearance more clearly.

****

The clock downstairs in the entryway later that

night chimed one o'clock, and McLaren eased his room door shut. The landing was dark and quiet, the last of the guests having come in over an hour ago and now sleeping. He tiptoed to the end of the hallway and grasped the railing as he leaned over. Light from a small table lamp splayed across the linoleum floor, the harlequin pattern looking bizarre in the dimness. With the black tiles merging into the darkness, the white squares of flooring appeared to be the only solid footing. No sound other than the soft ticks of the clock and a gurgling radiator wound up the stairs. The house had settled comfortably for the night.

He moved down the stairway, his bare feet hardly touching the carpet, most of his weight on his left hand as he inched along the banister. A step squeaked under his foot and he froze, fearful the sound would summon Jean. He stood in the faint light, trying to blend with the wall behind him, his heart racing. No one responded to the squeaky step; no one called out.

At the bottom of the stairs, he again paused, wondering which room to try. The guest lounge wouldn't have Jean's personal computer but perhaps the front room, where she'd been talking on the phone yesterday, would. He crept past the closed lounge door, watching his shadow stretch before him as he passed the small lamp, and stopped at the front room. He bent over.

No light shone from beneath the door. He laid his right palm on the door and turned the doorknob. It opened easily, without a sound, and revealed a black void.

McLaren slipped into the room and shut the door. He stood with his back against it, listening. No alarm sounded; no dog yapped. He snapped on his small torch and played the beam around the room. The windows seemed bedded down for the night, the curtains drawn securely to let in no chink of light. Or inquisitive eye. He let out his breath in one long, slow release.

The computer monitor threw back the reflection of the torchlight and he went over to it. He opened the desk drawers and carefully searched the contents, looking for letters or notes that would explain more fully the connection between Jean, Lanny, and Harvester. All he found were notecards, guesthouse stationery, postage stamps, bills and receipts, pens and pencils, paperclips, a magnifying glass, envelopes, and a ruler. He shut the drawers. Was he looking for something that didn't exist?

He moved the computer mouse and the screen jumped to life.

He read the titles of the word document folder icons displayed on the monitor desktop: Reservations, Business Bookkeeping, Private Events, Correspondence, Menus, Advertising, Tourist Sites. None of them looked promising. He moved the mouse cursor and opened the word file. Every file pertained to the guesthouse business.

When he double clicked the email icon a dozen mailings from Harvester caught his eye. He opened the first one.

From:Charles Harvester
Subject:Exterminating a Pest
Date:12 Nov
To:Jean MacNab

Jean—Things sound like they're progressing nicely. Good to hear McLaren's accepted the invitation and will be lodging with you. That's one less problem I have to deal with.

I'll be getting there close to when he arrives—don't know the exact date yet. I'm waiting to hear from my son, Emory, whom I will visit either on my way to or from Edinburgh. Part of my yearly Christmas routine, but I don't have to remind you of that!

I'll be well chuffed to see Emory again, make no mistake about that, but I think the best Christmas gift I'll ever have will be finally ridding myself of McLaren. We've hated each other since our days together in police school. I know I should've done something about it right after graduation, but anything that drastic would've pointed at me. Unfortunately, it's just grown worse for me every time I see his damned face or read his bloody name in the newspapers. You'd think he was some kind of rock star or super hero, the way the media get wound up about the cold cases he supposedly solves. I've never been so sick in my life, being subjected to all that crap. Well, I've got a little plan that will rid me of Michael McLaren for once and for all, so my new year will be something to cheer.
Thanks for your help with this. C

McLaren frowned as he re-read the email. Their uneasy history went back years, but he had no inkling that he'd affected Harvester so greatly. Was Harvester's little plan to murder McLaren?

He moved the mouse cursor to the Print command on the computer's tool bar, then eyed the printer, and stopped. He glanced at the door. It remained closed. There was no sound beyond it in the hallway. Did he dare take a chance and print the email? Would the printer noise wake Jean? But he needed the evidence…

Thinking better of the situation, he relinquished his grip on the mouse and opened his mobile phone. His hand shook slightly as he tried to position the email in the viewfinder. He took a deep breath, telling himself this was no way to help the police, should it come to that. His trembling ceased, his heart rate slowed, and seconds later he had a photo of the email.

Another email subject looked damning, and he double-clicked on it.

From:Charles Harvester

Subject:The Lure

Date:16 Nov

To:Jean MacNab

Jean—Smashing about the room for your guest. Thanks for playing the hostess. One other thing comes to mind: can you find the old man's home address and email it to me? I overheard McLaren talking about his family, and his grandfather in particular, during our forced mutual employment at Staffordshire years ago. Heard about it till I was sick of him and his bloody family. But who would've thought years later it would come in handy? I've got another little surprise planned for McLaren, once he gets there, but I need to know where his grandfather lives in order to set it up. Sorry I won't be able to see the two of them react to all this, but I'll get it second hand from him later, which is almost as good.

Thanks. C

McLaren's grip tightened on the mouse as he stared at the message. Why did Harvester need Neill's address? And what was the surprise that involved Neill and McLaren?

Unsure of Harvester's intended actions and

concern about his grandfather prompted him to photograph this email, too. He closed down the file, opened the next email and slowly read it.

From:Charles Harvester

Subject:Idea

Date:20 Nov

To:Jean MacNab

Jean—I've just about got it all set up, thanks to you. The old man can't be living in a better spot for my plan. Maybe there is a God after all! I will have it all together by December, when McLaren arrives there. Not much left to do. Lanny's got his instructions and he mentioned bringing in another bloke to help him. I'd rather it was kept between us three, but if Lanny needs help, that's fine. Just so it works. Keep your lovely eyes open and let me know if McLaren gets suspicious, will you? I'll be at the Station, of course, but a phone call can always get me if they need help. I may have to implement Plan B, but I doubt he'll give any of this a second thought. He's so egotistical he won't suspect he's been lured up there.

See you soon. C

McLaren sat in the darkness, the monitor alive and throwing shadows behind him. The house was silent, as quiet as the grave, but for the swift pounding of his heart. He glanced again at the door. Could Jean hear it in her room? It was an inane question, he knew, but his anxiety for his grandfather shoved his imagination into overdrive.

He grabbed his mobile for the last time that night and snapped a photo of the third email before returning it to its position on the dock. But he remained seated for another minute, the glow of the phone's viewfinder startlingly bright in the darkness. The emails incriminated Harvester as surely as any verbal confession, evidence of a nasty, premeditated crime. Enough evidence for a criminal charge and dismissal from service, never mind the prison time. McLaren brought up the three photos on his mobile, made sure they were readable, then emailed them to Jamie with an explanatory note.

After putting the monitor to sleep McLaren left the room. He got back into bed but was still awake when his alarm clock rang at seven.

Chapter Nine

Breakfast and checkout didn't come quickly enough for McLaren later that Thursday morning. He put on his best smile, thanked Jean for his stay, and forced himself to walk leisurely to his car. He'd never been so glad to see a place in a rearview mirror.

He left the busy M9 just north of Stirling, turning onto the A84. The road was a fairly straight shot northwest to his grandfather's house in Auchtubh and then on to Balquhidder. Yesterday, before he'd read those disturbing emails, he'd planned to stop in Callander for an early lunch and then side step to Lade Inn, at the foot of Ben Ledi. He had missed the beer festival, but he wanted to see the inn, have a pint of Rannoch in the area where his family had roamed. But the fear that his grandfather was in danger spurred him directly to the small village. He'd do the sightseeing later.

Traffic thinned out the farther north he drove and he pressed down more firmly on the accelerator pedal. Light rain fell, more mist than liquid, and he flipped on the wipers. They squeaked before they spread the water evenly over the glass, then settled down to a rhythmic slap. The land flowed past his window, rising up in heather-patched mountains, forests, and flat bogs. Higher mountain peaks merged into the white clouds littering the dark blue sky, with smears of snow in the elevated glens and along the rocky outcroppings. The wind howled off the mountain slopes and stirred the trees before bending the tough stalks of grass. A frozen burn caught the sunlight and winked at him.

Rock seemed to dominate most of the landscape, from the stony crag faces and boulders to the timeworn rock cottages and shielings, the small huts used by herdsmen as living quarters as they watched over their sheep on the hillsides. Rocks lined the riverbeds, their roughness smoothed by centuries of flowing water, their colors intense. Rocks formed the land, provided building materials and sometimes weapons. He glanced at a kestrel hovering over a section of moorland and wondered why he'd stayed away so long.

It was ancient land, the land of his ancestors, and he felt a strange tug of his heart and tightening of his throat. He couldn't contribute it to the concern over his grandfather's safety. It was a link with his heritage. He'd not been back since his parents took him away as an infant, but the tie welled up inside him as though he were a sailor back from a long sea voyage.

He found himself thinking of the lyrics to "Through Moorfields." He'd never sung it with his folk group, but he'd heard it often in his youth, his mother singing it at night as she sat around the fire or finished up with the tea dishes.

Through Moorfields and to Bedlam I went;
I heard a young damsel to sigh and lament;
She was wringing of her hands, and tearing of her hair,
Crying, 'Oh! cruel parents! you have been too severe!
~*~
'You've banished my truelove o'er the seas away,
Which causes me in Bedlam to sigh, and to say

That your cruel, base actions cause me to complain,
For the loss of my dear has distracted my brain.'

~*~

When the silk-mercer first came on shore,
As he was passing by Bedlam's door,
He heard his truelove lamenting full sore,
Saying, 'Oh! I shall never see him any more!'

~*~

The mercer, hearing that, he was struck with surprise,
When he saw through the window her beautiful eyes;
He ran to the porter the truth to be told,
Saying, 'Show me the way to the joy of my soul!'

~*~

And when that his darling jewel he did see
He kissed her, and sat her all on his knee,
Says she, 'Are you the young man my father sent to sea,
My own dearest jewel, for loving of me?'

~*~

'Oh yes! I'm the man that your father sent to sea,
Your own dearest jewel, for loving of thee!'
'Then adieu to my sorrows, for they now are all fled,
Adieu to these chains, and likewise this straw bed!'

~*~

They sent for their parents, who came then with speed;
They went to the church, and were married indeed.
So all you wealthy parents, do a warning take,
And never strive true lovers their promises to break.

He listened as the last line died under the hum of the car tires and the sweeping click of the windscreen wipers. The sounds of the road and the car crowded into the enclosed space, returning the moment to the ordinary.

The song seemed strangely fitting. Not because

he'd ever been in a similar circumstance but because it told of a separation. And even if the lovers in the song had been happily reunited, he doubted the outcome would be the same for him and his grandfather.

He dredged up the stories his mother had told him, recalled some of the clan history he'd read. Ian MacLaren had begun the family brewery in the early 1700s, sometime before the Jacobite Rising of 1745. Donald, a captain in the battle of Culloden, had escaped capture by the English after the Scottish defeat, but ended up with a musket ball in his leg and eventual imprisonment. He escaped in August 1746 on his way to his probable execution, disappearing into the mist near the Devil's Beef Tub near Moffat.

That much was fact. But fiction took over and the story had two endings. It was a matter of the listener's choice which to believe. Either Donald hid in a quagmire until he escaped at night to a friend's house, where he finally died of his wound weeks later, or he eventually returned to Balquhidder and remained in the village, disguised as a woman until amnesty was declared.

He didn't know which version he liked better. Both displayed Donald MacLaren's ingenuity and nerve. All he realized right now was that he was proud to be part of the family, even if his grandfather tried to disown him.

And what about the man? Was he really in danger? The last email McLaren had read puzzled him, invaded what little sleep he'd had after his sojourn in Jean's office. Harvester mentioned he'd be at the Station, but when McLaren phoned up the Staffordshire Station he was told Harvester wasn't at work and wouldn't be in the rest of the week. Had Harvester's plan altered since the email date 20 Nov and now? Just over a fortnight, but things did change. Was Harvester instigating Plan B, as he alluded to? It didn't much matter. McLaren tugged at the seat belt so it lay flat against his chest. The problem was that Harvester evidently was in the area and if he could be stopped…

McLaren's breath caught in his throat. If Harvester could be found, the threat to Neill might be eliminated. Of course, it might depend on Lanny Clack, too. If he had to get orders from Harvester, and Harvester wasn't around to give those orders, the kidnapping or whatever was planned, might not happen.

McLaren unzipped his jacket, suddenly flush with apprehension and desperation. He had to find Harvester. But where would he start? The only clue was from the email. The Station didn't make sense.

Although the temperature was a chilly twenty-eight degrees, he cracked his window, letting in the cool air and the fragrance of his land. Wet turf and grass, pine and wood smoke filled the car and his senses and he inhaled deeply.

When he came to Kingshouse Hotel he turned off, leaving the A84 and the rain, and driving west on a small road toward Auchtubh. His chest tightened as he returned to his grandfather's house, a large stone structure that dominated the village. A crenellated tower claimed the west section of the building, its arrow slits open and watchful. The slate roof shone from morning dew and frozen patches of light frost. Ivy lay thick on one wall and around the foundation, its dark green leaves ice-tipped. A remnant of another time, he thought, and his grandfather presided over its magnificent furnishings and few inhabitants with lord-like command and an ache for another century.

McLaren parked outside the massive front door. Now that he was here, he had doubts about his decision to come. He turned off the car's motor and sat with his hand on the car key, his gaze at the window in the front room. Did the curtain move? Had someone heard his approach?

McLaren's footsteps crunched on the gravel as he walked to the front door. Each step pounded into the quiet, booming out his presence. He paused, looking for the dog with which his grandfather had threatened him last visit. No opening gate or energetic growls warned him to turn and run. He reached for the brass knocker—a lion's head grasping a large ring between its teeth; the ring lay heavy in his hand. His fingers slid over the smooth surface, colder than Harvester's heart. How would he convince his grandfather his life was in danger? Would the older man even listen to him?

He slammed the brass circle against the plate affixed to the door. The bang reverberated loudly against the solid wood. Appropriate his grandfather had chosen the lion's head. The MacLaren clan crest featured a lion's head.

The cold of the flagstone porch invaded his boots, and he stomped his feet on the welcome mat. No response issued from the house. He knocked louder.

A wisp of wind snaked across the courtyard and swept past McLaren. He flexed his fingers—the cold threatening to stiffen them—and stared at the windows. No one peeked out, no light switched on.

He pressed the doorbell. No footsteps hurried to the door, no bolt slid from its metal cradle.

His heart thudded against his ribcage and he lost track of the number of beats or how long he stood there. He turned, debating if he should ring the house on his mobile or shove a note through the letter box, when he heard the sounds of metal skating across metal, and a latch clanking. Complaining door hinges squeaked and he turned to find a middle-aged man standing in the open doorway.

"Michael?" The word came out more statement than question, and the man stared at McLaren in frank surprise. When McLaren nodded, the man said, "I'm Brandon. Your dad's brother."

McLaren stood as if frozen in movement, undecided if a handshake or a hug was best. They were strangers, for all the family blood they shared, so he'd be more comfortable with the handshake, but wouldn't that seem cold?

He stared at his uncle, trying to merge the younger man of the family photographs with the decades-older person now standing before him. The eyes were the same, brown and hinting at humor within their depths, though the crow's feet were more pronounced. The brown hair had grayed slightly but was still full. A suggestion of McLaren's father shone through Brandon's lopsided smile, and even in the few words spoken McLaren could ascertain the timbre of his father's voice.

"Yes." McLaren extended his hand and felt his uncle's warm clasp. "I'm Michael." Relief flooded his veins and he grinned. "I-I've thought of you often, heard about you from my mum and dad." He paused, knowing it sounded inane, wanting to bridge the years in an instant, to be taken back into his family. He shifted his weight, unsure of what he should do.

Brandon opened the door wider and gestured toward the hallway. "Come in, come in. Don't stand there like a stranger, lad. You're family, aren't you?"

McLaren followed his uncle into the front room, large and wallpapered and warm from a fire burning in the grate. Reminders of the family and clan's past hung on the walls and perched on bookcase tops; the eyes of sepia-toned ancestors followed his movement across the room and watched him accept a cup of tea from Brandon.

He endured the minutes of small talk, the preliminary exchanges of how-have-you-been, opinions of the weather, updates on family members. It was an icebreaker, a method to connect after decades of isolation, a way to see if they would like each other. Although McLaren wanted to know his uncle, inwardly he resented the spent time. He needed to get to the subject that drove him to come.

"So, what brings you here?" Brandon finally said, easing McLaren's anxiety and moving the teapot on the side table. "Not that it isn't nice to finally meet you and talk." His right eyebrow rose as though letting McLaren in on a joke. "Another try at your grandfather?"

"Actually, I need to warn him about something." McLaren eased the cup onto the table and leaned forward. "I have very good reason to believe his life's in danger."

The trace of humor vanished from Brandon's face. "You're joking, of course."

"I've read some communication that makes me believe this."

"Well, when will this happen…and where? Here?"

He looked around the room, as if judging its defensive strength.

"I assume it's here. Grandfather doesn't go out much, does he?"

"You're thinking whoever this is will try something in the village?"

"In all likelihood, it'll be here at the house. I doubt if these people know Grandfather well enough to know his schedule." McLaren hesitated, picturing the scene. "Does he have a schedule?"

"Like, Tuesdays at the vicar's for a game of bridge, Fridays meander along Loch Voil? No. I and the house staff, such as there is, do the errands and the shopping. He goes outdoors for a stroll around the village or to putter in his garden. Occasionally he'll go into Callander or Edinburgh, but that's about once or twice a year. There are no set dates for those excursions. So, no, I can't see that anyone would be able to pinpoint him to an agenda. Even the gardening and strolling have no set day or time." He shook his head. "I can't believe this, Michael. It's too difficult to do. What is it, by the way? An abduction? Hold him for ransom?"

McLaren looked around the room. Most of the good pieces had been in the family for generations. Oil paintings, silver, tapestries. They would fetch something from a collector, probably, but some of it was a bit worn to command top price. "I believe so. Something about me as a lure…" He picked up his teacup but simply stared at the amber colored liquid. "It sounds daft when I tell it, but it scared me to death when I found out about it."

"You're certain it's about Neill? It can't be…someone else?"

"The only other person would be me. But my safety doesn't concern me as much as grandfather's."

Brandon poked the fire with the tongs, then settled back in his chair. "I'm not saying you're wrong, Michael, but it doesn't add up. Neill likes to play at being lord of the manor, but he has no ready cash. Oh, he's got things," he said, gesturing around the room, "but it'd take awhile to convert any of it into money. There are more richer men, much more accessible men to hold for ransom than Neill McLaren. You've got to be mistaken."

McLaren leaned forward again, his forearms on his thighs. "I agree I might be wrong, but are you willing to take that chance? The men whom I think are behind this are my enemies. They've been trying to get me for a while and something's always gone wrong."

"That sounds so much like a script for a film. How'd you get enemies? People don't usually acquire enemies, and certainly not on a level such as you're suggesting. It smacks of"—He pulled in his bottom lip, his brows lowering in his concern—"of drug deals and robberies gone wrong. You're…not involved in anything like that, are you?"

"No, Uncle. It's a hold-over from my police job. Sometimes there are a few criminals who can't let go of hatred."

"I'm sorry. I had no idea those things really happened. You're not in any imminent danger, though, I hope."

"As I said, I believe if my suspicion is correct the people are concentrating on grandfather. I'm in Scotland, a perfect place to carry out his plan because I'm away from my friends and ready help, and the man masterminding this has plotted this for months. He's got long arms and local ruffians to do his dirty work. He hates me and wants me dead. If he can get to me by using Neill, either as a lure or as ransom, this man will do it. What I learned a few hours ago suggest very strongly that Neill will be used in this scheme. I don't know how and I don't know if it's immediate physical danger. But I needed to let him, or you, know what may be coming quite soon. You can keep alert for strangers in the village or ringing your doorbell. You know of the danger, so you can act as a buffer between that and grandfather."

Brandon drew in a deep breath. "I think we're safe enough, Michael. I know you've come here in good faith, and I'm touched that you think enough of your grandfather to warn him, despite what he's done to you. Which I am in disagreement with, let me say. Dad has no great wealth that a kidnapper would want, nor is dad important in any political or religious way. He's not prime minister or an ambassador, nor does he keep a high office. Therefore, I can't see why he should attract the attention of which you're speaking."

"He's the lure, the bait to snag me. I thought I made it plain that I have men who are after me."

"You did. But even if that's true, I don't know why they would know where Dad lives. You didn't tell them, did you?"

McLaren frowned, his disgust nearly needling him into leaving. "Of course not. Who would I tell? And it's not the sort of thing you blab in a pub. I don't know how these men found out. Maybe they're tailing me."

"You said you were a police officer, didn't you?"

"What's that mean?"

"Wouldn't you be aware of someone following you? Especially here."

"You live in the village. You'd know if the same vehicle shows up, if strangers have been here since Monday."

Brandon nodded, his lips turning up at the corners of his mouth. "I see your point. Well, I haven't seen anyone I don't know. But I suppose if someone's really keen on staying hidden, he can do it. More so if he's a professional criminal."

They sat for a moment, McLaren imagining different scenarios and thinking of vehicles or people who might conceivably stick with them a little too long. A log in the fireplace snapped and settled lower in the grate. He glanced at the shift of light and shadow on the western window. More shadow than light lay on the glass surface. Perhaps storm clouds were rolling up the glen.

"Do you think I should tell Grandfather about this?" McLaren turned back to Brandon. "You obviously know him better than I do. Would he listen to me?"

"To be truthful, I don't think he'd even want to see you. If you recall this past Monday..." He grimaced, possibly embarrassed by his father's actions. "I'll tell him, of course, but I doubt if he'll speak to you. If he finds you've been here, well, that'll be bad enough. He won't talk to you. I know that."

"I thought he wouldn't, but I had to ask."

"You're not worried for your own safety, Michael?"

"I'm apprehensive, of course. I'd be a fool not to be. But I'm not going to deliberately get myself into a bad situation. My concern is for Grandfather. He could so easily be duped by some bloke's story."

"Yes. Forewarned, as you say."

"I can't stress strongly enough to be cautious. At least until Monday. I should be home by then and the danger to grandfather will be over."

"If there is any." Brandon gave a half smile.

"Assuming that I'm correct about using him to lure or trap me," McLaren went on, annoyed by his uncle's flippant attitude, "I won't be near enough for that scheme to work. If it's going to be effective, we have to be in the same vicinity."

"I'll keep an eye on him. I always do. There's not much we do together, really, but if I'm not here, one of the staff will be."

"You'll tell them about letting anyone into the house, then?"

"Certainly. Now, tell me about yourself. You asked about me when you first came in and I didn't learn much about you. How are the farm and your job?"

McLaren looked blank, reluctant to abandon the topic.

"The house is basically as my parents left it, though I've been tempted to update a few things. My job..." He didn't know how to respond. That it was basically a physical outlet for his anger and frustration, that he took pride in a well-coursed wall, that some days he was so tired and sore he could hardly get out of bed? He decided to side step the question. "I've more work than I can do."

"That's never bad, is it?"

"I suppose not, though I wish I could clone myself. All that money would be nice."

"Speaking of which." Brandon leaned forward, looking secretive. "I'd like to give you half my inheritance when dad passes."

McLaren blinked, clearly astonished. "You...don't have to do that, Uncle Brandon. It's a generous gesture, of course, but I've done nothing to warrant such a gift. You've worked for Grandfather. You've learned the brewery business and done all the running around that's been needed. The money's yours and I'd feel I was stealing if you gave me anything."

"I appreciate your feelings, Michael, but I wouldn't have suggested this if I didn't feel strongly about it. Colin, your dad, was the elder son. He would've received this inheritance if he'd stayed in Scotland and worked in the family business."

"But that's just it. Dad moved to Derbyshire. He wasn't connected to the brewery. He didn't even visit you to keep the link alive. You did all the work and took over when he left. The money wasn't dad's and it's not mine."

"I've given this a lot of thought, Michael, and this is what I want to do."

The wind whistled down the chimney, spreading the stench of ashes, as McLaren thought over the gift. He didn't want to hurt his uncle's feelings but he was embarrassed by the gesture. Nothing compelled the man to give the money away, of course. Well, nothing that McLaren knew. But would his uncle have offered if McLaren hadn't shown up? Had his appearance spurred his uncle into a guilty offer?

Brandon cleared his throat, bringing McLaren's focus back to the man. "I want you to know that I'm not doing this out of any pressure or sense of obligation. I *am* doing it because, well, Dad is incredibly bloody-minded with certain subjects."

"My dad being one of them."

"Unfortunately. My dad—your grandfather, that is—wasn't physically hurt when your dad left, but he carries that emotional wound still. Something died within him. Like a light went out of his life. I don't just mean the dream of passing the brewery on to your dad, though that was extremely hard for him to take. I think it was more that his authority as head of the family was cast aside. There'd been no discussion about you and your parents leaving. Your dad just announced it over tea one day. The shock nearly killed your grandfather." He leaned back, looking very tired and years older. "Oh, he survived. It wasn't like he had a heart attack. But he was emotionally hurt to think Colin would leave the ancestral home and business and Scotland. It was as if all those generations of ancestors didn't mean a thing to your dad."

McLaren nodded, his gaze on his uncle's hands as he grasped the arms of the chair. "I was too young to understand the ramifications, but I see now what my dad's decision did. I wish I could make it up to Granddad, but I can't come into the family business. That's just not for me." He slanted his head slightly, peering at his uncle in the growing gloom. "Do you understand?"

"Yes. It wasn't my intention to shame you into coming back, Michael. I just thought the way your grandfather treated you was abominable, and I want to make amends. It's the only way I know how."

"Sure. I understand. May I think about it? I don't mean to refuse your gift, but please understand I feel uncomfortable with this, too. If I could think it over and let you know, not meaning to throw your gift back in your face…"

"Certainly. I don't want to make you uncomfortable. Take your time." Brandon reached for the teapot. "Ready for more tea?"

McLaren glanced at his cup, drained the last of the lukewarm beverage, and shook his head. He stood up, pulling his car key from his jeans pocket. "I've something else to do before I end for the day. You'll be sure to tell Grandfather about the danger to him, Uncle Brandon…"

"Of course. I don't want anything happening to him. You're leaving already?" He looked astonished at the shortness of the visit.

"Yes, sorry."

"You just got here." He got up and walked to the door with McLaren. "Can't you stay for a bit? We've a lot of years to catch up on, what you've been doing. I know so little about you, Michael. I'd like to get to know you…for your own sake as well as for your father's."

"I'd like to stay and talk, but I can't today, thanks all the same. Maybe I can stop in on my way back to Edinburgh. We could meet somewhere…" He glanced at the stairway as they came into the hall. What if the older man heard their voices and was coming downstairs? Would he let loose the dogs, as he had threatened Monday? Had he mellowed since then, regretted his hastiness, and wanted to welcome McLaren back to the family? McLaren hesitated in the middle of the entryway, his gaze shifting from the stairs to the main room. He listened for his grandfather's footstep, wanting yet dreading to hear it.

"Yes. That'll be good." Brandon opened the door and stood to one side. A breath of wind brought the coldness into the house. "Well, I'll wait to hear from you then, shall I?"

"I'll ring in a few days and we'll get together." He stopped in the open doorway, unsure of what to do. He wanted to find his grandfather, tell him about the danger, make him listen, but his grandfather's previous behavior practically guaranteed McLaren's action would be foolish. "Well, I'll see you in a bit," he repeated, uneasy with the situation.

"Sure. It'll be like trying to hold back the tide, but I'll wait to hear from you. Just don't make it too long, Michael. I don't want to lose you again." He took a half step forward, then stopped, confusion on his face.

McLaren stared at his uncle's hand, then grasped his uncle in a hug. He held it for several seconds before murmuring his thanks, then walked to his car. When he turned to wave, he saw that the front door had already closed.

****

It was getting on to half past one, and he hadn't eaten since his early breakfast. McLaren backtracked his route, drove the nine miles south to Lade Inn. He stared at the mountain as he ate, imagined the area as it might have been centuries earlier, then finished his meal with a pint of Rannoch. Now that he'd been inside the family house and met his uncle, the tie to the beer meant more, gave the beverage more importance. After finishing his drink, he doubled back, driving to Balquhidder.

He turned off the A84 again and minutes later

passed Auchtubh. He didn't slow down; he'd said all he could say to his uncle. Loch Voil lay ahead, and his car tires skimmed over the Balvaig bridge in his haste to see his ancestral village. The majority of the houses straddling both sides of the road disappeared behind him, leaving him in less populated country. Scrub and tufted grass claimed the land as though forcing out the few houses that remained rooted to the soil. He could see ahead to the loch, shining before him like a donkey's carrot, and the rooftops of several houses along the loch's northern edge. Fewer dotted the land on the south side of the water, letting the land reclaim its wild history. He was in the Braes of Balquhidder, the land embraced by the hills sitting north and west of Loch Voil and Loch Doine. A beautiful, rugged land that held a wild, rugged past.

The village emerged from the glare of sunlight dancing on the loch water. He shielded his eyes, annoyed and immensely happy with the scene. Something tugged at his soul and he felt strangely alive. He passed a nineteenth century church, then stopped at one of the several bed-and-breakfast establishments crowding the road. After getting a room and unpacking, McLaren strolled around the village. No car'd followed him into the area, and he found himself whistling.

Balquhidder sat at the eastern end of Loch Voil, a skinny finger of a lake that separated the wild Braes of Balquhidder on the north from the lower lying marshy area of Invernenty. No commercial shops dotted the main road, only the handful of guesthouses and self-catering cottages. Beyond them, on the gentle rise of the hill, the old church stood. Keeping it company were the ruins of an ancient seventeenth century worship place and the gravestones of the old clans that had inhabited the area.

Above the glen floor, nearly fifty yards west of the church, a hill poked out from the twilight. *Creag an Tuirc*, McLaren thought, remembering the Gaelic name. The Boar's Rock. The MacLaren clan's ancient rallying point.

He wandered down to the near end of the loch. The terrain here resembled a tufted carpet, with clumps of calf-high brown grass blanketing the flat land. On either side of the water the thick stand of evergreens rose, dark against the dull green of the hills and the lighter gray of the mountaintops. Trailings of snow marbled the depressions in the hills, hugged the banks of the loch and river where the sun couldn't reach them. He walked back to his room, whistling and feeling more optimistic than he had in days.

His buoyancy crumbled the moment he spotted the torn Edinburgh Old Town pamphlet on the doormat, a stone positioned in the paper's center to keep the wind from carrying if off.

He pulled the pamphlet from its imprisonment and held it in the sunlight, as thought he needed every speck of light to see it. Why was it on his doorstep? Had someone left it there as a clue to Liza's whereabouts? If so, why not just leave a note telling him where she was?

He slipped it into his jacket, placing it flat against his chest, and sought out the bed-and-breakfast manager. He was in the dining room.

McLaren coughed quietly and the man looked up from the place he was setting. "Yes, sir? Do you need something?" He looked surprised and helpful at the same time, a trait, McLaren thought, that had to be practiced.

"Sorry to bother you. I wonder if anyone was here recently, asking for me." He tried to keep the urgency from his voice, tried to imply he was passing the time of day or inquiring after a friend who might or might not stop by.

The manager straightened and looked thoughtful. "No, sir. Nor did anyone query prior to your arrival or phone to see if you were coming or had arrived." He paused, his eyebrows raised. "Is that of any help?"

"Yes. Thanks."

"Are you expecting someone to arrive or phone you? I could take a message." He looked hopeful and clasped his hands across his stomach.

"No, I'm not." He was about to go back to his room when he asked, "Have any of your guests come in or left the guesthouse?"

"I don't know what you mean. I have one other person besides you staying at the moment. He's away in Inverness for the moment. He left yesterday and will return tomorrow. Is that what you want to know?"

McLaren nodded, thanked the man, and wandered into his room. He slammed the door behind him and sank onto the chair. It made no sense.

Again, the oddity of it all shouted to him. If the brochure were from Liza, why hadn't she written down where she was and if she needed help? He didn't doubt for a second that it was the same pamphlet she'd torn the Greyfriars Kirkyard piece from at the bus stop— there couldn't be two such things. Yet, if the piece was from her and she had delivered it, why be so secretive? How had she delivered it, and why not wait for him? And perhaps more important, how did the person know

McLaren was staying there?

That opened another set of chilling possibilities. Was he being followed? If so, why? The courier obviously knew about McLaren's connection to Liza. Did this pamphlet imply that Liza had escaped, and the courier thought McLaren could locate her?

He shook his head, trying to rid himself of the headache that had come on suddenly. The brochure had to have come from Liza. She was the only person who knew its significance to him, that he'd identify it with her. So there had to be a clue as to her whereabouts on the piece of paper. If not, he was back to the absurdity of the whole thing.

He bent over the paper, trying to discern a scratch or underscoring of a word, anything that would hint at Liza's whereabouts, but could see nothing. Then the brochure itself was significant. But only as a link to Liza. The clue had to be in the information about Greyfriars Kirkyard.

He pulled the scrap from his rucksack and stared at every photo and read every word on it. The main portion explained the history of the cemetery, the imprisonment of more than twelve hundred Covenanters south of the churchyard in 1679, the headstone to the dog who guarded his master's grave for fourteen years, and the famous Mackenzie haunting.

He shook his head at the conflicting images, remembering some of the mentioned points from his recent visit, hurried though it had been. He hadn't paid attention to any of those spots, but he made notes in his notebook before reading more about the graveyard online.

The information on the kirk and the cemetery made

no impact on him. Besides, the place was so large he had no idea where to hunt for Liza, if she was there. Which seemed absurd.

Covenanters and a poltergeist hardly held any significance, either. Was she hinting he should sit there all night to talk to the ghost?

But his questions turned serious when he read about Greyfriars Bobby, the Skye Terrier guarding his master's grave, his master who was Edinburgh police officer John Gray.

McLaren read the section twice, making certain he caught the significance. Or at least what he inferred to be important. Liza knew he was a former police officer—they'd talked briefly in her front room right after the hit-and-run. She also knew Jamie currently was a constable, a bobby. Was she asking him for police help? If so, where was he to send it?

Or was Liza giving him a different clue connected more directly to the faithful dog? She couldn't be at the dog's statue. That was at the junction of Candlemaker Row and George IV Bridge. Would anyone be imprisoned there? Were there shops or houses in which she could be kept? If so, which one would he search?

Maybe he completely missed the inference. She could be implying something else, like the church? Or even one of the cemetery's mortsafes, a low ironwork cage constructed over graves to protect bodies from the nineteenth-century grave robbers? He couldn't fathom that. It would mean she'd be sitting there, waiting for him. And if she could do that, she could get to Auchtubh.

Any of the other inferences were just as farfetched. She'd not be hovering at any of the mausoleums or monuments for the same reason. No. As far as he was concerned, at the moment, the pamphlet was a non-starter.

He tossed it onto the bed, half frustrated that he couldn't decipher the puzzle, if there was one, and half angry that he was no closer to locating Liza.

He brewed a cup of tea and sipped it slowly, going over the possible links. The photo of the stone wall and the mortsafes yelled at him. He set down his cup and grabbed the scrap, staring at the photo. Stone. Mortsafes. Cages. Was that a clue, that Liza was locked up in a stone edifice?

The paper sank onto the bed as he stared out the window. It could be, but was he reading something into it? And where would he begin to search? Edinburgh was a city of stone buildings. So were the villages around Edinburgh, around Scotland. Even here in Balquhidder, and in the countryside. Where the hell was he supposed to look, if he was correct?

He groaned, massaging his head, and stood up. He knew himself well enough to know he wouldn't be able to sleep if he didn't at least check out part of the puzzle.

He grabbed his keys, and a minute later was in his car heading back to Edinburgh.

****

Greyfriars Kirkyard and church stood silhouetted against the western sunlight, contributing another air of mystery to the site. In another hour or two, twilight would creep across the land. Night came early in December, late afternoon usually saw darkness and the moon creeping up the sky. But he had enough daylight to see properly and to find any hint to Liza.

He found himself retracing his route from

yesterday, but this time he kept to a leisurely pace, examining every item that could conceivably be referred to in the brochure scrap.

The Black Mausoleum of Mackenzie's ghost held no clue; neither did the Covenanters' Prison, the area formerly housing the prisoners and eventually merged with the cemetery as vaulted tombs. He forced himself to pause at each Scottish Presbyterian's plaque or grave in the stone wall, and examine the ground around the iron railings, even though the area disturbed him. The stories of the ghostly attacks played havoc with his imagination, but the Covenanters' history also disturbed him. And, he admitted, he'd just as easily believe Liza was killed or spirited away by the vengeful wraith, with all the knife wounds, scratches, and bitings it dealt its night visitors, as believe she left the message.

He searched the areas as quickly as he could, making sure no note or clue was there before moving on.

He gravitated to the mortsafes, thinking it the most likely spot for a hint of Liza. If any of the clues made sense, this one did, with its confining cage over the stone markers. Again he had to shake off the feeling of netherworld presence and upsetting history. He pulled his small torch from his jacket pocket and played it around the iron bars, examining all sides of the rods and flushing the tomb slabs with light. Nothing lurked in the shadows.

He walked back to the entrance. His last hint was Greyfriars Bobby.

The statue of the Skye Terrier sat on a carved stone pedestal just opposite the kirkyard's gate and in front of the pub bearing the dog's name. McLaren could see as he approached that it could neither hide nor shield any message, but he walked around the monument. The basin halfway up the pedestal's height might've held something at one point, if the note-leaver didn't mind the item getting wet, but nothing sat in it now. Besides, it was out in the open, very public. Frustrated, he returned to the cemetery.

He paused at the large marker listing some of the graveyard's more notable residents. Of the nineteen listed names, one was a woman. Mary Erkskine. He stared at the name, trying to link it with Liza's surname. But however he twisted the names around he could come up with nothing that made sense.

He abandoned the futile attempt and wandered over to the dog's burial spot. The red granite marker poked out of the heap of offerings left by sentimental visitors, various sticks and dog toys dotting the more numerous bouquets of flowers.

McLaren sighed but squatted before the tombstone. He had no intention of sifting through the shrine, disturbing the offerings. He stood up, about to leave, when a strip of a red, green, and blue fabric fluttered in the breeze. He stooped, his fingers automatically reaching for the tartan material.

He drew it from its half-hidden place behind the headstone and stared, disbelieving, at the fabric. Its edges were frayed, as if sitting for eons in the weather or being torn from a garment or bolt of cloth. It was also wrapped around a scroll of paper.

He slipped the loop of fabric from the paper. Although patches of snow still dotted the ground and the top of the stone, the paper sat clear of the wet soil. It was limp and damp with moisture, but unrolled easily enough. He laid it on his thigh and read the words.

It was an inked message, printed in block letters. He realized immediately he would never forget the three words, and though his name didn't appear on the paper, he knew it was addressed to him. *Tag. You're it.*

****

He drove back to his bed-and-breakfast in Balquhidder, hardly aware of the road or the countryside. The words danced before his eyes in a taunt that implied it would be more difficult to locate Liza than he'd imagined. But without another hint at her location, he was thwarted.

He parked in front of the guesthouse and stared into the twilight. Shadows stretched eastward from the building and base of the mountain range across the loch and over the village houses. It held a peace that belied the struggle within him. What should he do? Phone the police with this new development? But what did it prove? Nothing. Other than the fragment of Skene tartan, he had no positive link to Liza. There were probably thousands of Edinburgh residents who wore the fabric.

Perhaps the mystery and its solution would clear if he gave it time to perk. A walk might help. He still wanted to see the clan meeting place on the hill, too.

McLaren exited his car, breathing deeply of the cold air. His headache hadn't abated, but seemed less intense as he turned and trudged up the hill to the clan's ancient rallying spot.

The view from the Boar's Rock laid the village out in picture postcard fashion, the houses clustered among the trees and lochside. The spent heather, its purple and lilac colors withered to brown, claimed the higher elevations of the hills. But below, in the heart of the glen, the loch stretched smooth and serene, nearly black as it threw back the color of the sky.

A string of heavy gray clouds creeping eastward hinted that darkness would soon be complete. He had no desire to be caught on the hillside at night. The semi-blackness of Mary King's Close had tested his resolve to enter confined, dark places; nighttime in the forest wouldn't be much better.

Wanting to take home a link to his ancestry, he bent to pick up a small rock. It was the last he remembered before waking up in the snow.

Chapter Ten

His fingers dug into the snow as he rolled onto his back. The coldness wasn't apparent at first. He stared at the sky, black and star-strewn overhead. He lay still for several moments, trying to fathom where he was. His necklace—a leather cord strung with several wooden and ceramic beads—had slid up onto his neck. As he pushed himself into a sitting position, he tugged it back into place. His fingers lingered momentarily on the beads, the ceramic ones cold to his touch. It assured him he was alive and not dreaming.

Night had smothered the land; the moon hadn't yet risen. Swatches of snow shone barely visible against the dark ground. Gurgles, like slowly running water, sounded somewhere to the left. He stared into the darkness, trying to discern details of the landscape or a hint of where he was. All he was certain of was the snow, the cold, and the unending stretch of the unknown. Who had dragged him off the hill onto this flat ground?

He got to his feet; the world tilted and spun; he bent over. His right hand went to the back of his head. The flesh was tender and throbbed. When he removed his fingers the tips felt cold and slightly wet. From the snow? He patted his hair with his other hand. It was damp but not sticky, as was his right hand. He brought his fingers to his nose and sniffed. Blood. Had he fainted and hit his head on a rock? He got on his knees and felt through the snow where he'd lain. No rocks. He crawled forward and pawed through the snow on both sides, then pushed his hands through the snow in front of him. No rocks. McLaren sat back on his heels. How did he end up on the ground with a head wound?

Someone had hit him. Knocked him out and left him in the freezing temperatures. Which meant setting the scene to look like an accident. Which also meant his assailant thought McLaren would die of exposure and become another unfortunate victim of wintry misadventures. His assailant would be getting away with murder.

The question wasn't whether he had enemies in Scotland, but who had attacked him. Could Lanny Clack be here? He knew McLaren had spotted him outside Mary King's Close, had followed him underground. If Lanny had panicked, afraid McLaren was trying to apprehend him for the hit-and-run, would Lanny follow McLaren here? If he had done, on Charlie Harvester's orders, why wasn't McLaren killed outright? Why leave him alive?

If Lanny wasn't his attacker, it had to be either Jean MacNab or Harvester.

The implication chilled him more than the cold. It murmured in his head, blotting out the rustle of the tall grass and sighing of the wind. Was Harvester in Scotland? He was probably behind the botched hit-and-run attempt on McLaren's life, never mind that he wasn't the driver of the vehicle. If Harvester wasn't in Balquhidder, hadn't personally hit McLaren, had he orchestrated it? Why? To use him as bait for his grandfather? But that would mean kidnapping

McLaren, tying him up, and hiding him some place. Leaving him for dead on the snowy ground was not the norm for a kidnapper. So, again the question whispered to him: why not kill him outright?

McLaren wiped his fingers on his jacket and stood up. The land held no further information of where he was. No light shone, so he was either in the more desolate area of the moor or he was near a village that had bedded down for the night.

He was on flatland, and the gurgling sound suggested he was probably near the River Larig— assuming he was in the same area. If his assailant hadn't moved him far. But would the man have risked being seen? McLaren had been on the Boar's Rock when he'd been attacked. Even at dusk, the man would've taken a chance moving McLaren very far. So he had an accomplice to lift McLaren into a vehicle. Probably unloaded him after dark, McLaren mused.

He *was* on flatland. He was certain. In a glen. Mountains in front and behind masked the lower portion of sky, giving the blanket of stars a jagged lower edge. But what glen?

His mobile was no help, neither providing GPS location or placing a call. The signal evidently didn't reach to wherever he was.

The soggy ground clutched his shoes as he walked, and he stumbled several times. His hands plunged into the sodden soil as he righted himself, and he shook off the frigid water. The aroma of wet grass around him was strong. He trudged onward, no goal in mind other than reaching a house.

He lost track of time as he staggered toward an unknown goal. The wind curled around his head and bore into his ears. It whipped the grasses against his legs and pelted him with sleet. He covered his ears with his gloved hands but soon abandoned that stance. He needed his arms to keep his balance.

His shoes and bottoms of his jeans, heavy with water, hindered his progress, and the chill seeped through to his skin. He flexed his fingers. Fearful they would stiffen and freeze, he slapped his folded arms against his chest to force circulation into his blood. He couldn't do the same for his feet. Nothing dry or solid existed on which he could stamp. He prayed for an end to the glen and a place to rest.

Near a stretch of still water that he assumed to be a loch, a rectangular mass proclaimed itself against the blacker hue of the mountains. He trudged up to it, wary of its identity. He moved slowly, slipping constantly, unaware of the uneven ground beneath his near-frozen feet.

As he neared the form, he stopped. The moon broke from behind the mountain range and silvery light trickled onto the landscape, revealing the darker lump.

It was a cottage. Or ruin of a cottage. The roof was gone, probably centuries ago, he thought as he stood in the doorway and peered inside. Tall grasses and heather had taken root between the cast-off rocks littering the ground outside and inside the structure. But enough of the walls remained to give him shelter from the wind, and a fireplace and chimney claimed the gabled end of the far wall. He staggered into the house and practically fell onto the firm ground.

Hours seemed to race by as he lay there, his chest heaving from the trek across the moor. Hunger gnawed his stomach but he couldn't alleviate it. He cursed himself for not slipping an energy bar into his jacket pocket, then excused his blunder; he'd had no suspicion this would happen. He'd planned to be on the Boar's Rock for a few minutes only. Someone else had caused his situation.

The insight didn't placate him much. Hunger was hunger, no matter the reason for it. He rolled onto his side, bringing his knees to his chest, and broke a stem off a clump of heather. He chewed it more to fool himself into believing it was food than to actually eat it.

It helped only slightly. Either that, or numbness made him insensible to further feeling.

He shut his eyes, his thoughts on Dena and his grandfather. They seemed to speak to him: Dena commiserating with his situation, Neill jeering at his stupidity. His chewing slowed, then stopped. The heather stem sagged at the corner of his mouth as his breaths lengthened and deepened. The stars had altered their position by the time he sat up.

The darkness and cold momentarily confused him. His hand went to the heather dangling between his lips and he tossed it away. He brushed the snow off his clothes, trying to make sense of it and the place. Wind snaked down from the opening in the roof, bringing the scent of the marsh with it. McLaren nodded. He remembered where he was.

He dug into his jacket pocket and withdrew a book of matches. He lit one and in the brief flare of light looked around the area.

Sticks, cut wood, and a mound of dried grass were stacked in the corner near the fireplace. He brushed the broken pottery from the hearth, wiped his hand on his jeans. As the match went out and the night reclaimed the ruin, McLaren took a deep breath. Did something rustle in the corner? Was the cottage about to be overrun with something crawling out of the dark?

He fought the urge to scream and run onto the moor. He'd never survive the sleet and freezing temperature if he left. Ignoring his pounding heart, he grabbed several handfuls of grass and piled them in the center of the hearth. He then carefully placed twigs and branches over the grass in teepee fashion.

As he struck another match, he prayed that the flame would take hold, that the wood wasn't too damp. The match shook in his hand and he placed his left hand over his right fist, steadying the flame. A gust of wind curled around his body and the flame went out in a puff of smoke and an aroma of sulfur.

He shifted around on his knees, presenting his back squarely to the door. Not that it did much good, for the cottage was roofless and lacked one entire wall. But he bent over the matchbook and lit another match, guarding it with his body as though he protected his newborn infant. The flame flared in the dark and caught the dried grass, then lapped greedily at the twigs.

The wood snapped and popped. McLaren added larger twigs and branches to the fire, forcing himself to go slowly. He wanted a bonfire but knew he must build up to it. If he went too fast, the flames would be smothered and he'd be plunged into the darkness and cold again.

He moved slowly, making certain the piece of wood burnt well before adding a larger piece. Minutes later he sat back and held out his hands to the heat and light. The fire burnt well and released the aromas of burning pine and dry grass into the air.

McLaren settled against the edge of the fireplace, getting as close as he could to the blaze. It was the first time he could see the remnants of his struggle. Mud, of course, caked his shoes, as it did the lower halves of his jeans. Mud also spattered other areas of his jeans and some of his jacket. A darker smear, probably blood from where he wiped off his hand, arched across the bottom of his jacket. He sagged against the lintel, the rounded rocks of the chimney's edge pressing into his back. Donald MacLaren, his ancestor, seemed to take over the room.

The man had hidden in a bog, covered with turf, if one believed the tales. Donald had escaped and survived. But that had been in August, McLaren reminded himself. This was December. Much different. Still, the man had lived through his ordeal. McLaren was of the same stock; he'd live through his.

Perhaps he was in Donald MacLaren's cottage.

McLaren went to the doorway and looked outside. The sleet had stopped, the thin line of rain clouds moved eastward. Now that the moon had escaped its cloudy imprisonment, the land lay exposed. The glen stretched in silvery patches of water where the moonlight hit them, the mountains supplying a somber, steep backdrop. Glints of water twisted through the brush and fed into a loch. He assumed it to be the River Lairg, as he'd previously suspected, but there were hundreds of rivers in Scotland. He could be just about anywhere.

He settled back by the fire. Daylight would be time to see where he was. Maybe he was near an inhabited farm.

He flipped open his mobile phone. Wherever he

was, he was out of a cell tower's range. Exasperated, he closed it and shoved it back into his jacket pocket.

Cold from the rock wall and the ground bore into McLaren's body. He stacked some larger logs onto the fire, angled his back into the corner, and fell asleep. When he woke, daylight hugged the eastern horizon.

He got up, stretching from the cold and huddled position. The fire had dwindled to hardly more than embers but he added more twigs and fanned the coals into flame. As the blaze caught, he reached for another log.

A sliver of silver winked at him from the spot where the log had been. He moved aside a few logs so the firelight could illuminate the recess. Several silver coins lay on the floor, half covered by dust.

He picked up a coin and angled it toward the firelight. Silver and heavy, it measured perhaps an inch in diameter. A man's profile claimed most of the observe side, with the words "President of the United States" arched around his head. The man wore spectacles, a tie, and a suit coat. The reserve side depicted a longhaired woman in a diaphanous dress. She held a hammer or mallet in her right hand. The head of the tool rested on an anvil. A triangular object that McLaren couldn't make out stood behind her. The words "one peso" curved on either side of the woman's head, and "Filipinas" arches under her feet along the coin's lower edge.

The majority of the coins were this style, although an eagle and shield replaced the man on some of the silver pieces. "United States of America" and 1909 circled the coin's face.

McLaren pulled out the logs, tossing them across

the floor. A canvas bag, nearly rotted with age and exposure to the weather, lay half tucked behind a loose rock in the wall. He eased it out from the remaining sticks. A large hole along the bottom edge gaped open and another dozen coins spilled onto the ground. He felt the bag, making certain it was empty. His fingers traveled the length of a rigid object. He judged it approximately six inches in length and four inches wide. He loosened the cords around the neck of the bag, peered inside, and drew out a black leather notebook.

He blew off the dirt and grasped the book by its spine. Shaking it dislodged more dirt and bits of brittle paper. He laid the notebook on a flat stone by the fire and opened the cover. A label bearing the note Property of George Roper adhered to the inside. A small tear ran the length of the label and a corner was missing, but it suffered no other damage. He couldn't say the same for the rest of the book, however. The first few pages had been torn out or discarded; pieces of paper still clung to the sewn gutter. He leafed through the book and scanned the first sentences on each page. It seemed to be George Roper's diary. From World War Two.

Few pages still adhered to the sewn spine of the notebook. He counted them, turning them over and glancing at each sheet's front and back. Five pages. Five pages in a notebook that probably originally held thirty or fifty. Most of the torn out sheets of paper were in the later section of the book, giving the cover a loose, floppy fit when it closed. The existing five pages taunted him. What had happened to the other pages, and who had ripped them out? Better yet, why had they been ripped out?

The light was not strong in the cottage, and the

faded ink was hardly darker than the paper, but McLaren could read snatches of the entries. The words "Corregidor" and "The Rock" and "silver pesos" burned his imagination with the intensity of a fire. What happened seventy years ago?

He closed the book, stuffed it and the coins into his jacket pockets, and dumped snow onto the fire. It died in a series of hisses and wisps of smoke. He stirred the embers with a branch, making certain it was out, then left the cottage. There was enough daylight that he could see the terrain and hopefully make his way back to Balquhidder.

And to his room at the bed-and-breakfast. He needed to think, to piece together the strange events. If Harvester wanted McLaren permanently disposed of, why play around? If Harvester had failed to kill McLaren with the hit-and-run, if he or Lanny or someone else had knocked McLaren out and dumped him into the snow to die, why wouldn't they have killed him now, here? There were no witnesses to worry about. And perhaps more puzzling, how could Lanny or Harvester follow him to Balquhidder? He'd told Uncle Brandon to be alert to unfamiliar cars and people. Had McLaren failed to take his own advice? Had Harvester followed him from Lade Inn yesterday afternoon, climbed up the hill at the Boar's Rock, and struck him on the head? It seemed unlikely. Wouldn't he have noticed a car following him all that distance, heard someone climbing the hill?

If Harvester had followed him, perhaps he hadn't turned off at the village. Perhaps he used his mobile to phone Lanny and tell him where McLaren was headed. A different car and person could easily tail him when the first car gave up the chase.

The questions echoed in his mind, pounding more than his headache. Harvester certainly wanted McLaren dead, so why pussyfoot around? He could've shot or knifed McLaren at the Boar's Rock. Why hadn't he? Because he had some other use for McLaren? Because this was some sort of game or message?

He stopped several yards from the cottage and turned to look at it. In the morning light he could see it was most likely eighteenth century. The time period fit with it being Donald MacLaren's. Or, if not his, from someone of the clan. And if he was correct about the cottage, he was probably in Invernenty, the stretch of land near Loch Doine. About six miles west of Balquhidder.

McLaren glanced at his watch. Eight o'clock. Late sunrise in winter. He wandered down to the loch and sighted along its shoreline. It ran roughly east to west, which fit the geography of Loch Doine. Satisfied, he trudged off to his right, into the sunlight, hoping his assumption was correct. If not, he could be walking away from houses where he could get help.

The sunlight strengthened as the hours passed. The walking was slow and tedious, his shoes weighed down by water and mud. He reached the eastern edge of the loch where it narrowed into a river. He followed that and came upon a larger loch. Loch Voil?

He stopped and looked around as he fought for breath. The flat land offered nothing to sit on as he rested. He doubled over, his hands on his knees. His chest rose and fell painfully as he gulped in the cold air.

Minutes later, he walked on. The marshy soil gave way to the firm footing of packed earth and his eye fixed on a low-pitched roof that emerged slowly from the ground. Somewhat later, stone walls supported the roof and gave it height. A wire fence and wooden posts grew around a section of land adjacent to the barn, for that's what McLaren assumed it to be. A second structure, made of the same gray stone, looked to be a house. A stony courtyard stretched from the house and encompassed the land around the barn. As he got nearer he could make out bright yellow curtains in the window and a late model pickup truck beside the house. The lowing of cattle and a snatch of music, mingled with the aromas of coffee and steamy manure, floated out from the open barn doors. He ran his fingers over the bales of hay stacked against the structure's wall and stopped in the open doorway. The barn held the warmth of penned animals.

"Hello?" His voice sounded strange to him. Hollow and exhausted. The tone of a stranger.

The music stopped and a voice announced "Good morning. This is BBC Radio Scotland. Weather today for Edinburgh and the central region..." The listener turned off the radio. Metal cans clinked, rubber boots squeaked on stone, and a whistled tune broke the silence.

McLaren called again.

"Aye?" The voice, low and male, sounded rough from smoking or working over peat fires.

"Sorry to disturb you." McLaren clenched and unclenched his fingers to keep the blood flowing. "I've lost my way."

A figure emerged from the gloom at the back of the barn. There was a movement as he set down two large milk cans, then walked forward warily. He stopped just short of the shaft of sunlight slanting through an upper window. "Who are ye, then?" The fingers of his right hand curled around the handle of a pitchfork leaning against the wooden stall.

"My name's McLaren. Michael McLaren." He paused, hoping the surname would mean something to the man, would create a link of trust.

"Oh, aye?" The response neither welcomed nor banished McLaren. It merely acknowledged his presence.

McLaren debated briefly if he should mention his uncle or grandfather, wondered if their names would work any magic. Perhaps only if he was on ancestral MacLaren land. If he were in another glen where the MacLarens weren't very welcome…

The man responded before McLaren could decide. "Are ye up from the big house, then?"

"No. Though I'm kin to Neill McLaren."

"Aye, so?"

"He's my grandfather. Brandon's my uncle." He threw in the name as extra confirmation of his relationship.

The man stared at McLaren, perhaps considering the kinship or if there was a physical likeness in McLaren's face. A cow bawled, the noise breaking against the stone walls, and the man nodded and moved forward. "Are ye wantin' somethin' here?"

"I'm afraid I'm lost. I was wandering about the village last night…Balquhidder," he added, in case he was somewhere else. "Night fell rather quickly and I got disoriented. It caught me on the moor. I-I'm not sure where I am." He hoped he didn't sound foolish, show himself a berk if the village was close enough to hit with a thrown rock, as the saying went.

"Ye spent the night on the moor, did ye?" The man frowned, eyeing McLaren as if to ascertain the truth. His unspoken question resonated loudly in McLaren's mind: how could McLaren have survived the night in the sleet and wind?

McLaren answered the man's tactic question. "I was lucky enough to find an old cottage. A ruin near a loch. I built a fire on the hearth and stayed warm that way." He blew on his fingers; he could still feel the cold.

"Passed the night no better than one of your ancestors, huddled over the fire." The man smiled slightly, exposing a mouth of crooked or missing teeth. He ran his gnarled right hand through his hair, as though trying to smooth it down. The white wisps stirred in the wind racing through the open door. He pulled the edges of his grimy jacket together, hooking it closed by the button at his waist. Removing his gloves, he eyed McLaren's wet and muddy clothing. They seemed to support his story. The man nodded toward the open door. "Ye'd best have a cup o' somethin' hot, then. Tea or coffee with a wee goldie to get your blood leapin' again."

"Thanks, but I'd rather just keep going. I'm afraid if I sit down I'll never get up. Would you tell me where the village lies?"

"Balquhidder?"

"Yes. I've a room at one of the guesthouses. I'm anxious for a shower." He glanced at his dirty jeans, as though to underscore his situation.

"Ye're here. Well, near as. My farm lies on the south o' the loch."

"Loch Voil?"

"Aye. Ye've just a short tramp to go. Maybe a mile or so. I've never had cause to mark it off. But keep goin' east, like ye were doin'. Ye'll get to the village proper, right enough."

McLaren thanked him and practically ran up the road.

Chapter Eleven

McLaren stood in the hot shower, letting the heat pound his body. His muscles relaxed, and he flexed his shoulders and fingers. The cold and stiffness that had consumed him for twelve hours evaporated, leaving him feeling as though he might live after all. The back of his head was still tender and throbbed. His fingers found a gash beside the swelling but the blood had dried and seemed to be forming a scab. He dabbed some aftershave on it, thinking it was more show than preventive, hoping the alcohol would kill any germs still around the angry cut. If the sleet, mud and smoke hadn't infected it by now, he'd be lucky. He dried off and dressed. It was then that he realized he wasn't wearing his leather bracelet.

It matched his necklace. Dena had given both to him. He never took them off.

He looked around his room, opening dresser drawers, peering under the bed and through the sheets, felt inside the compartments of his rucksack. The bracelet wasn't there.

He sat on the edge of the bed. Of course he'd had it in Edinburgh. He remembered feeling it and seeing it after the adventure at the bus stop. And he had it when he left Jean MacNab's guesthouse. So how and where did he lose it? The only other places he could have lost it were Lade Inn, the Boar's Rock, Donald MacLaren's cottage, and that marshy moor.

He groaned, leaning forward and rubbing his head. Had the bracelet come off when he searched around in the snow? He'd never find it, if it had.

The sunlight slid onto the foot of his bed, nudging him to get on with his day. He left his room and wandered into the guesthouse's dining room. One table held a place setting, and he sat in the sun, sipping his coffee after he'd finished his meal. He wondered if he'd ever complain about summer temperatures again.

His mobile rang as he reached for a second slice of toast. He glanced at the Caller ID display and answered. "Jamie. You're up early."

"Not by choice. I have the information you wanted."

McLaren rubbed his forehead. Had he asked Jamie to investigate something? Had the attack wiped out part of his memory? What else had he forgotten?

"Mike?" Jamie's voice nudged him to reply.

"Yeah. This isn't the best time for this." He looked around the room. No one else was there. Was he overly cautious?

"You with someone?"

"No, but the owner could come into the dining room at any minute."

"You needn't make any incriminating reply, for God's sake. I was just going to tell you the connection between Lanny Clack and Jean MacNab."

McLaren nodded, recalling the photo in the Edinburgh guesthouse that showed the smiling faces of Lanny, Jean and Harvester. "All right. If I don't have to take copious notes, what did you find out?"

"Lanny, Jean and your ole mate Harvester are as

thick as thieves, which is more than a phrase."

"You're joking."

"Wish I were. Lanny has been convicted of theft, robbery, assault, and domestic violence, as I told you previously. He started out as a small time thug in his early teenaged years, as a lot of criminals do. But he's honed those skills to where he's now a member of a gang."

"The one that has that delightful skull graphic?"

"Right. The head of it—the gang, not the graphic— is a bloke you may remember from your time in the job. King Roper."

"Yeah. I recall the name. I never had any contact with him. I guess he never strayed as far south as Staffordshire."

"Consider yourself lucky. King Roper is one experience you don't want."

"I'd heard he was a nasty piece of work."

"You do have a delightful turn of a phrase, Mike. Murder, extortion, assault, smuggling, to name a few of his interests. He'd had a series of nasty run-ins with cops in CID here in Derbyshire. That went on for a few months, sent several officers to hospital."

"Are they all right?"

"Now they are, but it was touch and go for one chief inspector. Quite serious. No one knew if he'd live. He's made a full recovery, though, which got up Roper's nose."

"Glad to hear it—about the chief inspector and Roper's irritation. That piece of trash sounds like someone needs to step on him."

"You're echoing most coppers' sentiments."

"You say Lanny is part of Roper's gang. Is it based

in Scotland? Is that why Lanny is here?"

"Roper used to have his center in England. In Derbyshire, usually, though he roamed around if his current project called for a different location."

"Used to. What happened to cause the shift? You lads turn up the heat on Roper?"

"Not me, though it was my department. That chief inspector I mentioned. Geoffrey Graham. Well, his entire unit, actually. They were responsible for Roper's capture and subsequent prison stretch in Wakefield."

"The Monster Mansion in South Yorkshire." McLaren could imagine the prison. Fortress actually described it better. Walls several yards thick, living quarters for the country's worst of the worst, inescapable cells... "Don't tell me he's out."

"No. But with him in prison and the gang under a very hot magnifying glass, they decided to move their operation to Scotland."

"Away from English police jurisdiction and English law. They're probably hoping that Scotland's law is different, or they've not been heard of here."

"Or they've burrowed in some place and are hiding. Waiting for some big job."

"You think that's a possibility?"

"I'd say anything's a possibility with King Roper's gang. Scotland offers them a lot of area for concealment of contraband or preparing for some launch, and I don't mean a boat, necessarily. If you haven't checked lately, look at a map. You think any police force can cover all the country's lochs, shoreline, and glens? It's a bloody brilliant place to plan, reorganize, and attack."

McLaren nodded. Even in the region around Balquhidder there must be a dozen lochs, mountains, and rivers, all offering coves and recesses. "Do you know if King and George Roper are related?"

Jamie paused. "Sorry. The name's new to me. Who's George Roper? You run into him?"

"Not exactly. I found something that belongs to him."

"What?"

"A diary. I just thought the surname's too coincidental for them not to be related."

"Where'd you find a diary?"

McLaren told about the attack, waking up in the snow, and finding the diary in the cottage.

Jamie exhaled sharply. "For God's sake, Mike, what's going on? This is past a joke. You need to go to the police. Tell them what's going on."

"I don't even know what's going on. They're not going to listen to my few wild tales."

"If you've got wounds or bruising from the attack, they will. They can't ignore that type of evidence."

"They can put it down to me tripping over a stone or a drunken night out. There's nothing in the police code that compels them to believe me."

Jamie's angry retort sailed into McLaren's ear and he shook the mobile. "Can't hear you. Your signal's breaking up."

"The bloody hell it is. You're not Superman, Mike. You have one life, and I don't want to see it come to an end on some wintry moor. I want you to talk to the coppers."

"I'm telling you, I'm fine."

Jamie paused, and a hint of skepticism crept into his voice. "I hate to cast aspersions on a friend, and I know how stoic you usually are, but I'd like to assume you wouldn't needlessly put your life in jeopardy."

"You're right. You don't sound convinced."

"I'm trying to be, about both of us. Are you sure you're all right?"

"Yes, I'm sure. I'm mad, more than anything, and there's no medical cure for that."

"Maybe you should see a doctor. That's nothing to fool around with."

"I said I'm fine. Honest. Just a bit sore and stiff."

"If I had a penny for every time you said you were fine, Mike—"

"Have your lads learned anything?" McLaren interrupted Jamie's diatribe.

"Nothing concrete, unfortunately. But no one's getting much sleep until the gang members are rounded up. It's an uneasy time in our department."

"Do you have suspicions that Lanny's connection with Harvester and Jean MacNab are linked to King Roper's gang? Or, if not directly linked, to something criminal?"

Jamie sighed, sounding tired. "God, I hope not. I know Charlie Harvester isn't the world's most intelligent copper, but I hate to think he's that bent that he'd associate with King Roper. Lanny Clack is bad enough."

"Lanny could be the son of one of Harvester's mates. Maybe there's no criminal connection at all."

"You don't believe that."

McLaren mumbled that the odds didn't favor it. "Harvester's walked a bit too close to the line. Look at that case I investigated in October, if you need reminding."

"The Amy Jarvis case? The murder of the

university art student at South Wingfield?"

"Right. Harvester was chummy with that vigilante group. And while he may not have spoken publicly for them or had anything to do with Amy's death, he did know the group's leader."

"I thought coppers were prohibited from voicing any opinions of a political nature."

"I thought *murder* was illegal," McLaren returned before falling silent. He glanced out the window. How different the land appeared, whether seen in sunlight or night gloom. How different his emotions were. He neither battled his fears in the daytime nor gave them a thought. But sunset pulled his nightmares from the locked closet within his soul and mind, held them in front of him and taunted him. The landscape hadn't changed; only his perception had.

McLaren heard the clank of a spoon as it hit the sides of the teacup, and wondered if Jamie was stirring his tea.

"I don't know how Jean MacNab figures into the picture, Mike. She's sole owner of Saltire Guest House, as far as I can tell. She'd been married for four years— that was 1980 to '84, but her husband died in a car crash. Up near Inverness in December. Wintry road, snow, ice…you know."

"The '80s are too early for Lanny to come into the picture, Jamie. He's twenty, didn't you say?"

"Yes. Anyway, she could've met him through her insurance agent years later. She's had several fender benders."

"Is Stuart Forbes a friend of Lanny?"

"I wouldn't call them friends. Stuart owns Arthur's Seat Insurance Company, if you remember. He has no say-so in where his clients take their vehicles for repair work—"

"But he strongly suggests the place where Lanny works."

"Why do I even bother?"

"Go on."

"Lanny got to know Stuart through the car repair company. Might've done some work on Stuart's cars for all I know. Anyway, that's all Ross told me, although I suspect the Central Scotland Constabulary have a bit more on Lanny Clack than Ross is willing to tell me."

"So, if Jean MacNab is insured by Stuart Forbes's company, and takes her car repair work to Lanny's place of employment...yes, they could all know each other that way." McLaren's voice trailed off, betraying his exhaustion and frustration. "But we still don't know if this jolly threesome is actually tied in with King Roper's gang. Just because Lanny's a gang member, doesn't mean Jean or Harvester have connections in that direction."

"Like calling Dena and your sister coppers or police stoolies because you were a cop."

"Yeah." McLaren drummed his fingers on the table. A door opened in the back of the house and a dog yapped excitedly.

"Mike?"

"Yeah?"

"What's wrong?"

"This whole thing's coming together."

The yapping increased before the door shut.

"How?"

McLaren lowered his voice, as though he were

afraid of being overhead. "Harvester set all this up."

"Set what up? The hit-and-run, the attack at the Boar's Rock—"

"Not necessarily. Though those could be by-products. I mean getting me up here to visit my grandfather. When I was still in the job at Staffordshire, a few of my mates knew my family history. About my mum and dad, how my grandfather had practically disowned me. I learned recently that Harvester found out all that. He sent the letter or had Jean MacNab send the letter. The instructions were very clear I wasn't to ring up my grandfather, but to communicate through Jean MacNab, who would put me up for the week."

"You're certain your head isn't bothering you, that you don't need to go to hospital?"

"It's brilliant, Jamie. Listen. Harvester maneuvered me into staying with his friend, who could give him reports as to what I was doing."

"*Reports?*" Jamie made a noise like choking on his tea. "What the hell reports? You're not a criminal under surveillance."

"I might be to Harvester. He's hated my guts every since police school. He's just the sort to seek some sort of revenge and set it up carefully so it won't go wrong. He doesn't dare do it in England; it's too chancy he'd be a suspect."

"What do you mean suspect? Suspect of what…an accident?"

"Or my death. But two hundred fifty miles away in Scotland, he's far removed from any suspicion. He's arranged for a concrete alibi for the entire week I'm up here. When something happens to me, he can shed his crocodile tears, give a statement to the press about what a swell colleague I'd been, and keep his hands clean."

"You've alluded to this before. What's the reason for this elaborate charade? Why get you up here? It's an bloody expensive joke."

"As I said, Jamie, revenge is best served cold."

****

Back in his room, McLaren spread the silver coins on the bed. He would've believed a previous property owner had forgotten them, but the cottage had fallen into decay long before 1909, the date on most of the coins.

He opened the leather notebook and read the first intact page. It started in the middle of a diary entry, dated February 1962. The writer, presumably George Roper, referred to an event that happened twenty years earlier and made it plain he cursed his luck for having missed out on the original incident.

Every time this date rolls 'round I think of Frank. What a bloody lucky stiff! For once in his miserable life at the right place at the right time. Yanks always got the breaks—the prettiest birds, the highest pay, the easiest jobs of work. And not a year before this he thought his assignment to The Rock was gonna be boredom personified. How wrong can a bloke be! The Trout and the Japs, God bless them all. And Frankie's generous souvenir to keep me spirits up 'til I get the rest of the hoard. Till then, a trial by fire. A nice legacy for King and Cou...

The page was torn at the bottom, ending that entry. McLaren flipped through the rest of the pages, but found nothing else that explained the account. On the last page was a crudely drawn map devoid of country or other identifying marks other than Mac Ranaich. He stared at it, trying to fathom the location. It sounded familiar, but not as familiar as Balquhidder or Callander or Edinburgh. That it was in Scotland, he had no doubt. He'd never mistake Mac for a proper name if written on a map.

He opened his mobile and searched the Internet for the name. Dozens of entries popped up. Its proper name was Creag Mac Ranaich, a hill 809 meters in altitude. It sat north of the village, in the area loosely defined as the Braes of Balquhidder.

On the map, the artist had placed a small dot at the base of the hill, or what McLaren supposed was the hill—an upside down V. No other indication but a stray pen line half underlining the Braes of Balquhidder showed on the map. No penned X or circle or annotation gave a hint as to where the diary writer's souvenir might be stashed.

The silver coins on the bed seemed to whisper to him, to advise that he get more information before he jumped into his hiking boots. Just because he had a handful of coins didn't mean the X held more coins.

McLaren read through the notebook again. Nothing new presented itself. He turned back to the first page, to the label pasted inside the front cover. The signature smirked at him from the distance of half a century. George Roper.

The notebook sank to his lap as he stared out the window. Roper. He'd forgotten about George in the rush talking with Jamie. Could it be a coincidence? They had just talked about King Roper. And the diary entry had mentioned King. A nice legacy for King. At first reading, he'd assumed it to be King and Country. Wartime talk, for that's what he also assumed the entry to refer to. The date put it at February 1942. The reference to Japanese could also refer to World War Two. But what had a trout or a rock to do with this?

He entered the word *rock* into his smart phone's internet search engine. The usual results crowded the top of the list. He narrowed his search, this time typing in *the rock Pacific WW2*. The first article was on The Rock, the nickname of the island of Corregidor. He opened the article and read about the Allied occupation of the Island, about the vast amount of American and Philippine paper currency, silver pesos, gold bullion, securities, silver, and precious metals. All from city bank vaults, mining companies, and individuals of both countries.

With the impending Japanese invasion of Manila, the wealth on the Island had to be evacuated. The transfer of more than one hundred twenty-five tons of silver and at least fifty-one tons of government gold bullion took several days and was accomplished under cover of night. The gold ingots, coins, and other valuable metals were collected and transferred to several small ships. It was then transported to Corregidor Island during the night on December 27, 1941.

Now at The Rock, the wealth was transferred to the government vaults. These holdings consisted of $38,000 in U.S. Treasury checks, $3,000,000 in U.S. currency, $28,000,000 in Philippine currency, and 10,800 pounds of gold.

This solution didn't last long. The approaching Japanese invasion necessitated the evacuation of the holdings. Paper currency could be—and was—burned. But the gold presented another problem: it had to be disposed of. It could be sunk in the Bay, but it might be discovered and retrieved by the Japanese. Therefore, it would have to be removed from the island.

In one of those flukes of history, the USS Trout, which had delivered ammunition to the Island, needed ballast to replace the removed shells and torpedoes. The answer was the gold that needed to be evacuated.

Under the obscurity of night, U.S. and Philippine military personnel loaded gold bullion, securities, and some silver onto the USS Trout. *More than 600,000 silver pesos, contained in canvas bags, and six and a half tons of gold ingots were transferred to the submarine, a total of nearly $10,000,000.*

Due to the blackout and the haste of the operation, the transfer of the cargo to the Trout *could not be confirmed. Crewmembers caught the gold ingots as they were thrown to them from the pier. The bars weighed nearly forty pounds apiece. $23,000 a bar. In the confusion and dark, it would be easy to misdirect a bag of coins or an ingot...*

Were the coins on the bed from that frantic transfer of wealth? Was George Roper's American friend Frank one of the *Trout's* crewmembers? Had the lure of adding to his personal bank account been too much temptation?

How did George Roper get the silver coins, if they were part of that awful history of The Rock? Maybe more importantly, why? What were they going to do with the money? George's diary hinted at more, his lion's share, so there were more coins somewhere. Perhaps a few gold ingots, too.

McLaren leafed through the notebook pages again, as though another scan would produce more pages.

When had the pages been torn from the book? Who had done it and why, if he was wrong about Harvester's involvement? Had some rambler found the book and deciphered the location of the rest of the treasure? If so, why leave the book for someone else to find? The map had to mean something. Why else draw it?

An answer suggested itself. He phoned Jamie, hoping he wasn't about to sound like the Berk of the Year.

"Mike. Anything wrong?" Jamie's voice held the surprise of being called again so soon.

"No. Do you know who King Roper's dad is?"

"Are we back to this George Roper bloke?"

"Yes. I need to know if they're related."

"Hold on. I'll look at the police files…"

McLaren waited while Jamie brought up King Roper's file on the computer. Jamie's words trailed off for several seconds, then grew louder again. "I've good or bad news, depending on what you want."

"I'll decide that when you tell me."

"George and King were father and son. George was forty six when King was born."

"Late in life."

"Too bad it ever happened."

"Who said life was fair?"

"Probably not a copper. Anything else, Mike, or did you just want to pass the time of day?"

"If I did, it'd be with Dena. I need to sound you out on an idea, Jamie."

"Involving the father/son comedy team?"

"Not directly. Remember me telling you about finding the diary and the coins?"

"It wasn't that long ago, Mike. My memory's not

totally shot."

McLaren ignored his friend's comment. "I'll bet you my bank account that this World War Two diary and coins were planted for me to find."

"You think? You just said they were hidden."

"You've got to admit it's an awfully big stretch to believe I'd just *happen* to come upon the cottage that just *happens* to contain these things that are linked to blokes I just *happen* to know."

"In the normal course of your tourist day, yes."

"So, Harvester plants these things. He or his thugs knock me out, transport me to the loch area where I'll probably find the cottage and go there for shelter. It doesn't take a detective to figure out I'd then build a fire to keep from freezing, so they put the diary behind the stacked wood, making it look like it's hidden and that I found it."

"All right, I follow that and agree to a point. Harvester doesn't kill you, although he had the chance, because he needs you alive. But for what purpose?"

"The reason we use sniffer dogs. So that something leads the weary searcher to the missing object."

"And the object in this case is the rest of the Corregidor money."

"Yeah. Stolen that night of the transfer to the *USS Trout* in 1942."

Jamie let out a low whistle as McLaren continued. "Harvester learns about the money stash. Right now I don't know from whom—maybe that's not immediately important. Maybe King Roper's getting antsy because he's firmly and permanently ensconced in Wakefield Prison and he wants his gang to have the money. So King Roper gets word to a member of his gang, tells him about his dad's diary. Maybe King actually has the diary, left it with a mate. I don't know, but King knows where the diary is. His chum can't decipher the hiding place so he needs help. Maybe this chum contacts Lanny or Jean MacNab—after all, they're friends. One of them knows Harvester, knows he's pals with Lanny and Jean, figures Harvester's a detective who's a tad on the shady side of things, can solve puzzles—"

McLaren paused for Jamie's choice words, then continued. "So they let Harvester have a chance at deciphering it. Pal Harvester proves not to be such a brilliant detective after all. He becomes another statistic in the group who can't figure out where George Roper hid the money, so Harvester gets me up to Scotland to find it for him."

The silence that met McLaren's scenario was as deafening as if Jamie had yelled into the phone. The radiator gurgled and clanked out heat and outside a dog yapped.

"It makes sense," Jamie finally said, his words coming haltingly and low. "And it's a backhanded compliment to you, Mike."

"Harvester never gave me the time of day when we were in the job together. I'm astonished he honestly thinks I'm of the caliber to solve his little conundrum."

"Just don't get a swelled head."

McLaren touched his scalp wound and grimaced. "Little chance of that."

"I was trying to think of another set-up that would fit with everything you've told me, Mike, and nothing really works."

"So I'm not round the twist with this one."

"Unless I'm with you and we'll be roommates in

Bedlam, I can't see it."

"I don't know if that brings me comfort or unease."

"Whichever it is, don't do anything rash. You have my mate's phone number, don't you…Ross Gordon?"

"Your sergeant friend, yes."

"Don't be a hero. Use him."

McLaren assured Jamie he would and rang off. He grabbed his car key and sunglasses, slipped into his jacket and cap, and left the guesthouse. There had to be more to this saga, perhaps another note. Even if the clues were planted, they were authentic. It served King Roper and Charles Harvester no good at all if they faked anything. The real diary, perhaps supported by a letter or second clue, would give him another hint at the treasure's location. And it made no difference if King hadn't been born at the time of the diary entry. George Roper could've planned ahead and hidden the wealth for the child he hoped to have. McLaren had to find out.

The interior of his car resembled the inside of a refrigerator, having sat in the shade for more than twenty-four hours. He tugged his muffler more firmly around his neck and turned on the motor. He let it run for a minute before flipping on the heater. It warmed the enclosed space while he looked at a map of the area.

Approximately four miles from the village, Loch Voil and Loch Doine met at the narrow outflow of the latter. A tarmac road on the north side of the lochs would bring him close to this strip of water. The other alternative was to walk from the village and across the boggy land, as he had last night.

He exhaled loudly, not pleased with either way. The first route would probably give him a good bathing up to his neck; the second would merely dampen his boots and calves. His choice was a faster, closer, and wetter route or one that was slower, farther, and drier.

The radio personality announced the upcoming song and McLaren turned the knob, cutting off the banter. He eased out of the parking space, drove west, out of the village, and followed the shorelines of the two lochs.

The Buddhist retreat, Ledcreich, mutely announced the meeting of the two lochs. He drove past the establishment, recalling that it, as were other buildings, was put to the torch in 1746 as the Duke of Cumberland's troops repressive tactic at the end of the Jacobite rising. He let the historical image of flaming homes and fleeing villagers slip from his mind and parked off the road, leaving his car there and retracing his steps.

The neck of land between Loch Doine and Loch Voil could easily be boggy in the summer, he thought, glancing at the iced-over rushes and pockets of water. But most of the ground now was frozen, with an occasional patch of marsh still marginally soggy. Even when his boots broke through a thin layer of ice and he sank into the watery soil, the wetting was only ankle-deep. It was an easy route compared to the chilly swim he'd envisioned if the ford had been deeper.

He walked toward the loch, in the direction of the farm where he'd stopped yesterday, and entered the Tuarach, the low-lying ground where the cottage stood.

Sunlight spilled over the hilltop and the rose and indigo of the eastern sky became whitewashed with azure and milky hues. He put on his sunglasses, noted the time on his watch, and trudged eastward around the lower edge of Loch Voil. The sun had cleared the mountain range, and yellow-tinted light fell softly on the clumps of grass. Farther west, a kestrel hovered over a patch of ground. McLaren passed a high plateau in the distance and judged he had walked a quarter of the length of the loch. He looked for the village, now hardly visible on the loch's eastern end. The snow was nearly gone, but patches were pockmarked with his boot prints.

The wind shifted, blowing across the loch and bringing the biting cold he remembered from the previous night. He continued eastward, pulling up the collar of his jacket, and hunched his shoulders as he bent forward slightly. His breath puffed into the air in frosty clouds, rising overhead before they vanished in the sunlight.

The trek to the cottage was neither as long or as arduous as last night's. Daylight and drier clothes made the way more tolerable, and quicker. He strode up to the dwelling, his breathing accelerating. He was strangely pleased to be there again.

It didn't stem from connecting with Donald MacLaren, either.

McLaren walked over to the fireplace and moved the rest of the logs in the woodpile, stacking them on the other side of the room. No silver coin, notebook, or other object presented itself. He ran his hand over the stone mantelpiece but it was clean. He walked around the three walls, pushing and prodding the stones, hoping a loose one would fall and reveal a cache. He got on his knees and shifted the stone slabs in the fireplace. Behind one of those forming the inner hearth he found a scrap of paper.

He unfolded it. He'd left the notebook back in his

room, so he had nothing to which he could compare it, but the paper seemed to match. The handwriting also seemed similar. He scanned the entry, tucked it into his jacket pocket, and replaced the stone. Then he smoothed soil over the stone's surface and pushed it between the edges where it touched other stones. He placed a handful of dry grass and several twigs on the stone and lit it, watching it until it burnt out. Satisfied the hearth looked used and undisturbed—a nice touch to keep Harvester wondering if McLaren had retrieved the paper—he made his way back to the guesthouse.

After he showered and changed into dry clothes, he again read the entry on the sheet of paper, this time more slowly.

Roar not! Music soothes the savage breast though rudeness raves round you. Your future is here, a comfort at night or winter.

McLaren sank back onto the bed and stared at the ceiling. What the hell did music and rudeness and roaring have to do with that diary entry about the *USS Trout* and The Rock? Was he on the wrong track? Was this latest piece of doggerel something separate, penned by another hand? If so, why had it been secreted under the hearthstone? Why would anyone hide something like that?

He got up and filled the electric teakettle with water, turned it on, and slapped a teabag into one of the mugs on the coffee table. While the water heated, he looked at the hand-penned map again. Perhaps George Roper had written something more on it. He held it up to the lamplight, staring at every centimeter of the paper, but he could make out nothing. He passed the map slowly over the steam from the kettle, thinking something had been written in disappearing ink and would reveal itself when heated. Nothing emerged from the paper.

The kettle whistled and McLaren poured the boiling water into the cup. He let the teabag steep while he examined the actual map paper. It was pristine. No tears or holes marred the page. It looked as if it could've been drawn yesterday, or preserved under glass all those years. Evidently George Roper had taken care over the map, wanting it to last. Then why was there a pen mark under the legend *Braes of Balquhidder*?

He glanced at the rest of the map. No other stray line of ink marred its surface. Was the mark a clue, a sort of underline calling attention to the Braes? If so, what was he supposed to learn from the title of that region? It was a large area to search, a hill range north of Balquhidder village, if that was the action the cryptic clue implied.

He fixed his tea and sipped it while he peered more closely at the map. He saw a small dot near the end of the word 'Balquhidder.' A thin, short line of ink extended up from the dot. Was it another stray pen mark? He angled the map under the lamplight. It looked deliberately made, for the line ended firmly without trailing off. Further more, the dot was larger than a simple dot from a pen. It looked drawn on.

It also looked like a quarter note.

He set his cup down and moved to the stronger light at the window. Daft! Was he inventing meanings, looking for clues where there were none? What did a musical note have to do with The Rock or silver pesos or the Braes of Balquhidder?

But it did. He closed his eyes, suddenly afraid and excited, envisioning the sheet music for the old folk song. He'd just sung it yesterday as he drove to the village.

He hurried over to the bed and grabbed the scrap of paper he'd found beneath the hearthstone. The words popped out at him as though they'd been underlined or written more boldly.

ROAR not! Music soothes the savage breast though RUDENESS RAVES ROUND you. Your future is here, a comfort at NIGHT or WINTER.

He slowly sang the third verse, pausing as his eyes locked on the pertinent words in the message.

When the *rude wintry* win'
idly *raves round* our dwellin',
An' the *roar* o' the linn
on the *night*-breeze is swellin'
Sae merrily we'll sing
as the storm rattles o'er us,
till the dear shieling ring
wi' the light liltin' chorus.

He laid the paper on the bed. Did the message refer to a shieling on the Braes of Balquhidder? He supposed there could be one or two left, remnants of another century. Was that what the map and the message meant? The bulk of the silver stolen from the *Trout* waited in a shieling on the Braes? And the note drawn on the map was a hint that the Braes referred to the song as well as to the land.

Chapter Twelve

His tea grew cold as he thought through the song and the map marks from a different angle, but the paper scrap didn't mesh with anything but the song. At least nothing he could think of.

He emptied the teacup's contents into the sink, put on his jacket, and left his room.

The air held the bite of an advancing storm but McLaren didn't notice. He strolled around the village, hoping to talk to an older resident. He had to know if any shieling still existed in the area. He also needed to know about Frank, George Roper's wartime mate.

Several villagers were out. He could distinguish them from the tourists by their conversation topics and the workday tools they carried. McLaren bypassed anyone under the age of sixty-two. If any coins had been secreted in the area in 1962, any very young child seeing that might not remember. Someone ten years old in '62 might reasonably recall a stranger lingering in the area.

McLaren fought the urge to take the easy way out, to talk to owners of the tearoom or hotel or bed-and-breakfasts. Even if they were the correct age, he didn't want to supply them with fuel for gossip or alert them to his business. So he wandered back to the farm at which he'd inquired yesterday. The same elderly man was there, in the courtyard this time. He wore the same gray cloth jacket and blue cloth cap. His khaki-colored wellies were dark and stained with mud. He looked up as McLaren approached.

"Good day, sir." McLaren picked up one of the gloves that lay on the ground and handed it to the man. The leather seemed as old as its owner: dry and stiff from overwork. "I wonder if you could spare me a few minutes."

The man eyed McLaren, perhaps to see if he'd changed clothes since yesterday. He removed his cloth cap and wiped his forehead with his jacket sleeve. "What are ye needin', then?"

"I wonder if there are any old shielings in the area."

"Shielings? Why would ye be wantin' to know about a shieling?" The man's voice was wary, as though suspecting a trick. "Are you inclined to do a bit o' wild campin'? Ye just got cleaned up, man." A hint of a smile played around the corners of his lips, then vanished as he scratched his chin. "Aye, I mind one or two o' them still standin'. That cottage where ye spent the other night, now, it's not a shieling, aye?"

"Yes. Am I correct in assuming it's Donald MacLaren's cottage? Donald *mor nan mart*?" He added the Celtic nickname that translated to Big Donald of the cattle. It never hurt to reveal a bit of insider knowledge.

The man nodded, the smile now in his eyes. "That was a long time back, the 1750s. But the houses stood. Had to. Ye've come up agin' a wee bit o' our bleak weather and a bit o' wind. So ye should know what a Highland winter can do, even to tree and rock." He stared at the Braes rising north of the loch. "Wind, rain and ice can pick at a mountain, wear it down to a gorge or flat land. Can it not do the same with a dwellin'? That's certainly not as strong or solid as yonder ben."

"You're saying that no shielings have survived in this area."

"I'm not sayin' that. I'm sayin' that there are very few left. The modern folk dinnae follow the sheep or cattle to the summer pastures as they did. They've no use for the shieling. They stay put in their own comfy houses. But ye'll find one up on Creag Mac Ranaich."

McLaren glanced back at the village. "That's north of Balquhidder, isn't it?"

"Aye. 'Bout a half-day walk if ye were hikin' to the top o' the ben. But ye're just wantin' the shieling. It's no more than an hour's walk. Not that hard, even for a city dweller." The man paused and eyed McLaren's boots and jacket. "Ye'll do."

"Is the building easily seen? Do I have to wander off the track to spot it?"

"It's not along the path. Ye'll have to go a bit to your left."

"Will I know the spot when I come to it?"

The man shook his head. "But ye'll find the burn. Ye'll be followin' a line o' fence posts. They'll stop at the beginnin' o' the forest. Two hundred yards on, there's a wee path windin' to the left, into the forest. A muckle rock sits there. Take that path into the forest and cross o'er the burn. On the other side o' the burn is your shieling."

"That's the only one in the area, then."

"Aye. There's another farther north, near Ben Nevis and Benalder Forest, but Creag Mac Ranaich's got the only hut hereabouts."

McLaren said this one sounded like it would fit his

needs.

"You're the third man who's asked me about the shieling."

"Yes? When was this?" He smiled to show his disinterest. He didn't want to alert the man into thinking the shieling was important.

"Oh, I'd say the first was in the early 1960s."

McLaren felt his heart pound in his throat. "How are you so certain about the early '60s? That's fifty years ago."

"I remember it was 20 February, 1962. And I can be sure because 20 February is my birthday and that American astronaut John Glenn orbited the earth. He was the first Yank. Read about it in the newspaper. I always thought that was amazin'."

McLaren did a quick mental calculation. The diary entry was February 1962. George Roper hinted at a generous souvenir, which strongly hinted at the Corregidor money. That money could be hidden in a shieling in the area. "Is it usual for tourists or visitors to do hiking in the winter? I assume that's what that man had in mind if he asked."

"Not so many in February, but we get a few. If it's warm or we havenae had much snowfall we tend to get more. The less serious walkers, ye understand."

"He was a tourist, then?"

"At first."

"At first?"

"Aye. He came that day, stayed a while and hiked the ben. Stayed in the village. He left after several days—I dinnae remember how long—but came back in June two years later, when he took up residence in the village."

"He lived here?" McLaren wasn't expecting that.

"Toward the end o' the glen. In a small house. Not so grand, I'm thinkin', as the one he had in the city. Nothin' grand like the big house in the village proper. Your grandfather's home," he added, showing he still remembered McLaren's connection.

"You knew this for a fact?"

"No. But he had an air about him, like he expected the world to hand him things. Like he had money and was used to gettin' what he wanted. A way of talkin' to ye, if ye understand. I never saw the inside o' his house, but a mate o' mine did. Said it was full o' fancy furniture and knick knacks that must've cost more than my farm. Of course he couldnae work. Formally, I mean. Hold down an outside job."

"Why not?"

"He was a Yank. He was friendly enough but kind o' kept to himself. Never worried about money, lived well enough despite no regular job. But he had nice clothes and a car and stood a few rounds each week at the local. If ye'd asked me about him I'd have remembered straight away. Had a strange surname. Papadakis. Greek, I reckon. Nice laddie, though. Did his bit in the war. Army, I think."

"Do you remember his first name?"

The man withdrew a pipe from his jacket pocket, filled it with tobacco from the tin sitting on a milk can, and lit it. "Frank."

"Did Frank Papadakis live here long? Is he still here?" McLaren gazed at the village, as though wondering if he'd passed the man.

"Died a few years ago. Buried in the village churchyard, if ye care to have a look. Not many attended his burial. Oh, we villagers went, of course, but I mean foreigners didnae come. Could be because he was a foreigner, left his family in America. Could be he was the last of his line, too. I dinnae know."

"He wasn't married, then? Had no family?"

"None that I know. Or ever saw in the village. Seemed to be alone, as I said. Some blokes came to visit him a few times. But they were mates from the war. I know that because they'd sit in the pub and tell stories of their times in the service, sing songs. They were in different armies, of course. Different divisions. Papadakis was in the US Army Forces in the Far East. In the Philippines, under MacArthur, I believe." He stopped to draw on his pipe and watched the puffs of smoke fade into the wind. He seemed in no hurry to get back to his work. Perhaps he enjoyed McLaren's attention, or he just wanted an excuse for the break. McLaren could hear a voice calling from the house and a back door slam. Music seeped outside, from a radio or a record player, perhaps, and the voice spoke to a dog that yapped in answer. The older man maneuvered the pipe to the corner of his mouth. "Must be right. I heard their stories enough. Same stories, a' the time, each time they'd get together. As though they loved talking about the South Pacific campaign."

"You said I was the third person who asked about shielings, sir. Who was the other one?"

"Some tourist. He came after Papadakis had been livin' here for a few years. He asked around the village, took to walkin' the hills and snappin' photos with a grand camera. Must've cost him a handful o' quid. I didnae pay him much mind. He was gone after a day or two."

"Do you remember any of the others who visited Papadakis?"

"From the war?"

"Yes."

"Two chaps, one English by the sound o' him. Bath served in the Burma campaign under First Viscount Slim." His teeth clamped down on the stem of his pipe and he pulled on his gloves.

"Just those three men?"

"I never heard or saw anyone else. Papadakis and his two mates."

"Do you know either of their names?"

The farmer cocked his head slightly and squinted at McLaren. "Why are ye so interested? You mates with one them?"

"I'm writing a book about the area. About the village in particular. I'd like to include its history and interesting stories of residents." He smiled and hoped he'd said it smoothly and readily enough.

"Oh, aye? Well, that's interestin'." He took a few puffs on his pipe, perhaps dredging up the names from the past. "I recollect no other names. Even if I heard them, I've forgotten. They meant nothing to me."

"But the two men were British."

"Unlike Papadakis, aye. I think one must've lived near the village, though. Not in Balquhidder, or I'd have known him. But perhaps close by. They talked a lot about Callander. That I remember."

"Do you know why? You think one or both of them lived there?"

"One might have done. The wee lad."

"He was smaller than Papadakis?"

"Oh, aye. Like a jockey. I thought he rode the

horses for a livin' afore the war. Could do then, I suppose. Thin and wiry, but with a hard face, like he'd been in one too many fights and wouldnae hesitate a moment to kill the next chap he tangled with."

"Do you remember the other man, what he looked like?"

"He was the Sassenach. Tall like a tree. His eyes were dark and looked like they could throw daggers when he frowned or stared. He was bald, though he couldnae have been over fifty. I dinnae think he lived around these parts. Had an accent different from us."

"Did the small man have a local accent?"

"Not local, but maybe lowland Scots. Or the border country. Could be Carlisle or close by."

"And this third man…"

"Nothing like Geordie or Cockney or Somerset. Sorry."

"Anything distinctive about his speech? A stutter or lisp or rough voice?"

"You need all this for that book of yours?" Again the man eyed McLaren with what seemed to be a growing misgiving.

"Not at all. It just occurred to me as you were telling me about the three men that I could talk to them, get some war time stories from them, perhaps interview them to see if they knew Frank Papadakis' reason for living in Balquhidder instead of in America."

"And since he's breathed his last on his soil yer're thinkin' of talkin' to his mates. Aye, perhaps they'd know."

"Have you seen either of them since Papadakis died?"

"That I haven't. They've no reason to visit here."

"Just wondered." McLaren felt his hope slipping away.

He was about to leave when the man called to him. "I do mind something that might or might not help ye in your search for them."

"Yes?"

"That third chap...the English bloke."

"Yes?"

"He were a beefy chap. Tall and muscles like boulders. He had a tattoo on the side o' his face. Just in black, it was, no colors other than black."

"Do you remember what the tattoo looked like?"

"I'd never seen anything like it afore. All geometric, like a modern painting."

"Just a design, then. No graphic or word."

"Just the design. I found it strange yet interestin' to look at. Didnae look like a gang tattoo, like ye see nowadays. More like art."

McLaren said it sounded intriguing and he wished he could see it.

"I'd stake my life he were a Sassenach," the man added, his voice floating downwind and urging McLaren to stop.

He turned and looked at the farmer. "Why's that? You remember something about the locality of the accent?"

"No. Not a thing. Though I thought the three o' them could've competed for the parts of first and second murderer in *Macbeth* and it'd be a good choice whichever two got it."

"Then, what?"

"They had a few toasts they'd give over and over in the pub. I got to thinkin' they knew no others, or those few meant somethin' very special to them."

"Would they have toasted their regiments or the safe return of their friends from the war?"

"Might've done. But it wasn't like any other toast I've ever heard. They'd raise their glasses and the tall, muscular chap wi' the tattoo would call out 'To my little king.' The first time I heard it I thought he was salutin' George VI. But he said little."

"Did he say it in a disparaging fashion, as though he were demeaning the king?"

"No way! All three blokes were straight faced and stone cold sober."

McLaren thanked the man and returned to the village.

****

He stopped several yards from the b-and-b, in a clearing where he couldn't be overhead, and opened his mobile. He looked up the phone number of Saltire Guest House and waited for Jean MacNab to answer. He tore a page from his notebook and held it near the phone.

"Saltire Guest House. Jean MacNab, proprietor. May I help you?"

McLaren almost gagged as the honeyed tone came to him. He took a breath, mentally ran off a quick prayer, and changed his voice to a nasal whisper he hoped would pass for Harvester's. It should; he'd heard it for years when they worked together. "You alone?"

"Charlie?" Jean's voice queried McLaren more than her actual question did.

"Yeah. Can you talk?"

"Sure. Are you in town?"

"No. I got a call from Lanny. He needs a hand. But

he rang off without telling me where he was." He repeated his prayer, hoping Jean hadn't heard from Harvester or Lanny before this phone call.

She evidently hadn't. Her tone was bitter. "The twit. Sounds just like him. He have McLaren, then?"

"Yeah. Finally. Do you know where Lanny is? He doesn't answer his mobile."

"Doesn't surprise me. Probably turned it off or lost it. He's at the shieling. At least, I think he is. That's where they've got the woman stashed."

McLaren's throat tightened. His mind whirled as he fought to think straight.

"You hear me?" She paused, as though reconsidering the conversation. "Charlie?"

McLaren crumpled the paper and held it close to the phone receiver. He continued crinkling it and talked over the sound. "Yeah. He didn't change spots, did he? Still at…" He dropped his voice and rustled the paper more loudly.

"Awful connection, Charlie. I can't hear you. They've not botched that up. They're on the ben."

"Creag Mac Ranaich."

"Of course." Her voice sounded wary.

McLaren rolled the crumpled paper between his fingers. "Just making sure they didn't muck that up. Smashing. I know where to find him. I'll see you soon." He rang off before Jean could say anything more.

He pocketed his phone, smiling as he gazed up the hill. Harvester came in handy in the most unexpected times and places. Perhaps their years working together hadn't been in vain.

The shieling made sense as a hideout or as a spot to keep kidnapped victims, whether it be him, his grandfather, or Liza Skene. They could probably see anyone approaching the hut for dozens of yards. Anyway, who'd think of looking in Balquhidder for a missing Edinburgh woman?

He considered leaving a message in his bed-and-breakfast room, stating where he was going and when he was leaving. Harvester had a nasty habit of popping up where and when he was least wanted. But McLaren couldn't envision the man at the shieling. Keeping Liza hidden in a rock hut wasn't Harvester's style. He left the menial labor to underlings. And Lanny Clack was as close to the epitome of menial labor as McLaren had ever seen. Besides, who was there to know if he went missing? The b-and-b owner wouldn't know, and Jamie had no idea what he was about to do.

He turned away from the guesthouse and walked toward the kirk.

The climb up the hill was slick in spots. Skiffs of snow had melted and refrozen overnight, giving the top of the snow an icy mantle. Rocks poked out of the earth, black and mossy and lichen-covered on their northern faces. Dotting the ground like reverse dominoes. The soil around them had become sodden where the melt collected. Where the snow still lay pristine, sunlight glanced off the crystallized surface, breaking into prisms of light. Deer and hare tracks interlaced on the white surface but vanished in the brown grass and bracken.

McLaren followed the line of fence posts, stopping periodically to catch his breath and make visual notes of his route. It could be helpful on his return. He stopped in an expanse of heather, now brown and dried as the grass, then moved on.

Fifteen minutes' further hike brought him to the beginning of the forest. The trees stood sparse around the first hundred yards of the perimeter, as though they'd been newly planted a decade or so ago. The wire fence fell behind as he continued on, and another minute's walk brought him to a large rock. A footpath meandered off the main trail, cutting across the heather field to the left.

As he entered the wood the world took on a different feeling. Sunlight fell in sporadic patches, slanting through the boughs like searchlights. The air held the scents of damp earth, pine, and wet stone, chillier now that the sun could not warm it.

The light grew dimmer as he tramped deeper into the wood and he felt the first prickles of the old fear and panic. He concentrated on the directions the farmer had given him, forced himself to think of Frank Papadakis and his two mates.

King had been mentioned twice, now: first in George Roper's diary entry and then in the toast drunk nightly by the three wartime buddies. It hadn't been a slander against George VI, McLaren was certain. Not if the three men had been as serious as the farmer stated. He'd stake his life that the reference was to George Roper's son, King. Even if the boy hadn't been born yet, or even conceived, it wouldn't stop Roper from planning for his prospective son's future. Men did a lot of that in wartime when they saw mates die beside them, heard of men lost on bombing flights or aboard ship. Life was more precious then. A child, even the hope of having a child, grew in importance. The child would come from the soldier, carry some of the father's talents or likes, perhaps. It would continue the family for another generation.

There was no reason George Roper hadn't had these same desires and dreams. A toast to his as yet unborn son carried the solemnity of the future. If George were lucky, the infant would be a duplicate of himself. Who said you couldn't live forever?

McLaren pushed a bough out of the way and walked around a large rock. The wood was quiet but for occasional birdsong. He wondered if George had been pleased with his son, if he'd made plans for the boy's education, thought of father-son outings, wrote about what he'd done in the war to make King proud of his old man.

Perhaps some of King's pride in his father would come from George's participation in the Corregidor money scheme.

Frank Papadakis *must* have buried part of the money in the shieling. He'd had no job, so how had he supported himself? He could've lived off an inheritance, but if he'd stolen some of the silver coins that could have supplemented his Army pension enough to afford him a comfortable life style. He'd chosen to live in Balquhidder and bury the money close by because the nameless friend lived close by in Callander. Frank wouldn't have just come to Scotland on a whim; he'd had some reason. Same thing for choosing the village in which to live. Why Balquhidder?

McLaren came to the burn. The water had frozen in the shallower depths and around the edges of the rocks littering its bed. A path of large, flat stones had been laid to connect bank to bank. He stood by the river's edge, grabbed his mobile, and punched in Jamie's phone number.

Jamie answered with a cheery "Mike. What's going on?"

"Just walking around." McLaren looked at the hill rising steeply to his right.

"You must be having fun. Or drinking your way through the beers. Which's got your vote so far?"

"I need a favor."

"If you're out of money—"

"Can you look up some old Army records and send me some information on three individuals?"

The silence on the other end of the phone told him Jamie hadn't been expecting that. Several seconds passed before Jamie replied. "If it's not too involved. Who, what, and when?"

"George Roper."

"King's old man."

"Yeah. George Roper served under First Viscount Slim in the Burma campaign."

"Burma? When was this?"

"World War Two."

Jamie groaned and muttered that consideration was awfully scarce these days. "Who else?"

"There's another bloke who was in the same regiment as Roper. I don't have his name."

"Of course not. That would make it too easy."

"But he had the physique of a jockey, if you stumble across any photo of him. After the war he lived in Callander."

"You think that's his home town?"

"I don't know, Jamie. But Callander couldn't have been that large after the war. Surely it won't be hard to track down a bloke who served in Burma who resided in Callander."

"You won't say that if you had to do it. Anything else, I'm afraid to ask?"

"One more. An American named Frank Papadakis. He served in the US Army Forces, stationed for a while in the Philippines, under General MacArthur. He lived in Balquhidder after the war and died in 2008."

"How'd you learn that?"

"I looked at his gravestone. He's buried in the village churchyard. Born in 1924. That should help you a bit."

"Right. What do you want to know?"

"Photos of them, if you can get them. Either from their military records or police records—"

Jamie's voice held a tint of suspicion. "You know they're criminals?"

"I have a suspicion. From what I hear they at least look the part. George Roper had a tattoo on the side of his face."

"Like father, like son."

"What do you mean?"

"King has a Maori tattoo on his thigh. I've not seen it myself, but some chaps here at the station have."

"DCI Graham."

"Right. It's quite large. Done in black, red and cream colors, I believe. Or close to it. Evidently it's an authentic moko."

"A what?"

"You need to get out more, Mike. A moko. The Maori of New Zealand have these tattoos on their faces or shoulders or thighs. They're as individual as fingerprints. They're not merely a pretty design; they tell the individual's ancestry or personality. For anyone but a Maori to wear it is equivalent to what we call identity theft. It's taken very seriously by the Maori when someone requests to get the tattoo. Permission is granted by the chief."

"So George and King Roper are part Maori, then?"

"I wouldn't know. But I wouldn't be surprised if it's like everything else King's done in his bloody life."

"Stolen it from the Maori, you mean?"

"Theft is just one of his pastimes, as I said."

"Nice family, the Ropers." McLaren tried to picture what the tattoo looked like, but he had no idea. "Anyway, the bloke who lived in Callander evidently had the looks and perhaps the disposition of a man who'd not hesitate to slug a vicar if he didn't like the clergyman's expression."

"Lovely. Anything else besides the photos?"

"Send them to my mobile, if you would, Jamie."

"Sure."

"If you can get the name and address of the chap in Callander, send that on. Plus, I'd like the address of George Roper. Find out if they're living and if so, where. If he died, find when. I need that date. That should do it."

"It may take me a while. I'll have to do this off hours when the climate is better for personal projects."

"Just don't get caught, Jamie."

"You don't have to remind me, but thanks for the God speed. I'll ring you back as soon as I've got it."

McLaren crossed the brook, emerging from the forest twenty minutes later. Open grassland spread before him, treeless and dotted occasionally with boulders and outcroppings on the hill face. The long grass and ferns bowed in the wind, the dry stalks and seed heads rustling as they knocked against each other.

The sky stretched like a broad canopy in blue and gray, and seemed to touch the hilltops in every direction.

Several hundred yards ahead sat the shieling, a small stone cottage perhaps twenty by ten feet. The sod roof was intact but for the area farthest from the wooden door. The door and the hole in the roof where smoke from the fire escaped were the only means of light for the long-ago residents. The rock walls were solid; the two small squares on either end of the house had been plugged with sod years ago. A footpath, worn into the soil and overgrown in parts, wandered to the door.

An off-road vehicle was parked near the door. McLaren yanked his notebook and pencil from his jacket pocket and wrote down the number plate.

As he approached the shieling he heard voices. They grew louder the nearer he got to the structure.

He stood at the end of the cottage, where the roof had fallen in. The conversation was clearest there. He listened, hoping Lanny was one of the men. Shielings were not so plentiful anymore that there would be more on the hill.

The rock wall was cold against his back. Bits of turf, stuffed like insulation into the chinks between the rocks, had frozen into rigid saw-like blades, sharp and cold beneath his touch. He ignored the cold; the conversation was more chilling.

"What the bloody hell are we gonna do with her?" The male voice exploded from the confines of the rock structure, the anger evident even without seeing the speaker's expression.

"Why do *we* have to decide?" snapped another male voice. Though lower in tone and volume, the words crackled with underlying hatred. And perhaps a touch of rivalry.

"Because you, as usual, made a cock-up of the job."

"I don't see how you can say that, Fowler. I snatched her before she talked to the coppers. I saved your worthless neck. You were looking at a murder charge if you'd got nicked."

The man called Fowler snorted, a blast of cuss words following. "You're dreamin', mate. *You're* the yob who drove the car. I wasn't even around."

"Of course not. You were safely away from the scene, as usual. Never want to get your lily-white hands the least bit soiled in any way. Leave it for barmy Lanny. He's not got the brains for anything but the grunt work. Well, I'm not gonna carry the can for this. I snatched her and I did what I was told to do: prevent her and that bloke from talking."

"Aw, shut it. Cry on someone else's shoulder. And do it some other time. We're still in a jam. I'd wring your neck if I didn't need your muscles to cart her off." A silence fell between them and McLaren could hear a woman crying within the hut. There was the sound of metal hitting rock, followed by Fowler's heated voice. "Damned coffee's cold. What's the good of coffee if it's cold? Can't you do anything right?"

"I wanted to build a fire, but no, you wouldn't have it. It'd give away our position, you said. Who to? Nobody's lookin' for her. I've been listenin' to the radio in the car. No one's put in a missing person report. We're fine." A clatter of wood on stone sounded. "You got a match?"

"You git. There might be a hiker around. He'd see

the smoke."

"I'm bloody freezin'. Why'd we have to stash her here? No one'd look in my flat, and we'd be warm."

"And one of your nosey parker neighbors might see us toting her inside, or hear her blasted crying. You're gormless. Think it through before you say anything. Better yet, before you do anything. We're in the perfect spot. And we're going to stay in this perfect spot until we get word from Roper."

"That'll be a bloody great trick, Fowler, with him in the nick."

"He's got his network. You forget how he got word out about him going to Leeds General Hospital? He's got ways, Lanny. We'll hear from him."

"I still think it's time to put someone else in charge of the gang. Someone who can make decisions on the spot. It takes too long to get word back and forth from Roper. We need a man outside."

"And just who do you have in mind for this job? Wouldn't be you, Lanny, would it?"

There was something in Fowler's voice or his expression that must have warned Lanny off the subject. He muttered something McLaren couldn't hear. His voice picked up a bit in volume when he asked the woman if she wanted anything.

"Worry about yourself." Fowler's voice moved closer to McLaren. "Miss Liza Skene's not going to be with us much longer, anyway, so I doubt if she's worried about a cold cup of coffee."

"Just so it looks like an accident."

"Afraid someone'll look for you if we top her outright?"

"There are other ways than leaving a knife in her

back. Why can't we make it look like an accident?" Lanny's words rushed out as he warmed to the idea. "Yeah. An accident. Like she fell into a ravine up here, or died of exposure. It's bloody cold enough for the coppers to believe that."

"We'd have to knock her out and leave her in the snow or chuck her down the gorge. Make it look like she stumbled and hit her head. You willing to risk the cops won't find rope burns on her arms and think something's a tad fishy?"

"They won't think it suspicious if she dies by fallin' down a ravine. It's a cinch to walk to it and push her over the edge. Another careless hiker who stumbled off the rock face." His voice came stronger now that he was confident of the scenario. "Yeah. Like McLaren. We left *him* in the snow. Probably froze to death or got hypothermia or somethin'. A death that the cops couldn't pin to us. Same with her. An accident. No possible link to us, so no coppers breathin' down our necks. Harvester's brilliant."

The woman cried louder. A sharp retort, like a hand hitting flesh, a growled "Shut it!" and the crying stopped.

"So, what about it, Fowler? Brilliant, eh?"

The door squeaked open and McLaren ran to the end of the hut. Fowler's voice sounded as if the man stood beside McLaren.

"I don't know how I got into this. Doing jobs of work for two different blokes. Roper consumes enough of my time, then you hook me up with this other guy." He mumbled something beneath his breath.

"That's just it, Fowler. We pick up these odd jobs when Roper doesn't need us. Nothin' wrong with makin' a few extra quid on the side." Lanny fell silent and McLaren could hear the woman softly crying. "This was just the one-time thing. I doubt if he'll hire us again. We did our job; he's happy and we'll get our money."

"When? He's had time enough to give it to us."

"He'll pay us when McLaren's body is found, when an account of his tragic accident runs in the newspapers. That'll be proof enough and we'll get our money. End of association."

"How you ever got hooked up with this bloke is something I'll never understand."

Lanny laughed. "Mutual friend."

"If you've got any more friends like that, I don't want any part of."

"So, what about leavin' her in a gorge? Or make it look like a rock hit her on the head?"

"I'll think about it. I'm leaving now. I'll pick up some food, maybe make arrangements for her accident. I'll be back in a bit."

"Lock the damned door behind you. I don't want anyone burstin' in here and findin' me with…her."

"You've got the key, lame brain. Harvester gave it to you when he put the lock on the door last month. Remember?"

"I just though he gave you one, too."

"Yeah, well, he didn't. Probably didn't want to spend the extra quid."

"I'll let you back in. Don't be stupid. Now, go on."

The hinges shrieked at being moved. "Don't do anything more stupid than you can help, Lanny."

The door slammed shut, cutting off Lanny's retort. Seconds later the vehicle's motor started and Fowler drove off.

McLaren eased back to the door. Lanny's voice seeped through the hole in the roof.

"I didn't think it'd end like this, lady. I truly didn't. If I could make it different, I would."

"You could let me go." Liza's tone was sharp and wavered, her words hurried. "We could make it look like I hit you on the head with one of those logs. Fowler would never know you released me. I'll stay with a friend down south in Devon. I'll be out of the way, I'll keep quiet. He'll never know." She paused and McLaren wondered if Lanny was considering the woman's suggestion. "Please, Lanny. I won't go to the police. I'll never say a thing about Hurd or about this. Please! I-I'll give you money. £3,000. I've got that much. You could go away, get away from Fowler. Start life over. Please!"

"I can't. I'm sorry, but it'd be my life if Fowler found you gone."

"If that's not enough, maybe I could get more. Yes! My car. It's only a few months old. You can have that. Plus my ring. See?" She must have held a hand out to Lanny, for he whistled. "I've got a matching necklace at home. Real diamonds. You can have that and my other good jewelry, too." Her voice quivered, betraying her fright. "Please let me go! I'm begging you."

McLaren stepped in front of the door and pounded on it with his fist. The door shook in its wooden frame.

"Just a minute, Fowler," Lanny called out. "Why're you back? Forget something?" Lanny opened the door, muttering that Fowler's chief talent in life was pestering people. He never finished the remark. McLaren grabbed Lanny and pulled him outside. He uttered an exclamation before McLaren's fist slammed into his stomach. As Lanny grabbed his stomach and bent over, McLaren kicked the back of his knees. Lanny's legs folded and he crashed to the ground like a collapsed deck chair. Lanny bent his legs beneath him and pushed his palms into the grass, struggling to get up but McLaren slugged him again in the jaw, and Lanny crumpled, spread out on the ground.

McLaren dashed into the shieling. Liza Skene sat on the floor in the far corner, her hands, arms, and legs tied with rope. The hems of her trouser legs and her tartan muffler were caked with mud and her coat was matted with spots where water had dried. Her hair hung uncombed to her shoulders, her one barrette dangling over her left ear. She stared at him with eyes that were puffy from crying, yet held the fear of her capture and relief that he had appeared. He pulled out his pocketknife as he ran over to her.

"Mike!" Liza gasped, the words barely more than a whisper. "How'd you find me?"

"We'll talk about that later." His knife blade cut through the rope and he threw the pieces into the fireplace. "First thing is to get out of here and make sure you're all right." He gave her his hand and pulled gently. "Can you stand?"

She doubled her legs beneath her and pushed against the rock wall with her left hand. Nodding, she got to her feet. "A bit wobbly. If you can give me a few minutes…" The fingers of her left hand wove around McLaren's as she steadied herself. "Nice to see you again. Especially under these circumstances."

"I'm rather pleased, too." He rubbed her ankles and wrists where the rope had chaffed her skin. "Feel any better? Are you able to walk? It's a bit of a hike, I'm afraid."

"Don't worry about me, Mike. I'll make it. I could scale Ben Nevis if it meant my freedom."

"How'd they grab you?"

"Quite easily. I was walking down the street. It was dusk. Fowler came up to me from behind, showed me a knife and ordered me into their car. Lanny was in the driver's seat. I thought about screaming, but he nudged me with the knife, so I got into the car. I know I shouldn't have. I know that once a victim ends up in the abductor's territory the abductor has the advantage and it's harder for the victim to escape. But it happened so quickly; he seemed to pop out of nowhere. And the car was within a yard or so of us. He pushed me into it and we drove off before it really dawned on me what was happening."

"Why'd they grab you? Did they say?"

"I don't know for certain. But I infer it was to keep me from talking about Hurd's project."

"His *project*? The one he worked on at the library?"

"They never said which one, but I gather it was one of the ones Hurd worked on during his off hours, moonlighting for other people. It must've been secretive or important, or they'd not be so anxious to keep me from talking."

McLaren nodded. "Again assuming you knew about it. But they'd not want to take a chance Hurd spoke to you about it. If Fowler and Lanny knew you two worked together, they would easily believe Hurd might have told you something of it. Or that you helped him. Better safe than sorry." He rubbed her wrists, getting her circulation going again. "Those kind don't care if they're right or wrong about a person. It's best to eliminate everyone, clean up loose ends so the threat's gone."

Liza flexed her fingers and stamped her feet. "Lanny and Fowler argued a lot over that. I gathered that was why they finally caught up with me in the city. They kept squabbling over how much Hurd had told me, how to silence me so I wouldn't talk…" She trembled, as though hearing the argument again, or envisioning her fate. "I'm supposed to know something that's damning to them. That's the only thing I can think of." She grimaced and avoided McLaren's gaze. "I know what a berk I've been, that I should've fought or fainted or something, but it's hard to think when it happens so quickly."

McLaren squeezed her hand. "Don't beat yourself up, Liza. Not many people would do any differently."

"I do know another thing I'd do differently."

"Oh yes? What's that?"

"Not tell Fowler about that Edinburgh brochure."

"The one you tore to give me?"

"Yes. It was fairly soon after…my capture. He went through my handbag and found the brochure. I guess I shuddered or blinked, for he realized it had some significance to me. He…slapped and punched me until I told him about it, how I'd given you the part about Greyfriars."

McLaren swore softly and stared at her face, aware of the dark bruises that were shifting to yellow and purple hues. "Is…that all that happened to you?"

She nodded and gave him a smile. "He didn't do anything about the brochure for a while, but he kept it.

He'd look at it periodically, then he laughed and phoned someone on his mobile. This was before they moved me here. I think we were still in Edinburgh. It was some city setting, at least, because I could hear the traffic noises."

McLaren nodded at her muffler. "Is that when he ripped that?"

"Yes. He also wrote something on a sheet of paper. Then he rolled it up, tied it with the fabric strip, grabbed the brochure and left. I haven't a clue as to what became of them, but if they hurt or jeopardized you in any way, I'm extremely sorry. I guess I wasn't very smart. Or strong." She eyed him, frowning. "Did he use them against you somehow?"

"Yes, but I'll tell you about it later. Now, however, I think it prudent for us to get out of here."

Outside the door, Lanny still lay sprawled on the ground. McLaren pulled his mobile from his jacket pocket and punched in a phone number. "Why don't you tell the police where we are—just north of Balquhidder. Tell them to follow the trail behind the kirk, heading toward Creag Mac Ranaich. Come to the shieling on the other side of the burn. There might be a different route up the hill, something drivable. I know Fowler drove down the other side. They're familiar with the area, so they would know. Anyway, tell them what happened, and that they might want to pick up Lanny."

"You're not leaving?" Fear crept back into her voice and her eyes widened.

"No. I just want to have a quick look around the shieling. I won't be long." He shoved the mobile into her hand and went back inside.

He crossed the room and followed the same routine he had in Donald MacLaren's cottage. There was no woodpile to sort through, so he examined the rocks comprising the walls. He poked and nudged and pulled, replaced sod that became dislodged, felt around the holes of the few rocks he did manage to extricate. No coins, notebook, or piece of paper presented itself.

He did the same with the rocks serving as the fire pit. He pulled them from the haphazard ring on the ground, then examined the exposed soil. The odor of old ashes and partially charred wood assailed his nostrils, making him cough. Ignoring the stench, he restacked them. Nothing.

Chapter Thirteen

"I'm sorry, Mike." Liza handed him his mobile phone as he emerged from the shieling. "I can't get a signal up here. Or the company's having some kind of trouble."

McLaren nodded and pocketed the phone. He glanced at the stand of trees bordering the brook, at the ruined cottage and the rows of mountaintops that looked like ocean swells. The peaks appeared to change hues from chocolate brown to dingy gray, fading into the distance and mingling with low-hanging clouds. He'd assumed there would be no mobile phone service in this wild area, but he had to try. He had to contact the police. When they got back to Balquhidder...

Liza rubbed her wrists watching McLaren's every move. "What are you doing?"

"Making sure the police have something to pick up when they get here." He tied Lanny's hands and feet with lengths of rope formerly used on Liza. Giving the knots a tug, he nodded. "I'd hate for them to make a trip for nothing." He glanced at his watch, then at the sky. Somber clouds were building in the west and the air held the scent of snow. He grabbed her arm and gently nudged her. "Come on. I think we best be going."

"Where?" Liza looked at the knots as they walked up to Lanny.

"Back down the trail. To the village. You need

looking after."

Lanny moved his head slightly and groaned.

"Should we leave him some water?" They walked past the man and she turned her head, studying him.

McLaren pulled her along. "No. I'll call from Balquhidder. I know the mobile works there. He'll last that long out here." He glanced at Lanny's wool jacket. "He won't turn into an ice cube. The police will be here soon enough. I'll tell them it's urgent."

They hurried down the trail, wanting to put as much distance between them and the two men as possible.

Back in the village, McLaren insisted Liza use his bed-and-breakfast room to clean up. He sat outside, the cold wind racing across the surface of the loch and along the road. He angled his back to the cold and phoned the police.

He'd just finished talking to them when Liza stepped outside. She'd washed her face and hands and combed her hair, and seemed more relaxed now that she experienced some form of normalcy.

"How about something to eat?" McLaren stood up, looking hopeful.

"I won't say no." Liza fell in beside him as he walked to a café. "I honestly can't remember when I last ate."

"Didn't they feed you?"

"A sandwich, but that seems days ago. I think I drank more coffee and water than I've ever done. I had the impression that was their main staple."

"Well, choose whatever you like from the menu. Coffee and water are optional."

"Thanks." Liza glanced at the village. "This where

your family comes from?"

"The MacLarens, yes. But my grandfather lives elsewhere." He let the silence build between them, uncomfortable with the topic. "This is it," he said, coming up to the café. "Whatever meal you want. Don't be influenced by the time."

"What time is it?" Liza looked at the sky. The sun hovered near the western horizon.

"Does that make a difference what food you order?"

"No. I like breakfast any time of day. But I'm disoriented. Late afternoon, obviously, but what time? What day?"

"Thursday. Just after three o'clock."

"It'll be dark soon." Her voice suddenly sounded tired. Or perhaps she was dreading the approaching night, he thought.

"I can get you a room at the b-and-b. You could take off for home in the morning, if that's what's bothering you." He glanced behind him, to where the main road led east to Kingshouse on the A84.

"Oh. No. I didn't mean to sound... Oh, I don't know what I sounded like." She smiled weakly as he opened the café door. "Thanks. I'm starving."

After the late lunch, McLaren drove Liza to the nearest bus stop. She repeated that she was fine, that she'd be home in a few hours, and that she was eternally grateful for his rescue. He stayed until she boarded a bus to Edinburgh, made her promise she'd phone the next day, and then drove back to Balquhidder.

Back in his room he turned up the heat on the radiator, then showered, brewed a cup of tea, and sprawled out on his bed, the weariness and aches from the past two days screaming in his muscles. He wanted to search the shieling again, more thoroughly, interior and exterior. The money had to be there. All those clues in the diary couldn't refer to anywhere else, not with the hint of the song and the Braes' title underlined.

He rolled onto his side and stared out the window. Dusk was advancing quickly, the first star visible through the branches of a tree. Had Lanny or Fowler come upon the money while they'd been there? It was possible. But the two men hadn't the air of someone just finding a large hoard of coins. They'd still be arguing about the division of the treasure or where they'd taken it even if they'd been there since they snatched Liza on Tuesday.

And what about Lanny? Now that McLaren had seen Lanny's chin tattoo up close and personal, he had to admit he'd not seen anything like it. A Maori moko.

Did those tattoos mean anything? Not literally, for he was certain they did when the Maori wore them. But here were three people he knew of—George Roper, King Roper, and Lanny Clack—and they all sported a moko. Did King wear it because his father had? But why Lanny? Was it a symbol of acceptance, like full membership in King Roper's gang?

McLaren lay back in his bed and stared into the dark. Instead of magnifying his fears, the night cocooned him, and he fell asleep.

****

Fowler parked his off-road vehicle alongside the shieling. He'd been gone only an hour but shadows already stretched eastward from the hut and boulders and blanketed most of the ground. The sun touched the highest peak of the hill range to the west, transforming the slopes and valleys at their base to shades of indigo and violet. Gray light crept into the air, softening the edges of objects, blurring them in a near-dream. Lanny's trussed up body, however, was no dream.

"What the hell happened?" Fowler yanked the ropes binding Lanny's arms, then strode into the shieling without waiting for a reply. He charged back outside seconds later. "Where the bloody hell is she?" He pulled on the rope again, tightening his grip. The hemp bore into Lanny's skin.

He let out a yowl. "She got away, Fowler. I-it wasn't my fault."

"Yeah? Whose fault, then? Hers? She over power you with a rock? Get you down with a judo hold? All while she was tied up?" He kicked Lanny's shins, drawing another cry from the man.

"Fowler, don't! Please!"

"When did this happen? How long's she been gone?" He stared at the forest, trying to discern the path she took.

"She's not been gone long. I don't know exactly. Right after you left. Not five minutes from when you drove off. I swear. We can find her. She's probably still heading down the trail. She'll walk slow, wobbly, probably. We'll catch her up."

"If she had an hour start, we're not going to grab her on the trail, you idiot. We'll have to find her again. Either in Balquhidder or Edinburgh or her house. That's *if* she went there. She's probably thinking she can hide so she'll go to a friend's. Or check into a b-and-b or holiday camp under a different name." He ran his fingers along his jaw, trying to decipher where the woman would stay. "You're really somethin', you know that? Wait till Harvester finds out you let her escape." He kicked Lanny in the back.

"*Bloody hell!*" Lanny arched his back and grimaced, his eyes watering. "I couldn't help it, Fowler. I was ambushed. It was a trick. I didn't have a chance. There were a bunch of blokes. They all jumped on me. I couldn't do a thing."

"Where'd this army come from? The Royal Scots Guards? NATO? The infants' class at the local school?"

Lanny raised his head, as Fowler pushed the sleeve of his jacket up. Lanny's voice croaked, sounding frightened, the words quivering before the wind snatched them away. "You've got no right to treat me like this, Fowler. I won't involve you when I talk to...*hell!*" He rolled onto his side, trying to escape the blows.

"You better not mention my name. I had nothing to do with this. I was in Callander, as you well know. You botched the Mary King's Close incident and you botched this. How do you think he's going to take it?"

"He'll be mad as hell. He'll kill me but he'll keep me on."

Fowler stood over Lanny, shaking his head. "Wrong again, mate. He won't kill you, but I will." Fowler withdrew a knife from his jeans pocket, opened it, and plunged all six inches of its sawtooth blade into Lanny's stomach. He watched Lanny gasp and fold up like a pocketknife, the blood seeping from his wound and pooling beneath him into the snow, before yanking it out. He then pulled a leather bracelet from his pocket, glanced at it and tossed it onto Lanny's body. "Almost wish you'd be alive to explain that when the cops come.

Almost. But I'm chuffed pink to see you this way, mate." He kicked Lanny once more, then spat on him. This time Lanny didn't groan. A few minutes later, Fowler got into his vehicle and drove back down the hill.

****

Knocking on McLaren's door woke him an hour after he'd drifted to sleep. Confused, he looked at his watch, then out the window. The moon balanced on a branch of a pine tree along the road and someone walked past the guesthouse, the footsteps slapping against the tarmac. Just gone nine o'clock.

He staggered to his feet, ran his fingers through his hair, and shuffled over to the door. He grabbed the doorknob as he asked who was there.

"Mr. McLaren?"

"Yes."

"This is Ross Gordon," explained the soft Scottish accent.

"Oh, yes. The friend of Jamie Kydd." He opened the door and in the pool of light cast by the hallway light fixture saw a red-haired man of forty, dressed in tailored trousers, shirt, and tie. The business suit was implied, for Ross Gordon emitted Official Matters. "Come in." He stepped back, gestured toward the room, and shut the door after Ross took a chair.

"I know it's rather late, but I needed to talk to you."

"That's fine. It's not about Jamie, is it? He's not hurt or anything."

Ross shook his head, his expression still stern. "As far as I know, Jamie's all right. I'm here about the report you made this afternoon."

"The report?"

"About Lanny Clack."

"Oh, yes. I rang up the police station as soon as I got back to the village here. Several hours ago," he added, checking the time on his watch. "Well before we—Before lunch. It was rather late. The lunch, I mean, but I phoned as soon as I could. Ordinarily I'd have done it at the scene and stayed, but with no phone service up there—"

"I understand that, sir. My visit isn't about your rather unorthodox procedure."

McLaren frowned, clearly confused. "Not about... You found him up at the shieling, didn't you?" McLaren's voice rose in near panic. Had the man escaped? Was he still at large?

"We found him. That's not the problem."

"Then I don't see..."

"The problem is we found him dead."

McLaren's throat went dry and he rubbed his forehead, trying to ease the throbbing that suddenly filled his head. He lowered himself slowly into a chair, sitting opposite Ross. "What do you mean he's dead? I left him tied up on the ground outside the hut. He was unconscious but alive. There's some mistake."

"Hardly a mistake, Mr. McLaren. We arrived and found him bound with rope, a knife wound in his stomach, a wound from which he died. Have you any idea what may have happened?" Ross didn't sound overly friendly. In fact, he sounded tired, as though he envisioned another case comprised of long hours and little information.

"Not at all." McLaren explained that he'd been with Liza Skene at Hurd Dowell's hit-and-run accident, that he'd been looking for Liza since that time to assure himself of her safety and health, and that he'd found her in the shieling as he hiked the area. "All I did was free her and tie up this Lanny Clack bloke. I suppose I could've forced him to walk back to Balquhidder with us, but Miss Skene was a bit unsteady of her feet and I had to help her for a while." He paused, debating if he should be completely truthful. "And frankly I didn't want his company."

"Personal, was it? You angry that he'd nearly killed you in Edinburgh?"

"Not particularly. I didn't want Miss Skene to endure his company any longer than necessary. She was near the emotional breaking point, if I judged her correctly. She'd been through a hell of an ordeal, and I didn't see any benefit to prolonging her association with her kidnapper by taking him with us. I left him tied up, assuming he'd be safe for an hour or so until the police arrived. I escorted Miss Skene to Balquhidder, treated her to lunch, and saw her safely onto a bus to Edinburgh. That's it. Plain and simple."

"When did you discover Lanny with Miss Skene?"

"I don't know the time. I didn't think I'd need to confirm it later. But I phoned the constabulary as soon as we got to Balquhidder."

"When was that?"

McLaren exhaled heavily. Hadn't the man seen the report? Surely the time was noted on it. "An hour or so after we left the shieling."

"You just said you didn't know the time."

"It takes about an hour to climb to the shieling. I've asked in the village and that's the universal answer. We may have made it down more quickly, but with Miss

Skene's physical condition, it probably took about an hour."

"What was wrong with her condition? She suffer from hypertension or have any injuries?"

"I just stated," McLaren said, his voice rising in his anger and frustration, "that she'd obviously endured this captivity. She'd been physically assaulted and then tied up, for days. She'd been in this roofless hut, again possibly shortly after her kidnapping, and she sat on cold ground in bloody hell freezing temperatures and in snow. Of *course* she wasn't in the best shape to run a damned marathon or jog down the damned hill." He broke off, aware he was too angry for his own good.

"You know Lanny Clack was wanted for murder." Ross' tone assumed an edge to match McLaren's.

McLaren blinked. Why the detailed questioning? "Well, I saw a television newscast giving his description after the hit-and-run. Since the CCTV tape shows it's clearly him driving the vehicle that killed Hurd Dowell, I figured you wanted him for murder. If not that, then some other offense, such as culpable homicide." He hoped he had mentally translated the English 'manslaughter' into the correct Scottish equivalent.

Ross leaned forward, closing the distance between them. "You're sure you didn't get angry when you found him this afternoon?"

"*Of course* I got angry! Who the hell wouldn't? The bloody git killed a man, frightened a dozen others who were there, kidnapped Miss Skene, held her hostage—" He stopped before saying Lanny had knocked him on the head and left him for dead in the marshland along the loch, or that he was a threat to

Neill McLaren. He took a deep breath. "But I didn't kill him. I tied him up so he wouldn't escape, then phoned you when I could."

"An hour later." The voice was flat, unimpressed.

"Yes. An hour later. Maybe ninety minutes. I didn't write down the bloody time, but I phoned here, in the village."

"Why wait so long to ring us?"

"Pardon?" The suspicion that things were turning horribly wrong whispered to McLaren.

"Why didn't you phone right then? Did you want to put some space between you and the killing so you could establish an alibi?"

Chapter Fourteen

McLaren stood up, clenching his fists. His neck muscles threatened to erupt from the tension filling his body. He shouted, his voice bouncing off the walls. "I did *not* kill Lanny Clack. I admit I wanted to, but I merely tied him up. I gave Miss Skene my mobile to call the police, but we couldn't get a signal up there. The closest spot we could phone from is here. So I did. Look somewhere else for your killer."

"The trouble is," Ross said, his voice easing, "the Procurator Fiscal can't accurately establish time of death due to the cold temperature and wind. The body cooled quickly."

McLaren exhaled deeply and ran his hand over his chin. The stubble felt like sandpaper beneath his fingertips. He walked to the window and stared into the darkness. Though the bedside lamp gave off a pool of warm, yellow light, the majority of the room lay in gloom. As gloomy as his future seemed at the moment.

He turned and sat on the window ledge, his back against the pane of glass. The cold bit into his cotton shirt, helping to anchor him to reality in this nightmare. "Look, Sergeant Gordon, I appreciate that you've got a body on your hands and you're needing to find the bloke who killed Lanny, but I'm not your man. I have a witness that he was alive when I left him at the shieling."

"Yes? Who is that?"

"Liza Skene."

"The kidnap victim." The voice turned skeptical.

"She obviously was there, saw me tie up Lanny. When we were leaving, Lanny groaned. Miss Skene asked if we should give him some water. I said it wasn't necessary, that the police would be along soon after I phoned them."

"Is Miss Skene here?" Ross swiveled in his chair, staring at the door to the bathroom.

McLaren nearly snapped that he had higher morals than to go to bed with a woman he didn't know. He pressed his lips together, trying to keep his cool. "Miss Skene is not here. Neither in this room nor in this bed-and-breakfast nor in this village. We had lunch when she got freshened up a bit. Then—"

"Where did you have your lunch?"

"Pardon?"

"Did you have a picnic on the trail, or eat in Callander, or sit in your car?"

"We ate in the café here in Balquhidder. It was rather a late meal, but we were both hungry and couldn't wait for tea."

"Which café was this?"

McLaren gave Ross the name. "After lunch, I drove her to the bus stop and she boarded a bus for the city, I believe I told you not two minutes ago. Now, if you want to speak to her, either to confirm my statement about Lanny or about anything else, I suggest you phone her at her house."

"I will. I wanted your statement before I spoke to her."

"Have you had the knife fingerprinted?"

"We will when we find it."

"I thought it was left in the body…"

"I merely said Lanny died of a knife wound. I didn't mention we had the weapon."

McLaren acknowledged his assumption.

"Can you tell me about this?" He produced a leather bracelet encased in a plastic evidence bag.

The room dimmed and tilted. "Where…that's mine! Where'd you find it?"

"At the crime scene. Next to Lanny's body."

"You can't believe I killed him. That's what you think this suggests, don't you? That he ripped it off my wrist in a fight. I didn't kill him!"

"How else do you explain its presence? Did you lose it at the shieling and Lanny just happened to fall next to it? Did Miss Skene have it and toss it onto the ground while you weren't looking?"

McLaren rubbed the back of his neck and closed his eyes. He was in a whirlpool, in danger of being sucked down into the darkness and shut away from his friends and help. He heard Ross' voice as if in a dream, reverberating and distant. When he looked again at Ross, he tried to think of an explanation. "I realized I'd lost it a day or so ago but I didn't know when or where it happened. My fiancé'd given it to me, so I was anxious to find it, but that seemed an impossible task. I've been in Edinburgh and Callander, as well as walked the braes here. I can't understand how it came to be close to Lanny Clack, but I swear I didn't put it there or kill him."

Ross seemed to stare at the broken leather and the wooden bead that had come loose. A tree branch tapped against the outside of the windowpane, interrupting the quiet.

McLaren jammed his hands into his jeans pockets. "So, where do we stand?"

"Jamie Kydd vouches for you. Your record while you were in the job is impeccable, which doesn't imply you're lily white now." He grinned suddenly, the humor coming through in his voice, and tossed the bagged bracelet to McLaren. "You can stop thinking of names to call me. I've probably been called a few you've never heard of." His Scottish accent thickened momentarily. "*Och, mon*, I know who ye are. I'm returnin' this tae ye even though it's again' policy and should technically be held as a piece o' evidence."

McLaren eyed the plastic bag as though it were a trap.

Ross' tone returned to his normal speech. "You're in the clear. We're quite aware that there's no phone signal up at the shieling—don't worry about that. I'm sorry about the rough time I gave you just now, but I needed to test your mettle myself. I think I can safely let you roam the countryside."

"Thanks." Sarcasm seeped into McLaren's reply.

"I'm to pass on a message from Jamie, by the way."

"Oh, yes?" McLaren screwed up his mouth, expecting a lecture from his friend.

"He says to quit showing up the bloody English constabulary and come home. Those were *his* words, McLaren. I'm not going to evaluate *any* police force, especially English."

McLaren laughed and got to his feet. "Now I know what a released prisoner feels like."

"Oh." Ross paused just outside the door, the

lamplight throwing the near side of his face into relief. "Thanks for giving us the number plate of Fowler's vehicle. We've alerted our personnel, as well as other constabularies. I shouldn't think he'll go unnoticed for long."

"He needs to be bagged before he goes off the deep end again."

"Well, I needn't say how much you've helped us. We appreciate it."

"Just seemed like the thing to do at the time." He escorted Ross to the door, promising he'd keep in touch, and got ready for bed.

****

Saturday morning McLaren breakfasted and was on his way back up the trail before the sun cleared the crest of the hills. He walked quickly, wanting to get to the shieling before the snow blew in from the western islands. He exhaled on his hands and flexed his fingers. The cold worked through the leather gloves and into his bones.

He followed the line of fence posts and the footprints from his previous journey, still visible in the snow. As he plunged into the forest he was surprised the darker space held no terrors for him this morning. Perhaps because he knew what the wood held, or because he focused on the hut. He didn't pause to dissect his feelings. The need to explore was too great.

He'd peered at the map and the diary after breakfast that morning, making certain he had come to the correct conclusion. Harvester may have set the clues for him to find, but McLaren was convinced of their authenticity. He had no doubt about his route. And if he found Harvester following him, he could deal with the man when he had to.

When McLaren arrived at the shieling the snow where he had left the man seemed to shimmer before him. Dozens of shoe prints that had processed the scene and streaks of red mottled the uneven whiteness, and McLaren bent to peer at it. He pinched a portion of the snow and looked at it more closely. It was frozen blood.

He shook his hand, freeing himself of the crime residue. If he'd not known what happened, he might believe a fox or wildcat had made a killing here. Or a hunter had shot a deer. But he couldn't ignore the truth, and he felt partially responsible for Lanny's death. Maybe he should've taken the man with them.

McLaren shook his head and stood up. No. He would not wallow in guilt. Lanny had killed Hurd Dowell. And although the death penalty had been abolished in Scotland, Lanny probably wouldn't have escaped King Roper's clutches for long. It was conjecture on his part, McLaren realized, but Roper didn't leave loose ends. Look no further than South Yorkshire's little hospital escape. No, King had long arms. Lanny's days had been numbered; it didn't matter if King or someone else got to him first.

McLaren entered the shieling and looked at the same places he had yesterday, but slowing his search now that he could do it leisurely. He tried shifting rocks from their positions in the wall, moved the fireplace stones again, used a stick to poke the sod roof. No treasure proclaimed itself.

He examined the cottage exterior in the same manner, trying to budge stones and moving fallen debris. Again no treasure showed itself.

As he came to the far side of the shieling he saw

two sets of stone shelves dug horizontally into a mound of earth. Actually, they were more like bookshelves, for each unit was comprised of four large slabs of stone: three comprising the shelves and the top serving as a roof to hold up the sod. McLaren judged them to be about a foot wide, with chunks of large rectangular rock serving as spacers between the shelves. He stooped over and peered into the dim recesses. They were a foot or so deep.

In the shielings' heyday they served as storage for the families summering there. The interior of the dwelling was Spartan by any standard; extra space, such as these exterior shelves, would be welcome.

He knelt and peered into the shelves' dim interiors, then felt around with his hand. At the back of one of the shelves was a piece of paper. On withdrawing it, he saw it was a scrap on which was written a song title. It was small, hardly larger than one half inch by four inches. The paper had faded, leaving an overall yellowish tint and brittleness to the fragment. Two edges had curled and one was broken off. But the title was intact and readable.

"Rock of Ages."

McLaren frowned. Why hide a hymn title? Had one of the families who grazed their herds here left it, torn from a precious songbook? Was it part of Harvester's merry chase? Even if it wasn't, he still had no answer to his question. A hymn title seemed hardly significant. Unless the rock was.

McLaren stood up, his mind racing. The only rock of any significance and readily identifiable was the one on the trail up to the shieling. He'd passed it three times now. How many other spots like that could there be?

But was it too obvious? If Harvester had planted this old slip of paper, wouldn't he have figured out the title?

Maybe not, he reminded himself. Maybe Harvester's trail led to the shieling only; maybe Harvester didn't know about the hymn title. After all, it'd been shoved way to the back and so small he'd nearly missed it. Just because Harvester pointed him to the shieling didn't mean he had located the treasure. Perhaps the shieling was the end of *Harvester's* trail and he hoped McLaren would find or deduce something here that would reveal the money. Perhaps the hymn title was part of the original treasure trail from a half-century ago.

He grabbed his rucksack and crossed the burn, jogged through the forest, and emerged in the open moorland. The boulder sat at the edge of the wood, lichen covered and undisturbed since he'd last passed it.

The area was open and appeared to hold the only boulder, but he canvassed the vicinity. He parted tall clumps of grass and moved fallen boughs. No other rock large enough to qualify for the hymn title showed itself. Unless the rock was on the other side of the hill, this had to be the symbolic X on the treasure map, the spot where the silver coins were buried.

He widened his search, not looking for the rock this time, but for Harvester or a dogs' body of his. If the whole idea of this game was for McLaren to lead Harvester to the buried money, he'd be here watching, wouldn't he? Unless Lanny's death had scared off Harvester, or he was late getting to the shieling, perhaps helping Fowler hide.

That made sense. Harvester was the sort to stay in

the background, his hands on the reins, watching until the danger was over before stepping into the limelight and claiming the prize. He'd wait for a bit, giving the police time to vacate the crime scene with Lanny's body, then return and hope he wasn't too late to meet up with McLaren.

McLaren bent over and parted the snow and cast-off forest debris from the base of the stone. A hole had not been dug for it, as accommodated the huge uprights at Stonehenge. This stone was approximately knee-height and rested on bare earth. He grasped the sides near the top and tugged. It moved slightly. He positioned his right foot against the top of the rock face and pushed. The stone tilted several inches, then settled back into place. He embraced the rock and pulled. It shifted to the left, rolled onto its side, and rolled several feet before stopping against a tree trunk.

Small rocks covered the ground where the stone had sat. McLaren drew his mobile phone from his rucksack and snapped a photo of the area. Then he clawed at the rocks, pushing them away on either side of the enlarging hole. He again paused to take a photo, and took pictures at every stage of the excavation. He'd dug several inches when his fingertips scraped against metal. He scooped out the last handful of rocks and dumped them beside him, impatient to see what he had uncovered. His fingers tapped across the flat piece of metal and found a metal handle. He eased it up from the hole and sat it on the snow.

It was rectangular in shape, perhaps as large as a shoebox, and painted a dull green. Areas of the paint had chipped off or were scratched, perhaps where the rocks had bitten into it. A metal latch, the same color as the box, looked to be rusted shut.

McLaren pushed on the end of the latch. Its hinges squawked but the lid reluctantly opened.

The box nearly overflowed with U.S. currency, paper bills slightly scorched on one end. As though they'd been rescued from a fire. Still in the hole, beneath the box's location, silver coins and gold ingots winked at him. It was too much for him to transfer back in his rucksack. But he emptied the bills into his sack, then dumped in handfuls of coins and ingots. He'd at least make a start. He could get help to transfer the rest of the cache later. For now, at least, he had evidence of the hoard in case the police didn't believe him.

He fired off several photos of the money, box and immediate scene before easing the metal box back into the hole and dumping the small rocks on top. Then he rolled the stone back into place. He stood back and looked at it. Aside from the marred snow surface, it looked as though nothing had been disturbed. He scuffed the snow with the toe of his boot and spoiled the snow surface face for several dozen yards up and down the trail. Satisfied no one would be suspicious of the boulder, McLaren returned down the trail.

He'd just entered a section of dense ferns, thick-trunked trees and large boulders when a breaking twig alerted him. He stopped, the hair rising on the back of his neck, and stared into the gloom.

A man stood on the side of the trail. He was tall and thin as a flagpole, with dark hair. Shadow obscured most of his face but even from the shadowy depths below the forehead's overhang McLaren could feel the man's dark eyes staring. When he moved his head, sunlight revealed his smile.

McLaren took a step forward but stopped again. The wood felt suffocating, the air unusually cold. Bird song had ceased and the wind lashed bits of ferns and twigs against his legs.

"Mr. McLaren." The man's voice sounded cordial, bordering on enthusiastic, but McLaren detected hatred under the honeyed tones. "So nice to see you." He made no move, either to offer his hand or stand relaxed. The words might've played on a recording, for all the welcome they produced.

"Sorry, do I know you? Have we met?" McLaren ran the man's face through his mind but couldn't match a name to it.

"We have, but you might not recall it. My name's Ritchie. Fowler Ritchie." He waited, as though the name would propel McLaren into action.

It did. Almost as abruptly as the rock Fowler had swung at him Thursday evening.

McLaren stiffened, alert to a possible attack. "You and your pal Lanny knocked me out and dumped me in the Tuarach."

"Bravo! Doesn't take you long to add two and two and arrive at the correct answer."

"The police found your mate."

"You sure about that?"

"I rang them up, told them the location of the shieling."

"They may have him, but he won't tell them much."

"Are you sure? Science can work wonders these days. I can haul you in, hand you over as Lanny's killer."

"Sure. But only if you catch me."

Fowler opened his knife and advanced toward McLaren, his feet dancing like a boxer's. He grinned, apparently enjoying the game and the concern on McLaren's face. McLaren eased out of his rucksack and placed it along the edge of the trail.

"Looks like an explosive cargo." Fowler nodded almost lovingly at the pack. "The way you set it down, it must be nitro glycerin."

"You'll never find out." McLaren picked up a thick bough and waited for Fowler to lunge. His pocketknife was at the bottom of his pack.

The two men circled, as if in some strange dance. Fowler jabbed at McLaren, who warded off the man's hand with the stick. Again Fowler charged and again McLaren averted Fowler's knife. This repeated several more times before Fowler picked up a large rock. Laughing, he weighed it in his hand. "Good ole Lanny wanted everything to look like an accident. You found in the Tuarach, succumbed to exposure. That woman at the bottom of a crevice. 'Nothing to point to us, our hands clean,' I believe he said. Well, I'm not Lanny and I don't give a damn what the coppers think. I'll be out of the country and I doubt they'll waste their time or money hunting me." He tossed the rock, enjoying its weight when it smacked into his palm. "Sorry to rush this, but there's another apropos saying—time and tide wait for no man, McLaren. It's been nice."

He hurled the rock at McLaren's head, then rushed him with the knife. McLaren knocked away the rock, hitting it with the stick, but the knife attack came too fast for him to recover quickly enough. He flung up his arm, trying to divert Fowler's hand. The knife blade swerved from its intended target and sliced McLaren's jacket sleeve, faintly cutting the flesh of his arm. McLaren hooked his foot behind Fowler's knee and pulled. As Fowler fell, a movement to the side and behind McLaren diverted his attention. He glimpsed a hand grabbing the stick beside him, then felt the blinding pain as it smashed onto the back of his head. He groaned, fell onto the ground, and passed out.

Chapter Fifteen

McLaren's ringing mobile phone prodded him awake. He moaned, touched his head, and opened his eyes. The branches overhead puzzled him, and for a moment he though he was back in the marshland southwest of Balquhidder. But the ground beneath him was firm and dry, not cold and mushy. He pushed himself into a sitting position and fumbled for his mobile with his left hand. Something was wrong with his right arm. Why did it hurt?

"Yeah?" He hadn't glanced at the Caller ID display in his hurry to still the noise. "Who is it?"

Jamie's voice sailed into McLaren's ear. "Mike. You sound strange. You okay?"

"Other than my head split in two, I think so."

"What happened to your head?"

"It met a rock. I think." A twinge of pain shot through his right arm and he glanced at his jacket sleeve. It and his shirtsleeve were slashed, displaying a shallow cut several inches long on his upper arm. The blood had congealed but was still a shiny red. He touched it gingerly and grimaced again. "What's going on?"

"You need to call me back, go to hospital to have your head looked at?"

"No."

"If you got hit on the head, Mike—"

"I've had enough of hospitals to last me the rest of my life, thank you very much. October's escapade is still vivid in my memory."

"Good that you've got a memory if you got clobbered on the head. Look, if you're hurt, you need to be seen."

"I'm fine. Just have a splitting headache, no pun intended. Quit the damned mothering, will ya?" He glanced around the area. Hadn't he fought with some bloke before the blackout? Shouldn't there be a person lying on the ground? He turned to see behind him. He was the only person there. He crossed his legs, sitting 'Indian style,' and rubbed his arm. It hurt like hell. "Okay, what's up?"

"Too bad you're so far away. I'd drag you by your hair to see a doctor."

"Distance does have its advantages. Give."

"All right. You wanted me to look up some information on those three blokes."

"Right. George Roper and company. Find anything?"

"I sent the photos to your mobile, so you should have them already. The rest of the information took some digging, but I got it."

"Good lad."

"I got a mate to access the military records, which is how I got the information."

"You're getting quite good at lying, it seems."

Jamie groaned and said something derogatory. "Anyway, here's your data. George Roper died in 1973, age 48, when little baby boy King was two years old."

"Too bad the dates couldn't have been reversed."

"Roper lived in Manchester. 9 Thornton Square.

You were right about him serving in Burma in World War Two. He enlisted at the age of sixteen."

"Sixteen? Wasn't eighteen the age limit?"

"Officially, but with the rush to get men into the service, birth dates weren't always confirmed. It wasn't unusual for sixteen and seventeen year-olds to enlist, but if they were caught later, they'd be discharged immediately."

McLaren muttered that the Ropers seemed to be adept at avoiding the law.

"George Roper's buried in Edinburgh."

"You're joking."

"Nothing to joke about, Mike. You probably passed close to him several times."

"Why Edinburgh and not Manchester?"

"He was there and happened to die there. His wife didn't want him back, even in his less lively form, so she opted to leave him up there."

"They about to be divorced?"

Jamie shrugged. "From what I could find out, yes."

"It would tend to change your mind about going into the hereafter side by side."

"Young son King couldn't bring dad home to roost, as it were."

"What was George Roper doing in Edinburgh?"

"On holiday, I assume. It was May. I've heard rumors that he and the other war buddy had one of their reunions, but I can't verify it."

"Did you learn who this third chap is?"

"You *are* inquisitive. Yes. Tam Innes. He was born in Killin, but came back to Callander after the war and settled down there. Innes was born in 1922 and died in January 1974."

"What the hell's going on, Jamie? Two men, wartime friends, dying so young has got to be odd. They didn't die of something associated with the war, did they?"

"Like some disease or shrapnel or something? No. Roper died of a fall down a flight of stairs. Innes was hit by a bus in Edinburgh and died the next day in hospital."

McLaren exhaled heavily. "Isn't this too coincidental?"

"What do you mean?"

"Two mates of Frank Papadakis, both in Scotland, both die by accident and only months apart."

"You think Papadakis had a hand in the deaths?"

"I have no proof, but it screams to me that he did. Frank moved to Balquhidder in 1964. Roper dies in 1973 and Innes dies in 1974. Papadakis had time to plan their deaths, especially if they got together a few times during those intervening years. Frank died in 2008. That's over thirty years after his two buddies' demise. A long time to do something without them spying on him."

"I'm certain you have an idea what that something is too, Mike."

"My first thought is absconding with some of the money from Corregidor when the Japanese invasion was imminent, but they weren't in the same army."

"Not even in the same branch, Mike. Papadakis was U.S. Army, remember?"

"Yeah. And Innes and Roper served in Burma with their British regiment."

"So, how'd they get so chummy? Did they know each other before the war?"

McLaren said that was something he hoped to find out. "Or you, if you're bored at work."

"But all three men were in the same general area, Mike. Frank Papadakis in the Philippines and on Corregidor, and Innes and Roper in Burma. Maybe they met by accident. Not literally, but maybe they were all on leave at the same time, frequented the same bar or something." He waited for McLaren to agree, but when no response came, he continued. "It's happened. Not so far fetched."

"Well, perhaps that's not a crucial part of the story. They knew each other, so that's where we start. Do you know for certain that the Yank was on the detail either to burn the Corregidor currency or load the silver and gold onto the ship?"

"Wait a minute. It's in my notebook...Yeah. He was. It was a hectic time, as you can imagine, so I think that's how he got his hands on some of the wealth."

"Frank smuggled it back to the States, or directly to Scotland with someone's help, then he took up residence later. But why'd he contact Innes and Roper, and why tell them about the money? The British weren't involved with the evacuation of the wealth on Corregidor. It was strictly American and Philippine personnel. Why even tell Innes and Roper about the money he had stashed? He didn't need them after the fact."

Jamie cleared his throat. "Did he *have* to tell Innes and Roper?"

McLaren nearly choked. "I-I guess not, no. I just assumed, since they were mates..." He broke off, something nagging in the back of his mind. Finally, he snapped his fingers. "Of course George Roper knew

243

about the money. It's in his diary entry of 1962."

"Right. You told me."

McLaren reiterated about finding Donald MacLaren's cottage and the hidden silver coins and diary. "That would explain," McLaren said, picking up the current scenario, "why George Roper hid the diary and a few coins. He stole Frank's hoard from Corregidor and didn't want Frank getting his hands on the diary because it gave a cryptic clue to the money's location. Also, if George Roper stole Frank's hoard…which I'm sure he did, for how else would a Brit get his hands on Yankee money…he'd want to secrete it somewhere fairly close by. It'd have to be fairly easy to access, easy to remember, yet hidden enough so the casual passerby wouldn't discover it."

"Where is this location, or haven't you had time to unearth it yet?"

"I did. About…" McLaren glanced at his watch. "An hour ago,"

"That have any connection with your head injury?" Jamie's voice sounded worried.

"I don't know." He touched his arm again. It still throbbed. "My head connected with a rock, that's all I know. Damn."

"What's the matter?"

"Nothing. My arm hurts like blazes."

"Mike, I'm serious. Get to a hospital—"

"It'll be fine in the morning. I have my suspicion that this recent encounter came about from that hit-and-run encounter I had in Edinburgh."

"Where that man was killed?"

"Yeah. When I came up to the shieling, I overheard the rock thrower talking to the driver of the vehicle used in the hit-and-run."

"You're not serious, Mike."

"They didn't come right out with the name, but I suspect my friend Charlie Harvester is behind that assault and my current attack. After all, I know he, Lanny Clack, Fowler Ritchie, and Jean MacNab are all chums."

"Who's this Ritchie fellow? Another of Harvester's hit men?"

"Yeah. Fowler Ritchie and Lanny Clack. A warmer, more caring pair you'd be hard pressed to meet." He gritted his teeth as pain shot down his arm. He hadn't intended to move it.

"Why would Harvester do this? You two may not be drinking mates but you've existed for nearly eighteen months in a tense truce. Longer, if you count your time together in Staffordshire Constabulary. So, why now, and why would he choose Scotland to...dispose...of you?"

"I considered that the other day, Jamie. Scotland's far enough from Harvester's patch in Derbyshire so he won't be suspected."

"A lot of trouble for an alibi."

"As to why now...maybe he just got fed up with running into me. We all have our tolerance level, our breaking point. Something could've tipped him over the edge, too. I don't know."

"You've solved a few cold cases lately, Mike. Harvester's nose gets out of joint rather quickly, especially when he feels the limelight's diverted from his own genius. Could be that. You know—one too many newspaper articles. You're scoring where he isn't."

"Jealousy? Maybe. Anyway, he chose Scotland. Could be nothing more than he knew Lanny Clack, maybe he did Lanny a good deed once and is now calling in the favor."

"Harvester never did a good deed for anyone except Charlie Harvester."

"Well, I'm not going to analyze the bloke. I know he hired Lanny and Fowler. I heard the two of them talking in the shieling. Plus, I read those emails of Jean MacNab's. I don't especially care why Harvester's bent on ending my days. It's enough to know he tried."

"Devotion and single-mindedness can be carried too far."

"So it's logical to suspect Harvester conked me on the head."

Jamie let a few choice words about Harvester slip out. "Did you see him?"

"I was focused on Fowler and his bit of daring-do with the knife. But I saw someone grab a rock or a bough before the lights went out."

"And you're naming Harvester as the head pounder."

"It fits, Jamie. Look at the email communication with Jean. Look at how he used George Roper's actual diary and map to get me to lead him to the money."

"You two are strange bed fellows, Mike. Harvester leads you on this treasure hunt and you're leading him to the site. Why wouldn't he make it simple and have one of King Roper's gang decipher the cache location, leaving you out of it?"

"He probably doesn't trust them. He might be nervous stepping into a den of thieves."

"Hi, I'm a cop. Respect me and don't kill me.

Yeah. I accept that."

"Also, Harvester likes to control everything. He's a megalomaniac. The fewer people involved—namely, me—the fewer people he has to keep track of, has to direct, and has to worry about wandering away with the loot if they find the money on the sly. With just one guy to keep surveillance on, he's feeling bloody confident."

"Probably counting his pile of loot in his dreams. All right. As I said, it makes sense. But what about Fowler Ritchie? He tried to kill you."

"That's just a by-product of Harvester's Great Plan, I think. Fowler might be acting on his own, now that Lanny's dead, thinks he can watch me and get the money before Harvester legs it up the hill. They may have had a falling out, for all I know."

"Fowler will go up a notch in my estimation if he's parted from ole Charlie."

"Mine, too, I'm reluctant to admit."

"I, uh, told my boss about this, Mike."

"Why the hell'd you do that?"

"You know. To keep them up to date. Your case is getting more dangerous by the day."

"I can't argue with that." He winced as he moved his arm.

"I thought you needed to have documentation for all this. You know. Like when you were in the job."

"Cover my back, you mean. Especially if anything serious happens to me, then it won't reflect on you."

"That's not even funny—the slur on my character or the suggestion that you'll be hurt. Anyway, it seems the thing to do with Harvester, doesn't it?"

McLaren let out his breath, his mind taking him back to June of last year. Harvester sprawling in the rose bush, the constables and crime scene investigators standing in shock, unsure if they should go to Harvester's aid or pretend they hadn't seen the assault, fearing for their careers if they were called to testify. And McLaren's own hermit-like existence during the ensuing twelve months, his anger and mistrust, his near loss of his family, friends, and fiancée. He got up, the ground suddenly hard and cold. "Those dates, Jamie…"

"Which ones?"

"Roper and Innes' deaths."

"What about them?

"I wonder if Frank Papadakis killed George Roper to keep him quiet about the Corregidor money, insurance if he found out and was tempted to talk about it."

"To keep the loot for himself, you mean?"

"As good a motive as I've heard in a while. Georgie Roper meets with an untimely accident the next time he returns."

"Courtesy of Frank Papadakis' push down the stairs."

McLaren shook his head, interrupting Jamie. "We're on the wrong tack. Doesn't pan out. George's diary states he knew about Frank's loot. He wrote that he was about to get the lion's share. Doesn't that imply *George* had the money, that he stole it from Frank?"

Jamie picked up the story. "Okay. George Roper discovers where Frank hid the money. He steals it and hides it somewhere else. Roper then leaves a clue to the money's location in his diary, not wanting to forget."

"Can't believe he'd forget a thing like that."

"Perhaps he wasn't sure when he could get back, so he needed to make certain he knew where it was.

That's a hell of a lot of money to lose."

"Point taken."

"And being a greedy little bastard, George doesn't tell Innes, believing dividing a treasure two ways dilutes his portion."

McLaren's words tumbled out in a rush. "And Frank never finds out his money is gone. He pushes George down the stairs and pushes Innes in front of the bus to eliminate them, to stop them from blabbing about the Corregidor loot at a later date. He hadn't gone back to the spot where he'd buried the money so he didn't know George had found it and dug it up and hid it elsewhere." He smiled, satisfied with the plot.

"But if Frank realized the money was gone, he'd not have killed George and Innes. He'd have needed them around to tell them where it was hidden."

"Which is why," McLaren agreed, "the diary was still in Donald MacLaren's cottage these forty plus years later. Roper had secreted it there. He was dead. He hadn't had time to collect the money from where *he* had hidden it before Frank killed him. George and his wife were estranged, so he might've felt he couldn't tell her about the money and where the diary was hidden."

"And son King was hardly old enough to comprehend the secret."

"George Roper had no inkling that he was a marked man. If he had known, he might've told someone else. But Frank got to him first and stopped that threat to his money."

"Too late, as it worked out."

McLaren fell silent, thinking through the scenario. "I wonder if George Roper or Innes knew a father or friend of King Roper's present gang."

"What are you thinking?"

"We're missing the link between these two generations, Jamie. If we agree George Roper stole Frank Papadakis' money, hid it, and secreted the clues to guide the lucky treasurer hunter to the loot, and if we agree Mr. Personality Charlie Harvester got a hold of the diary and other clues in order to prod me into leading him to it—"

"How did *Charlie Harvester* get the diary and other clues?"

McLaren moved his feet and stretched. He was feeling the cold. "I can't see King Roper handing over everything to him with his blessing, and encouraging him to seek and find."

"King's greed makes Harvester look like a philanthropist in comparison."

"So, how did the diary et al fall into Harvester's possession, Jamie? Am I overlooking something obvious?"

Jamie moaned that he was mentally exhausted from digging up the three war buddies' past.

McLaren flexed his arm gently, hoping to keep it from stiffening. The wound didn't hurt as much now, but his muscle ached, as if it had been kicked. "I just thought of something."

"Yeah?" Jamie yawned. "What?"

"What if George, being a thoughtful dad, wills or somehow passes on the diary and other Corregidor items to son King? Maybe Innes got it after George's death and saw that King got it. Doesn't really matter, but King ends up with the diary and map. Souvenirs of dad's military adventures. Maybe Innes wrote out the whole story. Maybe the wife knew the story and told it to King. However King came by it, he had his father's diary."

"Plausible. Lots of kids have their parents' old military things."

"So, we've got two factions in this story. George Roper, Innes, and Papadakis, the blokes who stole the money and *know* where its buried, and we've got the later group of Charlie Harvester, Lanny Clack, and Fowler Ritchie, who *want* to know where that money is."

"How do you connect them?"

"Through the one person common to both. At least, one that I know of. Lanny Clack."

"Lanny?"

"Sure. Think about it, Jamie. Lanny's a member of King Roper's gang. Lanny's also a mate of Harvester's. What if Harvester approaches Lanny with this sob story about me, how he hates my guts, wants to get rid of me, and so on? What if Lanny, as a friendly helper, gets the diary and like items from King, strictly as a loan?"

"King would've done that. Probably said something like 'One less cop in the world,' or some such warm sentiment."

"Lanny then loans the diary and map to Harvester so *he* can set up the scheme, lure me here, nudge me into finding those items, and eventually lead him to the buried money." McLaren waited for Jamie to find the hole in the plot, to remind him of the crucial fact he'd forgotten, but only breathing came over the phone connection. "Well?" McLaren asked, unable to bear the silence any longer. "Where have I gone astray?"

"Nowhere, as far as I can see."

"Anything else suggest itself? Is there another way

for George Roper's diary to get into Harvester's hands?"

"Could do, but it's stretching the limits of believability."

"Such as?"

"Oh, estate sale, church jumble sale. You know."

"Harvester or Lanny just happen to buy this interesting albeit important bit of World War Two memorabilia, just happen to know George Roper through their personal acquaintance or knowledge of King Roper. I see what you mean."

"A little too coincidental to happen like that. No, Mike, I think you've figured it out. Lanny Clack has to be the hub in all this. He knows King Roper and he knows Charlie Harvester. No one else, at least no one whom we know, could've produced the diary. So now what happens?"

"I need to get back to my room and clean up a bit before I answer that. Damn, I'm stiff." McLaren got to his feet, grimacing at the effort. Every muscle seemed to complain at once.

"Ring me up when you've decided what's next."

"You going to come here?"

"No, but I like to be part of the story. Something to lull my grandkids asleep to in my dotage."

"First you need a kid of your own, Jamie."

"Always the nitpicker, aren't you?" He rang off after getting McLaren's promise to keep him informed.

Chapter Sixteen

The rucksack was nowhere in sight. McLaren walked around the small clearing, poked among the tall grass near the trail, thinking it might've been moved accidentally in the fight. He returned to the spot where he'd set the pack. No scuffed earth or trail through the snow indicated it had been kicked aside. It had simply vanished.

McLaren glanced at his watch. He'd not lain there that long. Perhaps fifteen minutes. Had Fowler picked up the rucksack? Did the person who slugged McLaren from behind have it? They were a team, no matter who had the bag, else Fowler would've yelled out when the second man appeared. It obviously wasn't Lanny, so it had to be Harvester.

McLaren's stomach tightened, as though he was about to be sick. Harvester wouldn't stop with the sack if he were after the entire hoard. Even if he weren't certain how extensive the treasure was, he'd not let McLaren out of his sight until he was sure of the extent of the cache.

McLaren shoved his mobile into his pocket and walked back to the village.

He cleaned up a bit, got his car, and drove into Callander. At Boots Chemists he bought a pocketknife, two nylon rucksacks, a packet of sterile gauze pads, a roll of adhesive plaster, and a bottle of antiseptic. At the local bakery he bought a tomato, cheese, and ham sandwich, a small bag of Galaxy Minstrels chocolates, and a bottle of pear/raspberry juice. Back at his room in the guesthouse, he dressed his cut and ate lunch.

Harvester's assumed involvement in this latest event stirred a memory in McLaren's mind. That email he'd read at Jean MacNab's guesthouse mentioned Harvester would be at the Station, that he'd be available to help Lanny. On reading it, McLaren had assumed it meant the police station at Ashbourne where Harvester worked. But that made no sense, not if the man needed to be close by to help. What other Station could it be? Something obvious to him and Jean. Some place, for the word was capitalized in the email.

McLaren took out his map and scanned the area around Balquhidder. The Station had to be in the vicinity if Harvester was to come to Lanny's aid quickly.

A minute's search showed him Balquhidder Station, northeast of Auchtubh. A smile spread slowly across his face. It had to be the correct place. Jean MacNab had rushed a bit too quickly over her reply to his question about the place no longer serving as a train depot, now catering to people on holiday. What better place for Harvester to hole up than in one of the holiday park's cabins or stationary caravans? Charlie Harvester, practically under McLaren's nose.

He rinsed out the empty juice bottle and pitched the sandwich wrapper into the wastepaper bin, slipped into his jacket and grabbed his car key, and slammed the door behind him.

The drive wasn't long, less than fifteen minutes, but it seemed like another world as McLaren drove into the resort. Tall trees and quiet enveloped him and he parked near the entrance. Now that he was here, what did he expect? To see Harvester walking down the road?

Inquiring at the office for Harvester probably wouldn't gain him anything. The clerk or the owner might be suspicious and, if they were safety-minded, wouldn't give out information on Harvester's accommodation. It was laudable but didn't help him any. But there was another way to spot the man if he were here.

McLaren opened his phone and punched in Harvester's mobile number. A cranky "Yes? What is it?" sounded in his ear, and McLaren thought how well he'd imitated that raspy noise to Jean MacNab. He took a deep breath, hating to have Harvester's voice so close. "I need help." He mentally said a prayer, hoping he sounded enough like Fowler Ritchie to prod Harvester into activity.

"What's wrong? Where are you?"

"At the Rock."

"The Boar's Rock?"

"Yeah. McLaren's leaving. What do you want me to do?"

Harvester muttered a few choice words. "You're an idiot, for one thing, out in the open like that where anyone can see you."

"No one's here. It's too bloody cold."

"All right. I'll be there in fifteen minutes. Keep McLaren in sight. Stop him if you have to. Oh, and to convince me you're not one hundred percent useless, did you get something from that woman and plant that note at the dog's grave?"

McLaren smiled but kept the humor from his tone. "Yeah, sure. What do ya think? That's why we got McLaren, ain't it?"

"Congratulations. Something went right. I'd give just about anything to've been there when he discovered he wasn't following Liza Skene. God, how long I've waited to pay McLaren back. I applaud your work. Now that we've got him, don't let him get away. See you soon." Harvester rang off and McLaren slid down in the driver's seat, his eyes on the park entrance, his heart beating faster than the wind-stirred boughs.

Harvester drove past McLaren five minutes later. The car wasn't the one with which McLaren was familiar, but the man had probably taken the train north and hired a car, as McLaren had done. Harvester took no notice of McLaren, his gaze on the road before him.

McLaren sat still for two minutes, making certain the man hadn't forgotten something and was returning. When he'd counted off the time, he eased up and glanced in his rearview mirror. No sign of Charlie Harvester. Fine, but what did that get him? The man still was free to carry out his plan. But at least McLaren knew for certain that Harvester was here, that he was involved in the murder scheme.

McLaren drove back to the village, unsure if he felt comforted or uneasy knowing Harvester was trying to kill him.

Back in his room at the bed-and-breakfast, he brewed a cup of tea. He hadn't seen Harvester walking around Balquhidder, but his car was parked below the Boar's Rock. McLaren uttered a prayer of thanks for his hired car, a different make and model from the one Harvester knew. He took a sip of tea and was reaching for the map when his mobile rang. He grabbed the phone and sat on the foot of his bed.

"Hello. This is McLaren."

"Michael, it's Ross Gordon."

"Should I be worried?" He kept his voice light, hoping his response didn't sound as cynical as it came out.

Ross laughed. "Not at all. In fact, that's the reason for the call. We found the murder weapon and you're in the clear."

"The knife that killed Lanny?"

"Yes. It took a bit of doing, but the lads located it in the shieling. Under the hearthstone, to be precise. Only one set of fingerprints was on it. Care to guess?"

"Fowler Ritchie."

"I doubt if you could've stabbed Lanny without your gloves smearing Fowler's prints. So we've crossed you off our list."

"I'll sleep better tonight for knowing that, thanks."

"The lab also found some fresh spittle on Lanny's jacket. Perfect match to Fowler's DNA. I can't believe it'd be conveniently sitting there if Fowler hadn't had a hand in Lanny's death."

"Thank God for his anger, then."

"Also, as a touch of icing on the cake, we checked mobile phone records. You, or someone, did make a call at the time you stated. I realize you could've given your phone to someone else to make the call, but the café owner confirms you were there. Also, your signature on the credit card receipt matches your signature at the guesthouse where you're staying. I don't doubt you were there when you said you were."

"That's nice to hear."

"Again, Michael, I'm sorry I put you through the wringer, but I had to see if there was a crack in your story. I should've just gone with Jamie Kydd's trust in you, but I had to investigate."

"No need to apologize, Ross. Any decent copper would've done the same. Thanks for letting me know."

"Fowler probably hid the knife because he didn't want it found with him. That'd be as damning as the fingerprints."

"Speaking of finding," McLaren added, "I'd appreciate someone official around when I go back to dig up the money."

"Money?"

McLaren told Ross about the Corregidor money and the tangle of people involved in it.

When Ross recovered from his astonishment he suggested he bring a constable. "Not only as another back to haul, if we have to, but he can watch for Charlie Harvester. That's if I get permission to come. I'm sure I will, so don't worry. But I have to notify my boss."

"Please do. I don't want you to be formally disciplined."

"I'd rather not endure that either, thanks."

McLaren hesitated, as though considering something. "If you can, better make that two constables, Ross. Fowler Ritchie might show up, alone or with Harvester. They're working together, unless Harvester's finished off Fowler, and also assuming Harvester's getting so close to me and the buried loot that Fowler's outlived his usefulness."

"Not to mention one less portion to divvy up."

"Not the first time that will have happened. But no other people know about it. And I can't see Harvester letting anyone else in on this. I think they're the only ones who might appear."

"Two of my men, then, for security, but no more. We don't want a squad tramping over the ben or advertising something big is about to happen."

They agreed to meet behind the kirk in one hour and McLaren rang off, feeling his adventure was nearly over. It would be good to get home.

Fifty minutes later McLaren walked to the kirk. The wind came off the loch, stiff with sleet and the scent of wet soil. He arranged his muffler about his neck, tried to ignore the cold pouring through his sliced jacket sleeve, and adjusted the rucksack higher on his back. He carried the second one under his good arm.

Ross Gordon and two police constables armed with shovels and nylon rucksacks greeted him on the far side of the building, nodding quietly so as not to draw undue attention. One of the officers took the second rucksack from McLaren, and they fell in line behind him and silently climbed the hill.

The route by now was familiar to McLaren, so he was surprised when the line of fence posts gave way to the forest and the path branching off to the left. The large rock sat where he'd left it, the soil and snow around it showing no evidence of anyone hunting there. McLaren slid out of the rucksack and walked up to Ross.

"The Corregidor money Frank Papadakis stole is beneath that rock." He gave Ross a brief accounting of the story and his own hunt for the money. "I lost most of the dollars when my rucksack was stolen after the fight. Also a gold bar and a silver coin. But there are enough bars and coins down there to make most anyone

happy, I think. Especially the American government."
He stood back as the two constables rolled the rock
away. One man stood guard and the other one dug.

"I know you'd rather be doing this."

The constable drew the box from the hole.

McLaren lifted his cut arm and shrugged. "I'll get
to play another day. Discovering it was the biggest
thrill."

The constable filled in the hole, replaced the stone,
and waited as Ross and McLaren counted the money
and put it into the rucksacks.

"Bloody heavy, isn't it?" Ross grinned as he lifted
a sack.

"It's the kind of weight I don't mind carrying,
though." McLaren grabbed a rucksack and slipped his
arms through the shoulder straps. He glanced around
the spot. The constable slowly pivoted on his heels,
scanning the wood and open land for any threat.

"Odd how that changes one's perspective on many
things. Constables, if you please." Ross stood lookout
while the two men seized the remaining bags. He gave
the place one last scrutiny. "Right. Let's go."

The trip back to the village kirk went smoothly.
Sleet belted them sporadically but the wind had calmed.
Neither was there a hint of Harvester or Fowler.

The constables went ahead to the police vehicle,
leaving Ross and McLaren several dozen yards behind.
As the constables unlocked the car and stowed their two
sacks inside, Harvester and Fowler emerged from the
other side of the kirk. Each man held a semi-automatic
pistol.

McLaren stopped short, holding out his arm to
retain Ross from moving. Fowler ran up to the police

vehicle and suggested the constables sit on the ground. Harvester grinned and greeted McLaren with a salute of his weapon.

"Well, McLaren. At long last." Harvester eased forward and snatched the two rucksacks. He dragged them several yards away before motioning to Fowler. "Not like our other encounters, is it? I've got the upper hand this time, mate."

"You've no chance of getting away with this." McLaren's old anger boiled inside him. "You're daft pulling something like this in the open."

Iron-gray clouds streamed across the length of the loch, rolling through the glen with the threat of a storm. The water rippled where the wind dug into its usually smooth surface, and the color of the sky reflected off the depths. Afternoon light, dimmed to a somber smoky hue, plunged the village and landscape into an early dusk.

"Not many people about." Harvester nodded to Fowler, who walked up to him, lugging the two sacks. "Even if they did see us and ring up the cops, we'll be gone before they can get here. That's the advantage of robbery in a village, McLaren. The law is stationed so far away." Fowler took one of the rucksacks and was slipping it over his shoulders. "Ready?" asked Harvester.

Fowler grunted and fastened the clasp across his chest. "More than you can imagine. I've been waiting for this moment for months." He raised the gun slightly and fired from waist level. The bullet slammed into Harvester's thigh, and the man fell to the ground, his hands gripping his leg, his head thrown back in pain.

McLaren started to lunge for Fowler, but Ross held

him back. Fowler ran toward the loch, firing at McLaren. The constables dashed after Fowler as McLaren hurried to Harvester.

Fowler ran to his car and flung himself into the driver's seat. The engine started with an angry growl and he slammed his foot on the accelerator pedal. The tires squealed as they dug into the ground. Chunks of soil and small rocks flung off as the car screeched down the road.

Harvester sat on the ground, holding his leg. McLaren had bandaged it with the items he'd bought at Boots. And though it wasn't a professional job, it stemmed the bleeding.

The rain, cold and heavy, had lessened slightly, but the clouds still threatened. McLaren, alone with Harvester, stood looking at the man's pain-ridden face. He'd had dreams about Harvester, wondered what he would feel if he ever had the upper hand and could vent his hatred of the man who had ridiculed his friend and ended his own police career. Now that Harvester sniveled at his feet, McLaren was surprised his hatred ran so deep.

Fowler obviously had no idea where the loch road led; he knew only that he had to escape. The car's headlights cut through the encroaching dusk, marking the snake of black tarmac hugging the loch. He passed a large building on his right, perhaps a hotel. The car flew past it and seemed to merge with the night. He jammed on the brakes when the road unexpectedly ended past Loch Doine. Seeing no exit there, he turned around and headed back toward Balquhidder. He stopped the car in a squeal of brakes and tires skidding on rock at the western end of Loch Voil.

He leaped from the car and ran up to the shore and scanned the area. No watercraft was moored any closer than several hundred yards away. He glanced behind him. The constables were coming up rapidly. Fowler waded into the water and started swimming diagonally to the far side. The constables yelled for him to stop, but Fowler kept swimming.

Down at the loch, Ross was busy with the boat and the constables, and McLaren considered leaving Harvester to run down to the shore. But he remained there; Harvester might escape if left alone.

Fowler had advanced into the deeper part of the loch when he began treading water. He sank slightly, then resurfaced, spitting out water and gasping for air. The rucksack, waterlogged and its contents causing the sack to shift, had grown heavier than he could manage. He tried to unfasten the clasp across his chest, to rid himself of the dangerous weight, but his fingers were clumsy in the frigid water. His legs felt immovable, made of iron and burdened by his heavy jeans. He went down again and took longer to break the surface of the water. Gasping for air, he yelled, his voice carrying across the loch and up the hills.

The constables reached the loch and shed their caps, jackets, shoes and gloves. One man waded in where Fowler had entered and the other man ran down the shore to a tied-up rowboat. He climbed in, jammed the oars into the oarlocks, and rowed toward Fowler.

The weather worsened in those few minutes, the sky blackening and the sleet pelting the water. Fowler's head was barely visible, a dark blob bobbing between the rising waves. At times his head was screened by waves; other times the head disappeared below the surface. The water swelled and ebbed, the waves rising and falling as the clouds broke overhead and the mixture of sleet and rain pounded everything.

Fowler fought with the clasp but by now his fingers wouldn't move. He twisted his upper torso, trying to slip his arms from the shoulder straps. They wouldn't budge; he'd fastened the clasp too tightly.

A cramp seized his calf muscle and he screamed. He bent down, his head submerged as he kneaded his leg. His head broke the surface as he gasped for air and shrieked in his pain.

Dipping and nodding, the rowboat rode the choppy swells as though it were a leaf floating on the surface. The boat was too light to make much headway in the wind. The man's weight pushed the stern down, and the waves and wind angled the bow upward at a dangerous pitch. He kept his oars in the water, trying to anchor his position as the other constable swam up and grabbed onto the gunwale at the bow. With the boat more level, the constable resumed rowing.

It did no good. Fowler had disappeared beneath the waves.

The constable rowed around the area in a tight circle, calling Fowler's name. He wiped the sleet and water from his eyes, trying to see, trying to get a location fix from the shore. The waves pushed him eastward, back to the land.

He gave in minutes later and guided the craft back to the shore. Ross ran over and helped the constable out of the water, then tugged on the bow to beach the boat.

McLaren exhaled, his muscles taut from watching the chase, then his gaze returned to Harvester. They would never know if McLaren murdered Harvester, set it up to look like Harvester tried to get away and died in a recapture attempt gone wrong. Harvester cringed from his wound. Could he be mentally disturbed? Was he obsessed with constantly trying to best himself, to get the limelight, to solve the tough cases? Was it more than the man's mean, even evil, nature? Was Harvester losing his mind?

Harvester moved and raised his head. His eyes, usually filled with disdain or loathing, had softened. Tears crowded in the corners, ready to spill down his cheeks. He leaned forward, as though about to get onto his knees. "McLaren?" The word came out in a blend of pain and plea, the yearning of his gaze underscoring his anguish.

McLaren stared at the man at his feet. What was he supposed to feel? How should he respond? A different man groveled before him. He remained still, trying to understand his emotions and Harvester's words.

"McLaren. Please. Let me go. As one cop to another, for the brotherhood we shared. Help me. If you do, I-I'll give you half the money. *Half!* Three quarters! Th-that's a hell of a lot of brass. You can do a lot with that. Y-you'll never have to work again. You'll be set for life." He took a breath and ran his tongue over his lips. They were wet from the sleet and rain. He tried to rise to his knees but buckled under the pain. "Listen." He raised his arm, as though to grab McLaren's hand. The effort was too much and he winced. He glanced at the drama still unfolding at the waterside, then turned back to McLaren. "Look. They'll never know if you let me go. They're busy at the loch. You...can get the sacks in the car, empty out part of the coins and gold bars. Stuff your pockets, hide it till they've gone.

They'll never know. I-I'll never tell." He gritted his teeth and took a deep breath. "Look," he said when his words had no effect, "I've got a plan. I-it can't miss." He tried to scoot closer to McLaren, but the pain stopped him. "You see, I'm best mates with Monty." He looked at McLaren, perhaps waiting for him to be impressed. "You can't not know who he is! Montgomery. Field Marshal Bernard Montgomery. The hero of El Alamein and North Africa. Responsible for plans to invade Normandy on D-Day." He waited for his words to sink in. "We-we're like brothers, McLaren. He'll do anything for me."

McLaren started to turn away.

"Didn't you hear me? Don't you understand? Monty's recovered the rest of the treasure. Th-there's a film about it. Watch it, if you don't believe me. It'll prove I'm telling the truth. *Casablanca*. Yes, that's it. You'll see all about the money. He'll divide it with us. He will!" He broke off, the sounds of the returning car soaring into his speech. He hurried on. "If you just tell them you were mistaken about everything, that this is…really my money, that you were helping me get it back, I'll never trouble you again. You can take my gun. It's worth a lot of quid—" He broke off as a wave of pain consumed him.

The pistol lay on top of the rucksack beside McLaren. All he had to do was grab the weapon and shoot Harvester. An accurately placed bullet or two, a made-up story, and he'd forever be rid of the thorn in his side. He bent and picked up the Sig Sauer. It was a well-made weapon, just about top of the line. Expensive and deadly. He hefted it in his hand, remembering the rock Fowler had weighed in the same manner and thrown. Was it true, an eye for an eye? Was death by a gun the same as death by a rock? Did it make any difference to the victim or to the killer?

McLaren glanced back at Harvester as a whimper of pain escaped the man's lips. Why did he hesitate? Hadn't he always dreamt of this moment, of this revenge?

He took a step toward Harvester. He was so near that he could hear Harvester's labored breathing, see the dark smear of dirt against the darker, wet clothing. McLaren raised the gun, sighted along the barrel and focused on Harvester's head. His finger wrapped around the trigger.

Harvester raised his head and in that instant must've realized he was a breath away from dying. He curled into the fetal position, his hands still grasping his wounded thigh, and tried to hide his head, to sink out of sight. The wet earth didn't receive him. He curled tighter and sobbed.

McLaren stared at Harvester. He saw both sides, now—the policeman and the criminal. Whether lunatic or genius, fear overwhelmed Harvester and he whimpered again for McLaren's help. McLaren felt the cold of the metal trigger beneath his finger, then he walked slowly back to his room, repulsed with the scene.

Chapter Seventeen

The sleet and rain changed to snow in the early evening hours, dusting the ground and rooftops. A cold wind curled through the glen and eastward to Auchtubh and south to Callander, frosting everything it touched with white. Snow drifted over the rural roads and swirled in wraith-like wisps over the A84, but the major storm didn't break for another twenty-four hours.

Inside his house, Neill McLaren sat before his fire, the yellow light throwing black shadows across the floor and into the dark corners. The shadows merged with the darkness, as though implying that darkness comprised most of Neill's entire world. He sank back into his chair, his arms resting heavily on the chair arms. It hadn't always been so. Sparks of light and laughter illuminated parts of his life. If he closed his eyes, he could remember them, hear the laughter.

His grandson's birth had been a spark of light. A gleam of hope for the future of the family business. That future hadn't evolved as everyone had assumed, leaving Neill angry and, if he admitted it, frightened. Three hundred years of labor and sacrifice to end like this, their name and work eventually passing to the hands of a stranger?

Neill's gaze dropped to the black and white tiles of the floor. A giant chessboard, he thought. Like his life, played out in a series of maneuvers to marry whom he wanted, hire whom he wanted, make business deals, create a demand for the product. His entire existence focused on one point. When had he ever done anything for anyone, paid attention to anything other than the brewery? How many music concerts, art exhibits, walks through moors and forests, fishing trips with Brandon had he missed? How many chances to become close to his family, to really know them, had slipped away?

His fingers drummed on the chair's armrest. He expected everyone to have the same passions and dreams consuming them. Was he lucky Brandon mirrored the passions and dreams, or had those expectations pushed Brandon into a business for which he didn't care? Had he ruined his son's life?

Neill got up and set another log on the fire. The disturbance sent a flurry of sparks up the chimney. Sparks of light, glowing with hope.

He shuffled to the window, suddenly feeling tired. The snowfall had nearly stopped, a few flakes drifting to earth but adding no depth to the whiteness blanketing the ground. The village lay silent under the clouds but for the yap of a fox. He'd left his tracks in the snow outside the house. Perhaps his grandson Michael was like that: making his own tracks regardless of the family company. Why wasn't his path as important as Neill's?

The fire snapped and Neill turned, leaning against the wall. Perhaps his grandson showed as much determination to be a cop as Neill had in continuing the brewery. Perhaps Michael showed more resolve. He'd chosen a difficult and dangerous career. He should be lauded for it, not shunned.

Neill smiled, Michael's voice and face coming

back to him. He would phone him, invite him back for Hogmanay. They'd ring out the old year and begin the new one together.

****

McLaren and Ross lingered over dinner in the local restaurant. Harvester had been taken to a hospital for mental evaluation, and the money was in police custody. "Stolen goods awaiting return to the lawful owner," as Ross had termed it.

"When you said you wanted help"—Ross picked up his coffee cup and wrapped his hands around the warm china—"I had no idea what was coming."

"Neither did I," McLaren said. "I don't see how anyone could've known."

"Well, it's a story to tell the grandkids. Buried treasure, a deserted cottage, clues in a map…I doubt if I'd have found any of it, Michael. I'm thankful the task fell to you."

"You not keen on deciphering puzzles?"

"Not that. If I'd been handed this case at the start, and heard research was part of it…what?" He frowned, looking at McLaren. "What's wrong?"

"The last thing you said."

"About what?"

"Something about if you'd had the case."

"Oh. I don't know. Just that if I'd heard research was so important to the case—"

"Damn! What a bloody, egotistical berk I've been!" McLaren slapped his palm against his forehead.

"What's the problem, lad?"

"You said if you heard research was part of it. Heard. Spelled as the man's name. Hurd. And research."

270

Ross blinked, clearly confused.

"Hurd Dowell. At the beginning, when this started with the hit-and-run in Edinburgh, I of course thought it was about me."

"Because you suspected you'd been lured up here to meet your grandfather?"

"Right. So I let that trick color my thinking for everything else. I assumed I'd been the intended victim, not Hurd. But I forgot he'd been a research librarian."

Ross shook his head. "Sorry. I don't understand the significance."

"Liza Skene told me Hurd had been working on a project during his free time. What if that project came from Charlie Harvester? Look." McLaren took out his notebook and pen, and drawing a mind map of the scheme as he explained it. "There was the original group of men from the war: George Roper, Frank Papadakis, and Tam Innes. They were all involved with the money and diary."

"Dating back to Corregidor. Right."

"The big stumbling block in my thinking was how to get the diary into Harvester's hands. Lanny Clack accomplished that. He was the link. He was in King Roper's gang *and* he was working with Harvester. I believe Lanny got the diary from King Roper and loaned it to Harvester.

"That would've been the end of the story, but King Roper, being the career criminal and murderer that he is, doesn't quite trust Lanny or Harvester. Especially because Harvester's a cop, no matter what he tells Lanny about wanting to kill me."

"So, Lanny employs Hurd to research the Corregidor money for King Roper because Hurd is a research librarian." Ross nodded, evidently satisfied with the scenario. "King figured Hurd would locate the whereabouts of the stolen money and King could get it before Harvester did."

"That's how I figure it. But then the old fly in the ointment appears. Lanny doesn't particularly like King. That's not surprising for any of us to hear because most of King's gang members don't like him, but they stay with him because he pays well. Lanny, being a loyal friend, though perhaps none too bright in the intelligence department, tells *his* best friend Harvester what King's up to."

"That there's a potential double cross with the Corregidor money information, that King's trying to locate the loot before Harvester does in spite of Harvester having the diary."

McLaren nodded and took a drink of beer. They and an older couple were the only diners left in the room. It had just gone ten o'clock and snow fell lazily, blazingly white from the exterior lamplight. McLaren wondered if either of the diners had served in World War Two, if they'd heard of or been involved with the Corregidor episode. They looked to be the correct age. Ross' voice pulled him back from his thoughts.

"So, Harvester has Lanny kill Hurd with the car, making it look like a hit-and-run accident. This pushes King Roper out of the treasure hunt game. His prime researcher has just been eliminated and Harvester seems to hold the trump card."

"If you ever get any sense from Harvester, he can confirm it, I suppose." McLaren exhaled loudly. That day could be a long time coming. Harvester had been babbling about returning to Corregidor under authority of *bona vacantia*, or vacant goods, and demanding to search the Bay for other jettisoned coins. Never mind that reality told a different scenario to Harvester's fantasy. McLaren shook his head. Poor old Harvester. He'd have an uphill battle convincing the U.S. government they didn't own the money.

He shoved aside his mental image of Harvester and made another notation in the mind map drawing. "Anyway, the car accident was intended to stop Hurd from researching the Corregidor money and stop him from telling King what he knew. Liza Skene and me coming up to him and talking to him had nothing to do with me as the victim. I just happened to talk to them."

"Then, Hurd was already in Lanny's target sight when you came by."

"I think so. Of course, you can check phone records, but I believe Harvester phoned Lanny on his mobile to tell him where Hurd was. Harvester had to silence Hurd once the research finished, so Harvester would keep tabs on him. Maybe Harvester was across the street in a shop so he could see Hurd. But I think that's how Lanny knew where Hurd was so he could run him down."

Ross waited until the waiter had refilled his coffee cup and left before replying. "No wonder you got the wrong impression. With the scheme involving your grandfather and the nicely laid out diary and map, then the attempt on your life at the Boar's Rock, well, anyone would think the car accident was part of it."

"And Lanny, under Harvester's orders and probably with Fowler's help, did transport me to Invernenty Glen and left me to find Donald MacLaren's cottage so I could stumble upon the diary and get on

273

with the chase."

Ross took a long drink of coffee, as though needing the caffeine to anchor him to reality. "All this…Hurd's murder, Fowler's drowning, Lanny's murder, your knife wound, Harvester's hospital admittance. All this because one man during World War Two got greedy, and got two of his mates involved in the web." Ross took out his wallet and reached for the bill. "Too many people in the way. As you were eventually."

"Just in the way," McLaren said, his voice low. "But not for long. Harvester caught up with me here."

Ross stretched, his fatigue evident in his voice. "I'm just thankful the good guy won."

****

McLaren left Balquhidder early the following morning. The snow had tapered off around midnight, leaving a thin crust of white on the ground. Blue sky stretched over the glen; there was no hint of wind.

He brushed the snow from his car's windscreens, threw his overnight bag into the back, and walked up to the Boar's Rock. The view was magnificent: a long stretch of Loch Voil cradled by the steep hills, the stands of forest dark against patches of new snow, the streaks of high, white clouds. He looked at the rock mound commemorating the clan's ancient rallying point, rubbed his bare hand over its surface. Centuries of fighting, hardship, and heartache were symbolized in the monument. But love and happiness also were encased. Perhaps families had stayed together and found contentment where they could.

McLaren picked up a small stone from the ground. He ran his fingers over its smooth surface. The perfect souvenir. An ideal reminder of all the rocks he'd encountered. He leaned against the monument, gazing at the loch, mentally writing his list: the Corregidor Rock, the Boar's Rock, Donald MacLaren's rock cottage where he found the diary and map, the rock shieling where Liza had been kept prisoner and Lanny Clack lost his life...

He placed the rock into the back pocket of his jeans, slowly, carefully, as though it might break. He patted it to assure himself it was there, then walked down the hill and to his car. He settled into the driver's seat, aware of the rock pressing into his lower back, yet needing to feel the connection to his family and his past.

As he turned onto the A84, heading for Edinburgh, the village slipped behind him. He started to sing "Lenachan's Farewell". But a different lyric formed in his mind. The tires hummed on the tarmac as new words and a new title suggested themselves. "McLaren's Farewell", he thought.

> *Fare thee weel, my native land,*
> *Heather moors and alder tree!*
> *Sweet the sight but hard the fate*
> *0' the lad who parts wi' thee.*
> *Tho' my grandsire's heart is stone,*
> *And disclaimed me as his own*
> *Still, I'm free the hills to roam,*
> *Mair content I canna be.*

~*~

> *Rock for shieling, rock for homes,*
> *Rock-named fortress in the sea,*
> *Rock for Clan and gath'ring cry,*
> *Keeping life and spirit free;*
> *Misty glens urge me to stray*

I slow my step, I turn away;
Here nae langer I maun stay
Mair content I'll never be.

He smiled. It was fitting. He would be back to celebrate New Year with his grandfather. He was content.

A word about the author...

Books, Girl Scouts, and music filled Jo A. Hiestand's childhood. She discovered the magic of words and the worlds they create: mysteries, English medieval history, the natural world. She explored the joys of the outdoors through Girl Scout camping trips and summers as a canoeing instructor and camp counselor. Brought up on classical, big band, and baroque music, she was groomed as a concert pianist until forsaking the piano for the harpsichord. She also plays a Martin guitar and has sung in a semi-professional folkgroup in the US and as a soloist in England.

This mixture formed the foundation for her writing. A true Anglophile, Jo wanted to create a mystery series that featured a British police detective who left the Force over an injustice and now investigates cold cases on his own. The result is the McLaren Mysteries.

Jo's insistence on accuracy—from police methods and location layout to the general "feel" of the area—has driven her innumerable times to Derbyshire. These explorations and conferences with police friends provide the detail filling the books.

In 1999 Jo returned to Webster University to major in English. She graduated in 2001 with a BA degree and departmental honors.

She has employed her love of writing, board games, and music in other ways by co-inventing a mystery-solving game, P.I.R.A.T.E.S., which uses maps, graphics, song lyrics, and other clues to lead the players to the lost treasure.

Jo founded the Greater St. Louis Chapter of Sisters in Crime, serving as its first president. She is also a member of Mystery Writers of America. She also enjoys photography, reading, change ringing, and her backyard wildlife.

http://www.johiestand.com